D1175826

LEGENDS
AND
LIARS

LEGENDS

AND

LIARS

MORGAN RHODES

RAZORBILL

RAZORBILL

An imprint of Penguin Random House LLC, New York

First published in the United States of America by Razorbill,
an imprint of Penguin Random House LLC, 2023

Visit us online at penguinrandomhouse.com.

LIBRARY OF CONGRESS CATALOGING-IN-PUBLICATION DATA
Names: Rhodes, Morgan, author.
Title: Legends and liars / Morgan Rhodes.
Description: New York,: Razorbill, 2023. | Series: Echoes and empires
Audience: Ages 12 years and up. | Summary: Joss and Jericho team up with their greatest enemies—including two of the most powerful mages in the world— to bring an end to the queen's empire of lies.
Identifiers: LCCN 2022051265 (print) | LCCN 2022051266 (ebook)
ISBN 9780593351734 (hardcover) | ISBN 9780593351697 (epub)
Subjects: CYAC: Fantasy. | Magic—Fiction. | LCGFT: Fantasy fiction.
Classification: LCC PZ7.R347637 Le 2023 (print) | LCC PZ7.R347637 (ebook)
DDC [Fic]—dc23
LC record available at https://lccn.loc.gov/2022051265
LC ebook record available at https://lccn.loc.gov/2022051266

ISBN 9780593351734

Printed in the United States of America

BVG

1 3 5 7 9 10 8 6 4 2

Design by Rebecca Aidlin and Alex Campbell
Text set in Fournier MT Pro

To our memories,
the good and the bad, the happy and the sad.

ONE

The witch moved through the crowded restaurant, drawing the eye of everyone she passed. She had long, dark brown hair, pale white skin, and lips as scarlet red as the dress that hugged her slim body. Diamonds sparkled at her ears, throat, and wrists. She could easily pass for the young wife of a politician or businessman, meeting her friends for dinner. Most would view her as beautiful, elegant, fashionable, and entirely harmless.

They'd be dead wrong.

She didn't look to the left or right. Her attention was fixed on only one person.

Me.

I didn't try to smile. I didn't wave my hand in greeting. Instead, I focused on hiding my fear, since it wasn't the least bit helpful tonight.

My gaze shifted from the witch to the tall young man who accompanied her. Black eyes. Dark hair. Broad shoulders. A tense, square jaw. The tattoo of a dagger on the side of his neck, visible above the collar of his black leather coat. Contrary to the witch's benign appearance, most casual onlookers would immediately assume Jericho Nox was dangerous, and instinctively want to run in the opposite direction. For me, however, the relief at seeing the Blackheart stole the air right out of my lungs.

Shortly after we'd arrived in Cresidia, a city six hundred miles north of Ironport, Jericho had disappeared without a word. And then five long days had passed in utter silence. I'd convinced myself that his evil boss had punished him for failing his latest mission. Or worse . . . killed him. But then, earlier today, I received a message to meet him and the witch here tonight. Alone.

Jericho scanned the restaurant vigilantly, his expression impenetrable steel. The table I'd been taken to upon my arrival was in a private alcove set slightly apart from the rest of the restaurant, through a carved stone archway. Just beyond the archway, the restaurant bustled with waiters and, most importantly, a dining room full of patrons. There was no way I'd ever meet with this witch without knowing there were a hundred witnesses present.

She took a seat across from me, and I tensed. I'd be perfectly happy if tomorrow this witch was executed for her long list of heinous crimes. I'd make sure I had a front-row seat. Tonight, however, her death would do me no good at all. Elian needed her help. And, in more ways than I cared to admit, so did I.

"Jericho, please make the introductions." Her voice took me by surprise—it was as sweet and smooth as honey. I guess I'd expected her to sound as shrill and cruel as her reputation.

The Blackheart took the seat next to his boss. I tried to read his expression, but it gave me no clues as to where he'd been for five long days.

"Valery," he said evenly, and his familiar deep voice betrayed not even a whisper of emotion, "this is Josslyn Drake. Josslyn Drake, this is Valery."

He'd called me simply Drake so many times that my first name sounded strange on his lips. Not strange in a bad way. Just strange.

Valery gestured for a waiter to approach. He had a bottle of red wine already in hand, and he poured two glasses from it without being asked—one for me and one for her.

"I took the liberty of ordering this for us," she said.

"How thoughtful of you," I replied dryly. "No wine for Jericho?"

"I prefer that my employees don't drink alcohol."

"It's fine," Jericho said. "I'm not thirsty."

I wished that we'd had time to talk before this, to help me get my bearings when it came to meeting his boss. What she knew, what she wanted, what she planned to do next.

"Have you visited Cresidia before, Josslyn?" Valery asked when the waiter moved away from the table.

Small talk didn't seem to suit the occasion, but I'd do my best to endure it.

"No," I replied. "I've rarely traveled far from Ironport all my life. At least, not until recently."

Ironport was in South Regara, and Cresidia was in North Regara. While Ironport was straightlaced, business minded, and highly respectable with its gray-and-silver skyscrapers, and meticulously groomed green spaces, Cresidia was known more as a vacation destination—with luxury shopping, glittering hotels, and sandy beaches. I'd spent most of my time since our arrival on one of those beaches, staring out at the sparkling blue sea, piecing together everything I'd seen and learned over the last month that had shattered the life I'd always known into a million jagged pieces.

"The life of a prime minister's daughter," Valery mused. "How very limiting that must have been for you."

I fought to hold on to my calm expression. "Actually, my life felt quite limitless. Until last year, of course."

She nodded, her expression serene. "Yes, of course. My deepest condolences on your father's death."

My fingers itched to grab the steak knife in front of me and shove it through her eyeball, straight into her evil brain.

"I'm trying very hard to be polite to you," I said tightly. "Really, I am. But I'm sure you must understand why that's going to be a challenge for me."

She studied me for a moment, a glass of wine poised in her perfectly manicured hand. "Jericho tells me that you know everything."

"I know enough," I bit out. Then I chose to ignore her and focus on the Blackheart for a moment while I gathered my poise and control again. "Where have you been for the last five days?" I asked him bluntly.

Jericho blinked, his jaw tense. "There was something I needed to take care of."

"What?"

His black eyes flicked to mine, a silent warning in their depths. *"Something."*

"I needed Jericho to retrieve this for me," Valery said as she reached into her handbag to pull out an object, which she placed on the table. It was a small golden box covered in geometric etchings.

My breath caught at the sight of it, and my confused gaze shot to Jericho.

"You may explain," Valery said to him with a casual wave of her hand.

Something tight in his expression eased just a little as the Blackheart nodded. "Val wanted me to pay a quick visit to Tobin to get the memory box back. She'd heard through the grapevine that he was planning on selling it. He'd already put feelers out to see how much it was worth on the black market. I got there just in time to retrieve it."

"I thought you said it didn't matter," I said, my throat painfully tight. "That the memory magic could be contained inside any object."

"I was wrong," he replied.

I glared at him. "You were wrong?"

He shrugged. "It happens occasionally. Apparently, the symbols on the box are specific to this piece of contained magic in particular. Live and learn."

I realized then that the black leather coat Jericho currently wore was the same one that Tobin, a Queensguard who secretly worked for Valery—aka a traitor to the Empire—had forcibly taken from him. The box had been in his pocket at the time.

"Nice coat," I said.

"It sure is," he agreed. "Glad to have it back."

I wasn't sure I wanted to ask my next question, but I really wanted to know the answer. "And is Tobin . . . still alive?"

Jericho didn't speak for a moment. "I'm sure he's still alive in the hearts of the people who loved him. If those people actually exist, which I highly doubt. But generally speaking? No. Tobin is very dead."

I didn't have to ask how Tobin died. I could guess. By Valery's command. It was how she dealt with difficulties. She'd wanted the memory box stolen from the Queen's Gala by any means necessary. And now she had it, only three weeks past the original deadline. Missing its valuable and vitally important contents, of course. But she had it.

The witch watched me carefully for my reaction to all of this. Perhaps she expected me to be appalled or squeamish or frightened at the suggestion that Jericho had killed someone on her orders. She would be disappointed.

Tobin had shot Jericho in the chest and then shoved both of us into a walled prison without sparing a moment of concern for either of our fates. And I wouldn't spare a moment of concern for his.

So, now I had my answer about where Jericho had been for five days. Time to deal with the present and what it meant for my future.

"What did you tell her?" I asked Jericho.

He met my gaze directly, his expression now unreadable apart from a nearly imperceptible tightness along his jawline.

"Everything," he replied.

The single word held a mountain of gravity.

"Everything?" I repeated as calmly as I could, my heart pounding.

He nodded. "Part of my job, Drake. I told Val about our meeting with Rush, consulting with Lazos in the Queen's Keep, then learning about Elian and his rather unfortunate curse . . . and, of course, about you. She knows the memory magic's stuck in your head and that we haven't found a way to get it out so she can deliver the intact merchandise to her client. Also, that you've seen a variety of disturbing scenes of Lord Banyon's sordid past, including the night he burned the palace city to the ground."

Well, great. That pretty much summed it up.

"That's . . . a lot," I said uneasily.

"Indeed, it is," Valery agreed. "It must be fascinating to get such deep insight into the warlock's infamous past."

I almost laughed at that. Luckily, I wasn't in a laughing kind of mood.

"That depends on your definition of the word fascinating, doesn't it?" I replied.

"I suppose it does," she allowed with a nod.

I hated that my deepest, darkest secrets were already out on the table, and I hadn't been the one to control the narrative. Of course, I didn't blame Jericho for this. Valery controlled him with her magic—magic she'd literally carved into his skin two years ago—giving him very little free will when it came to resisting his boss's command.

"What exactly have you seen?" Valery asked.

"Lots," I replied, taking a moment to center myself. I watched the witch, trying to read her reaction to the revelation that the magic she wanted was stuck inside of me, but saw nothing alarming or reassuring. "Jericho told you that we tried to find a solution through Rush. Through Vander Lazos."

She nodded. "He did. But you still failed."

I bristled. "I didn't ask for this to happen. It's the last thing I ever would have wanted. Only three weeks ago, I believed that all magic was evil."

She raised a brow. "And now?"

"Now I know that magic is like a knife, only as deadly as the witch or warlock who uses it." It was an analogy that Jericho had used, and I found it helped me understand it much better. Elemental magic was benign, neutral. But people could choose to be evil.

"Mages," Valery said. "We call ourselves *mages*—both collectively and individually."

"Sure. Whatever you say." I didn't come here to be lectured. Still, I tucked the information into my constantly expanding mental file on the subject.

Valery now studied me with the curiosity of a hungry cat who'd cornered a helpless rabbit. "How frightening all this must be for someone who's been so protected from the world of magic all of her life."

"It's definitely been an education," I allowed. "Jericho said that he'd mentioned Elian to you."

"We're not talking about the prince right now. We're talking about you, Josslyn. You, and the problem you've created for me."

I bristled. "Not on purpose."

"That doesn't matter at this point. The result is the same as if you'd willfully stolen from me."

I took a breath and raised my chin. It required a great deal of effort for me to pretend that this woman wasn't ready, willing, and able to literally carve this magic out of my body. But I wasn't going to cower before her and beg for mercy. I knew how power worked, and if I showed her any fear, she would know she could control me as easily as she controlled Jericho.

"To me, there's a bigger problem than an impatient client," I said evenly. "If Jericho told you about Prince Elian, then you know that Queen Isadora is a liar, a hypocrite . . . and a murderer. She executes witches and warlocks—*mages*—who don't deserve to die."

Valery studied me. "I don't really care what Queen Isadora does or doesn't do."

I didn't even try to conceal my shock at this statement. "You don't?"

"No, I don't. What I care about is my business, my clients, and my reputation. I plan to meet with Prince Elian tomorrow to discuss his rather curious situation."

Well, that put it rather mildly, didn't it? I thought.

"Can you help him?" I asked aloud.

"I can't answer that question tonight. Tonight is about you,

Josslyn. More specifically about what you've witnessed of Lord Banyon's past."

"Why do you want to know?"

"Consider it a test."

I hated tests, always had. Especially ones I hadn't agreed to take in the first place.

"If you're so curious, you'll have to hire a witch—or mage— that has air and earth elementia to properly extract this magic," I told her evenly. "Then you're welcome to experience an echo or two for yourself, if you like."

"There's a problem, Drake," Jericho cut in. "Mages like that are incredibly rare. One in a million. Actually, more like one in a billion. The last one who fit that profile got himself killed during the raid on Banyon's compound two months ago. We think he was the one who created the box in the first place before it was confiscated with the rest of the warlock's treasures. Lazos was stringing us along, making us think there was a way out, and keeping us from learning he'd lost his magic after what happened with the prince. But Banyon's memories . . ." His expression turned grim. "Seems like they're stuck inside of you."

While I had accepted having a front-row seat for occasional, random flashes of the warlock's fascinating and frightening past, the thought that this was an ongoing issue without an end date wasn't welcome news.

"Shit," I whispered. I took a deep drink from my glass of wine, draining it in one gulp.

I already knew there was an alternate way to extract these

memories from me. My death. The unspoken threat of it now hung over the table like a foul odor.

"We'll find an answer," Jericho said. "I just need a little time. Where's your client right now, Val?"

"Here in Cresidia," she replied, sliding her index finger around the rim of her glass.

"Who would even know a box like this exists? Who would hire you to steal it in the first place?" I'd been trying to figure out the answer to this very important question since the very beginning. "If Banyon made this box, he would have kept it secret. He wouldn't want his memories falling into the wrong hands. Unless . . ." I kept coming back to the same hypothesis, again and again, since it clicked for me. "It's him, isn't it? Your client has to be Lord Banyon himself."

"Is that what you think?" Val cocked her head, seemingly amused by my guess.

"I'd know if Banyon was Val's client," Jericho said darkly.

"Would you?" I challenged.

"Yeah, I would."

Valery shook her head. "This only proves how very little you know about my world, Josslyn. How interconnected it is, how deep the valley goes. There are dozens of people, if not hundreds—including the queen herself—who would pay a fortune to access Lord Banyon's captured memories. The chance to see what he has seen; experience what he's experienced. All the delicious truth and none of the useless lies."

"Yeah, it's been a real treat for me so far," I replied dryly, then lifted my chin to meet her gaze directly. "Are you going to kill me to extract the magic for your client?"

Immediately, I felt the heat of Jericho's glare. I'm sure that he didn't like how blunt I was, but I needed to know, and dancing around questions like this wasn't going to get us anywhere.

"I've promised Jericho that I won't do any such thing, Josslyn," Valery replied. "He assures me that he will find a solution to our mutual problem."

"I will," Jericho confirmed.

He sounded far more confident than I felt, especially since his boss had all but confirmed she'd been considering murdering me.

Jericho knew Valery much better than I did. Two years ago, she'd literally given him a second chance at life, but indentured servitude had been the price. I wanted him to have the freedom to choose his own path, his own future, without being magically coerced to be a Blackheart—a thief, assassin, and general errand boy—for an evil witch with a long list of rich, corrupt clients.

An evil witch who was rumored to be an immortal goddess of death.

I wanted to scoff at such a fantastical and frightening possibility, but after everything I'd seen, everything I'd learned, my scoffing days were long over.

"Well, thanks," I allowed as casually as I could. "In the meantime, you need to help Prince Elian. You have that special dagger that makes all the difference when it comes to death magic. That's why I think you can help the prince break his curse."

"You told her about my dagger," Valery said.

"Didn't I mention that?" Jericho replied.

"No."

"Must have slipped my mind."

"Clearly." Valery was silent for a moment. "Josslyn, why do you care if the prince is cured of his unfortunate . . . ailment?"

Many reasons, but I wasn't going to go into all of them here and now. "Because he's the flesh-and-blood proof that the queen has done exactly what she condemns others to death for."

"You want to destroy the Empire."

I considered that for a moment. "No, just the queen."

"And then, what? Prince Elian will take the throne and ensure that the hidden truth about mages and elementia is finally revealed to the world?"

I shrugged. "I'm not thinking that far ahead at the moment. Right now, all I want is for Elian to be restored to his former princely self. And I firmly believe you can do that for him."

Valery poured herself more wine. No food had come to the table, not even any bread. I could smell braised chicken and roasted garlic, delicious scents just beyond the curtained alcove, as tables of patrons enjoyed meals that would make my mouth water if this had been any other night. A violinist strolled casually through the restaurant while playing a pleasant melody that I barely heard. My focus didn't stray from the witch for a single moment as I waited for her to speak again.

"Tell me about the echoes, Josslyn," she finally said. "Tell me exactly what you've witnessed. The fire sixteen years ago? I've never personally dealt with memory magic before, and that infamous night fascinates me. Let's start there, shall we?"

We were back to this. It felt like I'd seen everything from

Banyon's past, but I knew it was only bits and pieces of the gigantic puzzle of the queen's fiercest and most dangerous enemy. A warlock who'd pledged his life to destroying the Empire and giving power and freedom back to those who could channel elemental magic.

I glanced at Jericho to see that his expression had tensed at the mention of that night—the night that claimed the lives of his parents, who'd perished in the blaze, orphaning him and his younger brother.

My gut told me to hold back, to not reveal much to this witch. She knew too many of my secrets already. "He summoned fire magic to escape his imprisonment. It got out of control. The queen says that Elian died that night, but he didn't. He was resurrected by Vander Lazos two weeks prior to the fire. That's pretty much it."

"I see. That is a start, I suppose. Now, I'd like to show you something." Valery reached into her handbag again, pulling out a dagger, which she placed next to the memory box in front of her. It was fully gold, and the length of a dinner plate, with symbols etched deeply into the sharp blade.

For a moment, I couldn't believe my eyes.

"Is this it?" I whispered.

"Yes," she confirmed.

The confirmation momentarily stunned me silent, and I sat there in sudden and utter awe of this ancient piece of dangerous magic. I felt something from it—a tingling sensation that I could only compare to static electricity, but more of a pleasant awareness than anything that could ever be described as painful.

It reminded me of what I'd felt when I'd first come across the memory box at the Queen's Gala.

"This dagger's true origins are a mystery, even to me," Valery said. "All I know for sure is that it helps to strengthen and hone my natural-born magic. It also works as a useful tool to pull the truth from unwilling lips."

I shook my head to clear it, drawing in a deep breath as I placed my hands on either side of my untouched plate, and forced myself to meet the witch's gaze. I had to keep my head clear and not allow myself to become distracted by shiny, golden things.

"The truth is my goal, Valery," I said firmly. "And, I believe, if you'll help Elian—"

I didn't even see her move until it was already over. And I didn't feel any pain until the blood began to flow, bright red in the candlelight.

My blood.

I stared down at the golden blade that now pinned my hand to the table.

Jericho was on his feet. "Valery, what the hell are you doing?"

"Sit down," Valery hissed. "Now."

Jericho sat down heavily in his seat, as if he had no choice.

I frantically met his gaze. "Wh-what—?" I managed, but I couldn't raise my voice above a raspy whisper. I couldn't summon the breath to scream for help.

"Look at me, Josslyn," Valery said.

Not a single person even glanced over toward our alcoved section of the restaurant. Conversation continued without missing a beat. Waiters delivered platters of food and drinks to tables without slowing a step. No one realized what had just happened to me.

I tried to speak again, but now I couldn't find enough air to form a single word. I only felt the searing agony of the sharp blade impaling my hand.

"Enough, Valery," Jericho snarled. "You said you wouldn't hurt her."

"No, I said I wouldn't kill her," Valery said evenly. "I command you to be silent, Jericho. You know it's torture to resist, so don't bother trying." The witch then met my pained gaze. "Tell me everything you saw the night of the palace fire and leave nothing out."

Hot tears splashed to my cheeks. I grasped my wrist, trying to hold my pinned hand steady. The pain made it hard to think or process anything. I couldn't stop shivering, and black dots swam at the sides of my vision. For a moment, I was sure I'd pass out, but the irresistible pull of Valery's voice kept me conscious.

I'd had no intention of telling her more about the echo—or series of echoes—I'd experienced from the night of the fire. But her words now had weight to them, a weight I could feel down to my very bones. A razor-sharp sensation dug into my throat, wrenching my attention away from my hand.

The words gushed out of my mouth as I told her what I'd seen—watching as Banyon moved down the streets of the palace city, leaving fire and carnage behind him. And earlier, before the fire, when he'd still been imprisoned—faced with the queen who hated him for refusing to raise her heir from the dead as she believed he could.

"Elian is Lord Banyon's son," I told her. "It's the queen's darkest secret. One of them, anyway."

"Jericho told me that already," she said, dismissing this epic revelation with a flick of her hand. "You said that Lord Banyon's wife and infant daughter were brought before him."

I jerked my head in a nod. "It was her revenge—she had High Commander Norris cut his wife's throat in front of him. And—the daughter . . . Banyon's daughter . . ."

Stop! I told myself. *Don't say any more!*

"Did the queen have the child killed as well?" the witch asked.

Fighting the urge to reply was like holding fire in my mouth and allowing the answer to burn straight through my tongue.

"No," I gasped as hot tears slid down my cheeks.

Jericho gripped the edge of the table, his knuckles white. "Damn it, Val. Stop this. What difference does it make sixteen years later?"

"I'd think that you'd want to know everything about that night, Jericho."

"Not like this."

"Tell me more about the child." Valery's words penetrated my mind just as her dagger penetrated my flesh and bone.

"She had a birthmark—a heart-shaped birthmark." I couldn't stop myself from brushing my fingers against my neck.

"Like yours," Valery said.

"Exactly like mine." I coughed and felt a trickle of hot blood slide over my bottom lip. "It was me. I'm Banyon's daughter. He believed they killed both me and my birth mother, so he lost his mind with grief and burned down the city and everything in his path. That—that's all I saw of that night."

Jericho's eyes were wide with shock. Tears blurred my vision, and I had no strength left to say another word. I'd said enough. So much more than enough.

Valery nodded. "Remember this lesson, Josslyn, and it won't have to hurt this much in the future." She stood in a single graceful motion, sweeping her long dark hair over one shoulder. "Bring Prince Elian to me tomorrow, Jericho. I look forward to speaking with him."

Jericho didn't say anything for a painfully long moment. "What about Lord Banyon's daughter here?"

The edge of a cool smile touched her lips. "Bring her too."

With that, the witch yanked the golden dagger out of my flesh and bone, turned her back on my shriek of agony, and left the restaurant.

TWO

"Meeting's over," Jericho said. "We're out of here."

Before I could say—or shriek—anything in response, the Blackheart had me on my feet and headed for the exit. He grabbed a white linen napkin and wrapped it around my bloody hand. Moments later, we were outside the restaurant and in the cool evening air. I wasn't sure how my feet were still moving, how I was still vertical, but I was. Jericho gripped my upper arm, directing us down a wide cobblestone sidewalk full of well-dressed pedestrians leisurely moving in every direction, with the gentle sound of live guitar music floating through the air.

Jericho knew the truth.

Of course, I'd meant to tell him. But I hadn't found the right moment before he disappeared. No one knew my secret, except for Elian. Between the pain in my hand and the guilt of what I'd been forced to reveal, I couldn't find the words to speak. A truly rare occurrence for Josslyn Drake.

But I needed to know where we were headed. Where would a trained assassin who'd been raised from the dead take the secret daughter of his worst enemy?

"Where are we going?" I forced out after a few minutes.

"Somewhere" was his curt reply.

Clearly. But he didn't elaborate, and I currently didn't have the strength to press for more information. It wasn't long until we arrived at a building lit up by thousands of flashing pink and white lights, and a sign declaring its name DELUXE. Well-dressed men and women stood on the front steps, laughing and talking loudly amongst themselves. A few of them glanced over with frowns as I clumsily staggered up the steps, with only Jericho's grip keeping me from sprawling unceremoniously in front of them.

Moments later, we were inside a crowded, smoky interior with a massive crystal chandelier hanging from a ceiling three stories high. The Blackheart then guided me into what looked like a banquet hall. Dozens of round tables, flowing bottles of wine and spirits, loud, upbeat music, and thunderous applause directed at the raised stage at the far left. On the stage, a half-dozen beautiful women performed a synchronized dance in front of an orchestra while holding fans made from long, colorful feathers. They blew kisses to the audience when they finished and were met with enthusiastic cheers.

Jericho brought me closer to the stage, signaling toward one of the dancers. She immediately left the others to disappear offstage, only to reappear a few seconds later pulling a diaphanous shawl over her sexy, sequined costume. She appeared to be in her early twenties with light brown skin and black hair drawn back from her pretty face in a high, tight ponytail. Her eyes were thickly lined with black coal, and her lips were coated in vividly fuchsia gloss.

"Jericho Nox," she said, without even glancing at me. "It's good to see you."

"Likewise," he replied. "I need a favor, Daria."

"Oh?"

"My acquaintance here is in immediate need of your expertise. Can you help?"

Finally, Daria scanned me with disinterest until she got to my bloody, wrapped hand. Then her eyes widened. "What happened?"

Jericho answered for me. "Valery happened."

Daria drew in a sharp breath. "You know I don't get involved in Valery's business."

"I promise, she won't mind this one time."

Still, she looked squeamish at the prospect. "You promise?"

"Cross my heart."

It still took her a minute. "Fine," she said reluctantly. "Let's make it quick. I'm back onstage in fifteen minutes."

"You are the best," Jericho told her.

"Yes, I am. You owe me one. But don't worry, I know you're good for it." Daria punctuated this statement by grabbing the Blackheart's coat, pulling him closer, and kissing him passionately on his lips.

When she was done, Daria hooked an arm through mine. My first inclination was to resist, but I didn't. My hand burned. And something in my heart was burning at witnessing their kiss. Which was ridiculous, of course. Jericho and me . . . well, there *wasn't* a Jericho and me. Not officially, anyway. Sure, I'd started to feel something for him while we'd been in the Queen's Keep, and there *had* been that incredibly memorable kiss between us.

But there had also been a seemingly endless series of problems we'd been forced to endure together, and tonight's was only the latest on the list.

Seeing him kiss Daria was a good reminder that Jericho already had a life here. And that life, of course, included other girls. Other beautiful girls.

Other beautiful girls that were not me.

I'd known the Blackheart for a very short time—only a few weeks. Therefore, I chose to believe that the sharp kick I felt in my chest wasn't caused by jealousy. It had to be bonus pain from getting stabbed by an evil witch. That was all.

Besides, he'd just learned that I was Lord Banyon's daughter. I should probably be grateful that he hadn't turned his back on me the moment we left the restaurant.

Daria led me away from the banquet room and into a small vacant room at the end of a hallway. Jericho trailed behind us.

"Sit here," she said, directing me to an emerald-green leather sofa in front of a huge, gilded mirror.

The sickly-looking, pale-faced girl staring at me confused me for a moment until I realized it was me. The blue of my contact lenses was a near perfect match to my regular eye color. I took them out only to clean them and had worn them without fail to cover the amber shade my eyes had turned after being infected by memory magic. Amber, honey brown, molten gold—it depended on the moment, the time of day, and whether I'd just channeled the memory magic to experience an echo. It was proof of the magic trapped inside of me. Most people instinctively ignored such physical signs of contained magic out of subconscious self-protection or plain old ignorance. But some did know what it meant. And for that reason, and for my own safety, I continued to wear the blue contacts when in public.

Daria unwrapped the bloody napkin as I cringed and gritted my teeth. I didn't want to look, but I couldn't help myself. All I saw was a mess of red gore. Jagged, torn flesh. And, even more horrifying, the glistening white edge of bone. A wave of nausea hit me, and I gagged.

"Are you trained in first aid?" I asked weakly, when I managed to compose myself.

Daria laughed. "Hardly."

"Daria's a witch," Jericho offered. "She can summon earth magic."

A witch.

My first impulse was to pull away from her. As much as I'd learned about magic these last few weeks, it was difficult to forget seventeen years of fear that had been burned into me.

"Like Tamara," I finally said.

"Similar," he agreed.

"Who's Tamara?" asked Daria.

"A witch who healed me recently," Jericho told her. "Bullet to the chest. Nearly died. I won't go into the gory details."

Daria's eyes widened. "You're lucky you found someone so powerful to help you."

"Can't argue with that."

She shook her head. "I'm not nearly that powerful."

"You underestimate yourself."

"Just being realistic. Luckily, this isn't a bullet through the chest. I'll do what I can." Daria sighed as she straightened my fingers. I swallowed down a cry of pain. She studied my face, frowning. "You're Josslyn Drake, aren't you?"

I tensed, a breath catching in my chest. "No, not me. I'm told I look like her a bit. I wish. I mean, she's gorgeous. Right?"

There was a time, not so long ago, when being recognized would have thrilled me. Times sure had changed.

Jericho groaned. "It doesn't matter if she knows who you are, Drake."

I shot him a glare. "Doesn't it?"

"Do you want her to heal you or not?"

"Of course I do."

"Then, just . . . roll with it."

"I'm rolling," I bit out. "Watch me roll."

"Great."

Daria shook her head. "Don't worry, I won't tell anyone that the former First Daughter is here at Deluxe, especially not with someone like Jericho. I mean, who would believe me?"

"Vaguely insulted by that," Jericho grumbled.

"Are you ready?" Daria asked me.

When I nodded, she pressed my mangled hand gently between her palms, closed her eyes, and a soft golden light began to emanate from her touch. I watched this warily, my heart beating triple time at being this close to someone channeling healing earth magic.

I'd seen it before when Tamara had healed Jericho in the Keep. I knew she wasn't evil, that this magic wasn't evil or harmful or destructive, so I tried to lean into this, to embrace it.

The only problem was, I hadn't properly prepared myself for a fresh onslaught of agony.

Daria's summoned elementia entered my wound, and it was as if I'd voluntarily plunged my hand into a pot of boiling water. I cried out and tried to pull away from her.

"If you don't want to have a nasty scar, then you need to hold still," she urged.

Before I could yelp out anything in reply, a different golden light appeared. This was just as familiar to me, even more so than the healing magic. It was the bright golden smoke that signaled an incoming echo.

I'd feared this magic. I'd dreaded this magic. And, slowly, I'd come to grudgingly accept this magic, since I knew it wouldn't hurt me if I didn't fight it. It only ever wanted to show me something important, even if I wasn't ready to see it.

One thing I knew about the memory magic, though, was that it refused to be ignored. It would make me experience an echo whether I wanted to or not.

So, even now, even as the witch attempted to heal my injured hand, I didn't try to resist as the sparkling, smoky ribbon engulfed me in mere moments, spinning me away from the hallway, away from Deluxe, to another place and time. My head swam and I tried to shake it, tried to get my bearings. The pain had vanished completely, and my hand now appeared undamaged. But I knew this wasn't real. An echo was like walking through someone else's dream. It didn't change reality. It merely opened a window to the past.

The scene before me cleared, the golden smoke receded, and

I found myself in an unexpectedly familiar room. It was the large study at the prime minister's residence, which had floor-to-ceiling windows that gave a beautiful view of the expansive and well-manicured gardens at the back of the building. Currently, it was night, so little could be seen outside apart from the thick foliage under a black sky studded with stars. But it wasn't the room that stole my breath; it was the two people who stood before me.

My father—the only father I'd ever known—Louis Drake, dressed in a stiff, tailored tuxedo, a stern and displeased look on his face, which was most certainly caused by the person he faced.

Me.

"This dress is perfect just as it is," I was telling him, my hands clenched at my sides.

"It's too short and it's too tight. You're only sixteen years old, Josslyn."

"I know how old I am!"

"You're representing the Empire tonight. As my daughter, you're representing Her Majesty herself. There will be reporters there. Photographers." He rubbed a hand over his forehead, clearly frustrated. "I don't have time for this. Not now. Choose something more appropriate; we're leaving in ten minutes."

"I hate you!" With that, the sixteen-year-old version of myself stomped out of the study. I cringed at the painful sound of the three thoughtless words that would haunt me to this very day.

It was the night of the Queen's Gala. Last year's Queen's Gala.

The night my father had died.

Even then, even during our fight about my short, sexy dress,

I knew he'd been stressed about something other than my fashion choices. I'd assumed it was because he despised social gatherings like this, the same ones I adored. It was his duty to attend, but it was my time to shine—the more reporters and photographers, the better.

Seeing this scene unfold before me had stunned me for a moment, but now I realized that it didn't make sense. This was *my* memory, not Lord Banyon's.

But how was that possible if these were *his* echoes?

Uneasily, I turned to search the corners of the dark room where I knew he had to be hiding.

When the door slammed behind the younger version of me, another door opened—a door leading to a small storage room—and Lord Banyon stepped forward into the meager light.

My gaze shot to my father, who, shockingly, didn't seem the least bit surprised by the warlock's sudden presence in his private study.

"I'm sorry you had to witness that," Louis Drake said wearily.

"She's very willful," Banyon replied.

"That she is."

"But you love her."

"With all my heart and all my soul."

Banyon nodded. "Her words are only those of a rebellious teenager. Don't take them to heart."

"I never do." My father chuckled and shook his head. "It's not the first time she's said such things to me. I know she doesn't mean it."

"I'm glad to hear that."

I listened to them in a haze. This couldn't be real. It had to be some sort of figment of my imagination. Perhaps I'd passed out from the pain of the healing magic, and this was only a dream. My father and Lord Banyon didn't know each other. They *couldn't* have known each other, not well enough for him to visit my father at his home, and not while I'd been standing in the same room with them!

"She doesn't get such stubbornness from either myself or Evelyne," my father said, and sighed. "She must have inherited it from you."

Banyon's lips quirked. "You think I'm stubborn, Louis?"

"You're the most stubborn person I've ever met in my life. If you weren't, you wouldn't have come here tonight."

"I didn't want to wait another day to show you this." Banyon drew a folded piece of paper out of his jacket pocket and placed it in front of my father, where he now sat at his desk.

My father scanned the writing on the page, frowning deeply. "Is this what I think it is?"

Banyon nodded. "Just as I've always believed, the queen and her predecessors have perpetuated the claim that mages make up only a minuscule percentage of the population. But it's a lie. This list is only a small sampling of family bloodlines that are touched by magic. You recognize a few names immediately, don't you?"

"I do indeed," my father said grimly.

"Royal council members, members of Parliament, wealthy, personal friends of Issy herself. All potential mages." Banyon tapped the paper urgently. "Issy hides this secret—she protects those who have value to her, while condemning those who don't."

My father shook his head. "Names written on a page mean nothing. This isn't inarguable proof."

"That's why I need your help. You're close to her, closer than anyone else. She trusts you. She considers you family after all this time. You can learn more, find more tangible evidence that I'm right about this."

My father stood up and turned toward the window, his arms crossed over his chest. "She would have me executed for treason if she believed I'd had even a single conversation with you. And this is most certainly treason that you're suggesting."

"No, this is fixing what has been broken for centuries. If I'm right, there are witches and warlocks out there who have no idea who and what they truly are, who fully believe the Empire's lies, who would not even give a moment's attention to a spark of magic within themselves for fear of the repercussions. I believe that there are hundreds of thousands—perhaps even millions—of mages in the Empire. And if they knew the truth, if they learned that the queen they serve would execute them for something they can't even control—well, that's the kind of thing that can irrevocably change a person's perspective. That can put them on the right side of history. *Our* side, Louis. A truth like this can't be concealed forever. A truth like this can't be rewritten or erased. It will eventually be revealed one way or the other. And it must be revealed if we are to put a stop to the queen's tyranny. The moment you learned what she did to Elian, what she allows my son to do when his hunger rises . . ." Banyon hissed out a breath. "You know that this can't continue, Louis."

My father remained utterly silent for several long, heavy moments, his expression haunted.

"I want to tell Josslyn the truth about you," he said quietly. "And I want to tell her tonight."

Banyon inhaled sharply. "Based on what I just witnessed, she's still far too young and immature to understand."

My father shook his head. "You don't know her like I do."

"You'd really want to burden her with a truth like this?"

"A truth like this can't be hidden forever," my father said, echoing Banyon's previous words.

"She's not my daughter anymore," Banyon said firmly. "She's yours. I made my peace with that a long time ago. Do what you must when it comes to Josslyn. And do what you must when it comes to finding the proof required to expose the palace's lies. I have work of my own to do now." He pressed his hands to either side of his head. "There's something here, locked in my memories. Something big, something beyond even what I have begun to understand through my investigation of these bloodlines."

My father frowned. "Memories are faulty at best."

"In their original container, they certainly are," Banyon agreed. "But there are other means of objectively accessing the past. I know one thing for sure, and I've known it for years: Issy holds tightly on to a secret, a secret that I believe could shatter the Empire. I plan to discover exactly what that secret is while there's still time."

"Still time?" my father asked.

Banyon's jaw tightened. He seemed to be deliberating whether to answer. "I'm dying," he said finally. "This disease is incurable, even through magical means."

Silence fell for several heavy moments.

"How long do you have left?" my father said grimly.

"Long enough for me to end Issy's reign, one way or the other." Banyon raised his chin. "Choose your side, Louis. You are either with me, or you're against me. But know this: nothing—*nothing*—will stop me now."

Before I could hear my father's answer to that chilling statement and ultimatum, the golden smoke swept in and swept me away in mere moments, and I found myself in the hallway with Daria still holding on to my left hand.

I looked up at her, stunned by what I'd just witnessed.

"Your nose is bleeding," Daria said, alarmed.

"Drake?" Jericho asked, frowning. "Did you just . . . ?"

I nodded shakily as I quickly wiped my hand under my nose. A light nosebleed was a normal side effect of channeling the memory magic.

It wasn't a dream. It was most definitely an echo. My father . . . and Banyon—they'd been working together against the queen. The warlock was aware that I was his daughter. And a year ago, Banyon knew he was dying from an incurable disease.

It was only then that I realized I was healed—apart from a pale pink scar on the back of my hand and on my palm. I stared down in amazement, running my fingers over where the wound had been, then flexing and unflexing my fist. There was no pain. No indication, other than the thin line of the scars, that it had been a mangled mess only minutes ago.

"I'm sorry I wasn't able to avoid leaving a mark," Daria said, chewing her bottom lip.

"It's okay," I assured her, although my mind was still a million miles away. "What you did is absolutely incredible. Thank you."

And I really did mean it. I knew that a couple of small scars were a small price to pay for surviving Valery's dagger.

"Anything for a friend of Jericho's," she said, smiling now.

"Thanks, Daria," Jericho said warmly. "You're a lifesaver. Or . . . a hand-saver, anyway."

"You're very welcome." She seemed to be waiting for more from him, perhaps another kiss, but when none came, she said her goodbyes and left us to return to the stage.

"Let's go, Drake," Jericho said with much less warmth in his voice now. "I'll take you back to the motel."

I was about to tell him I needed a minute to recover from my first personal experience with earth magic and from the ground-shaking echo, but then I realized he was already walking away from me. His bedside manner sure left a lot to be desired.

I finally caught up to him in the crowded, chandeliered foyer, which I now realized was a bar—long black-lacquered bar tops lined either side, with bartenders handing out wine and cocktails to their patrons. Still, Jericho didn't slow his steps, and it wasn't long before we were outside of Deluxe, headed toward the city square, a man-made park in the exact center of Cresidia. I tried to hold my tongue for as long as I could, knowing that he wasn't going to be in a great mood after the revelation of earlier this evening, but I needed to talk to him.

"Jericho, stop for a minute, would you?" I grabbed his arm, which was as hard and tense as steel.

He reluctantly turned to face me. "What?"

"I need to tell you about the echo I just experienced, because . . . well, I definitely need a second opinion on it."

He spread his hands. "So, we're just going to pretend that everything is normal between us, Drake?"

I needed this out of the way. I needed to deal with this so we could move on, which I hoped was still possible, even though I was afraid it wasn't.

"I'm not sure that normal's a word I'd use to describe either of us," I replied.

"At least we agree on that much."

"I know I should have told you." I wrung my hands and began to pace in front of the famous gigantic water fountain that was shown in nearly every travel advertisement for the city. Toss a coin; make a wish. I didn't have any coins, but I had plenty of wishes for it if I did.

Jericho hissed out a breath. "When did you learn the truth?"

He wasn't trying to change the subject or walk away from me. I took it as an encouraging sign. "At the palace. The first night, before your interrogation. I didn't know before that; I never would have guessed it in a million years."

He took this in. "So, this means that Elian's your brother."

I nodded. "Half brother."

"Does he know?"

"He knew before I did. He's overheard a lot of things over

the years, things he probably wasn't meant to overhear. This was one of them." I raised my chin. "Do you hate me now?"

Jericho frowned at me. "Why would I hate you?"

"Because you hate Banyon."

"Not sure what that has to do with you." He sighed at my pointed look. "No, Drake, I don't hate you. It sure would make everything a lot easier if I did, though. Would I have liked to hear the truth from you before my boss violently forced it out of you with her magic knife? Sure. Do I get why you didn't want to share this brand-new revelation about your family tree with me? Completely." He hissed out a breath, and his black-eyed gaze locked with mine. "I get it, you know. I had a big secret I didn't want share with you either. Remember?"

My throat thickened. "I remember."

His jaw was tight, and he turned to study the fountain. "You should hate me for that."

"I don't hate you, Jericho. I already told you it was Ambrose who killed my father. You resisted Valery's command as much as you could, and it would have been enough for him to live through that night. You aren't the reason he's dead."

"Ambrose," he bit out. "Piece of shit, that guy."

"Huge and steaming," I readily agreed. "Don't worry, I haven't forgotten about him for a moment. He'll pay for what he did."

Jericho eyed people passing by who were enjoying the night, oblivious to our comments about the current prime minister. On the side of a tall hotel to our left was a massive, spotlighted billboard advertising the Queensgames, now only a month away.

"Tell me about the echo," he said.

Something tight inside of me eased by a fraction. "Banyon was . . . he was working with my father. Trying to, anyway. He was trying to get proof of his theory that there's a larger percentage of people who are from a magical bloodline in the Empire than the queen claims. Many of them are in the queen's social circle and even in her council. It's not the random scattering that she's made everyone believe. That's, like, a lie that's been cultivated for generations. And he thought that if he could speak to those people, maybe he could convince them that the queen was wrong, if they knew they would be executed despite doing nothing wrong."

"Louis Drake and Lord Banyon were working together," Jericho said in disbelief.

"It's a surprise," I allowed.

"To say the least."

"But it's true. I saw it with my own eyes."

"How did Banyon think he could prove something like this?" he asked.

"He had a list, but my father said it didn't prove anything. Then Banyon said something about memories, and how to make them less faulty—he didn't say it explicitly, but clearly he was thinking about making the memory box. He believes there's a huge secret locked away somewhere in his memories, a secret that the queen is keeping—one that could change everything."

"So that's why he made the box. Thought it was only vanity, or whatever. Seems like he was planning to go on a hunt through his own past to find this secret. Any clue what it is?"

I shook my head. "Other than the truth about Elian . . . but that can't be it, because Banyon already knew about him. And a handful of other people did too—even my father did." I paused. "I think that was why he even took a meeting with Banyon. He learned what the queen was doing and he couldn't accept it. He might have been her prime minister for nearly two decades, but my father wasn't evil. I know in my heart he never would have wanted to intentionally hurt anyone."

"Unlike Ambrose," Jericho said.

"Yeah. Unlike Ambrose." My mood darkened several shades at the mention of that monster's name again, but I pushed away my hatred for him since it didn't help me at the moment. "Have there been any sightings of Banyon since the raid on his compound two months ago?"

Jericho shook his head. "None that I've heard of. Why?"

"He told my father that he was dying from an incurable disease." I swallowed hard. "That was more than a year ago now."

"When was this echo you experienced?" he asked.

"The night of . . . last year's Gala." I absently ran my fingers over the new scar on my palm, the pain from the wound now only a distant memory. "I saw myself in the echo, Jericho. My father wanted me to change my dress. And I told him I hated him." I drew in a shaky breath. "When I left, he told Banyon that he knew I didn't mean it."

"Of course you didn't." The Blackheart's gaze grew haunted, and he shook his head. "I'm sorry, Drake. I'm so sorry that you had to experience the night of his death again."

"Me too," I agreed heavily. "But because that night happened,

I'm standing here with you tonight knowing the truth, and with Banyon's memories stuck in my head."

Memories that he thought held the answer to exposing the queen's lies.

"Best not to think about any of that tonight, Drake."

I almost laughed. "Sure. Easier said than done."

"Got to rest up for meet-and-greet number two with the boss, remember?"

"How could I forget?" I replied tightly.

We left the city square, and I let my thoughts drift until we reached the nondescript, definitely *not* luxurious gray stone hotel I'd been staying in—with three rooms paid in full by Jericho just before he'd disappeared.

"I'll be back at noon," he said. "Goodnight, Drake."

When he turned away from me, I grabbed his hand to stop him. "Wait."

He eyed me warily. "Something more to say?"

My breath caught at the feel of his warm skin in the cool night. There was a lot still to say between us—we'd only just scratched the surface. But that wasn't why I'd stopped him. Something had occurred to me.

"The night at the palace when I saw the truth about . . . me," I said. "About Banyon . . ."

He waited, his brow furrowed. "What about it?"

"That memory was a serious shock in too many ways to count, but I wanted the truth. I . . . I asked for the truth, and the truth is what I got. Maybe I have more control over these echoes than I think I do. Maybe I can find the secret for myself."

"Maybe." Jericho considered this. "But even if you could flip through fifty-plus years of that warlock's memories like some ancient paper book, how would you even know where to start?"

"Excellent question," I had to admit. "And, to be fair, the echo at the palace might have just been a fluke and I didn't really summon it at all. Pretty much every memory has been a truth bomb, but this one just hit differently."

He shook his head. "I don't know, Drake. Maybe you can control this magic. Maybe you can't. I'm not exactly an expert on the subject."

When it came to experts on the subject of magic within a fifty-mile radius, only one currently came to mind. "Valery might be able to help me," I ventured.

Jericho raised a brow. "Val nearly killed you tonight."

"She stabbed me. She didn't kill me." Still, even though the pain was completely gone, I shuddered at the fresh memory. "She seemed very interested in learning more about the memory magic, to put it mildly. What did she call it? A test? And . . . I am seeing her again tomorrow, aren't I?"

He studied my hand, lit only by a flickering streetlamp, his brows drawn together. My breath caught as he ran his thumb along the scar on my palm, which I might always have to remind me of tonight.

Finally, his gaze locked with mine. "Sorry to break it to you, but Val's not going to volunteer to be your magic tutor, Drake, if that's what you're thinking."

I shrugged. "Then it'll have to be you. Go get some tips from your boss, and then you can help me start sorting through Banyon's echoes. Also, you need to find out if anyone's seen the warlock in the last two months."

He eyed me, bemused. "Gee, let me write all this down before I forget your order. Anything else?"

The final words of tonight's echo repeated in my ears.

"I'm dying. This disease is incurable, even through magical means."

"How long do you have left?"

"Long enough for me to end Issy's reign, one way or the other."

"Maybe there's a reason there have been no recent reported sightings of Banyon," I whispered. "Maybe he's already dead."

"I hope he's not," Jericho replied grimly.

I eyed him with surprise. "Really?"

"Really." He pushed a smile to his lips, although there wasn't a single shred of humor in his pitch-black eyes. "If he's dead, that steals my chance to rip out his heart while it's still beating. That's been my shiny, happy dream for sixteen long years. His being your birth father doesn't change that in the slightest."

My chest tightened. "Jericho . . ."

"Get some sleep, Drake."

The Blackheart turned and walked away from me, disappearing into the darkness.

THREE

My mind refused to let me sleep, instead going over the events and revelations of the night. As jarring as it had been to realize that my father and Banyon were acquainted and possibly working together, it gave me the sense of clarity I'd desperately needed.

The memory magic I'd originally seen as a curse could hold the answers to questions that few had ever dared to ask. If I did have control over the echoes, then I needed to find what Banyon was searching for.

Sure. Simple.

Well, maybe not, but it was a glimmer of hope. I could become an agent of change. I was a rebel, working against the queen. A champion of the truth.

I liked the sound of that.

I didn't blame Jericho for wanting Banyon dead, even knowing there was more to the warlock's story, that he wasn't just an evil villain who indiscriminately killed innocent people. I wanted to make Ambrose pay for my father's death, not to try to understand why he'd hired Valery to have him assassinated.

Forgiveness wasn't an option for me when it came to him, and it never would be. So, I absolutely understood how Jericho felt.

Banyon might already be dead. Logically, it seemed like the most likely answer. But somehow, I didn't think he was. Despite what Valery had said to deflect the question, I still wondered if he was here, in Cresidia. Jericho disagreed, but this answer made the most sense to me when it came to the warlock.

No matter where Banyon was, right now, I was the one with his memories in my head. Vander Lazos had given me a few meager lessons on elementia when I'd been stuck in the Keep, including how to keep from drowning in the memory magic. I'd initially tried everything in my power to resist it, but that only made the proverbial tidal wave higher and more powerful. He'd suggested mindfulness and patience—two things I didn't come by naturally, even on a good day. But I'd started to lean into it when I saw the golden smoke approaching, and that had helped ever since.

If I'd summoned the truth about my birth father and mother that night at the palace, then it had to be possible for me to control the echoes. What little I knew about memory magic told me that it was meant for reliving certain memories, not being randomly hit with them when you least expected it.

If it was possible, then I needed to figure it out. And quickly.

I spent most of the night trying to summon an echo at will, just as I had at the palace. I sat in front of the mirror, staring into my own eyes. I'd taken out the blue contact lenses so they were their current golden color.

"Show me the truth," I said to my reflection. "Show me the queen's secret."

I repeated this for an hour—even lighting a candle and staring at the dancing flame, which seemed to have been a trigger for summoning echoes for me before—until the only thing that happened was that my eyes watered and my head started to hurt.

Frustrated, I shifted my focus to spend some time trying to sense the natural-born elementia within myself. I was Banyon's biological daughter, after all. He, infamously, was the most powerful and feared warlock in the Empire. And a witch had very recently told me that she could sense magic in me too. It only made sense—I was part of his bloodline, after all.

Banyon could summon a powerful inferno. But, after hours of concentration, I couldn't even seem to summon a spark. By then, I wasn't sure if I was disappointed or relieved by this result. A mixture of the two, for sure.

Maybe I wasn't a witch after all. And maybe what had happened at the palace was a fluke and I was nothing more than the current container for this magic, just like the golden box had been.

I studied myself in the mirror, alarmed by the disappointment on my face.

"It's okay," I reassured myself. "We'll try again tomorrow."

The next morning, at exactly one minute to noon, I left my minuscule and entirely forgettable motel room and stepped into the bright light of day. The first person I saw was Jericho, currently engrossed in a conversation with his brother by the metal gate leading to the main street.

Viktor glanced over at me and gave me a curt nod, which I returned. Seeing them standing together like this reminded me how similar they were in so many ways—both tall, dark haired, and painfully attractive. Viktor, however, had his hair cropped shorter, his face clean shaven, and absolutely no tattoos visible.

I'd come to much prefer the brother with the tattoo.

"What do you think they're talking about?" A familiar voice drew my attention to my left, where Elian leaned against a wire fence. My half brother's hair was a few shades darker blond than mine. His irises were as dark as Jericho's, which reflected the extra helping of death magic he'd been given six-teen years ago. He had a naturally royal air about him, like someone born to privilege and affluence, who'd never wanted for a single thing in his life.

"Probably you," I answered honestly. "Are you sure you want to meet with Valery today?"

"I'm sure." His brows drew together. "She's my only hope."

Unfortunately for him, he was right about that. However, I didn't say this out loud.

"How was your dinner with her last night?" he asked.

When the motel manager had delivered the short message from Jericho to my room yesterday afternoon, including the address of the restaurant, Elian had been visiting with me. He hadn't asked to join us at the fateful dinner. For all his problems and the urgency of his situation, Prince Elian seemed to possess one thing that I didn't: an endless supply of patience.

I absently rubbed the scar on my palm. "Let's just say it was . . . educational."

He raised a brow. "Educational."

"*Very* educational." I studied him for a moment. He didn't

look terribly royal at the moment, wearing dark jeans and a black T-shirt, which Jericho had given to him from his own minimalistic wardrobe. I'd arrived in Cresidia with only the clothes on my back—which were great clothes, actually. A designer dress and expensive high heels, all provided by Her Majesty when I'd been a short-term VIP guest at the palace.

I'd sold the clothes to a local consignment shop, settling for a fraction of what they were worth. But with that money, I'd been able to buy a tiny wardrobe that had gotten me through the week. Today I wore black leggings, lace-up, rubber-soled white sneakers, and an oversize emerald-green V-neck tunic with gold flowers embroidered on the sleeves.

Not exactly the height of current fashion, but comfort and functionality were priority numbers one and two for me.

Well, make that priority numbers two and three. Getting answers and learning the truth about the queen's big secret was number one.

"Can I ask you a question?" I said to Elian. At his nod, I continued. "Have you ever showed any sign of magic? Of being a warlock like Banyon?"

Elian's expression grew thoughtful. "After I learned that he was my father, I asked Vander Lazos about it. He said not everyone with a witch or warlock as a parent will have access to elementia. If you don't notice anything by the time you turn seventeen, it probably won't happen. I turned seventeen two weeks before I died." He shrugged. "I never got the chance to ask him any more questions."

"Too bad. He knew nearly everything about elementia. He would have been a great magic tutor."

"I don't think my mother would have liked that very much."

"Who cares what she thinks?" I said venomously.

Elian grimaced. "I know how much you hate her. She's made some horrible choices during her reign. But she bears a heavy burden as queen, heavier than you even realize. The same burden I would have as heir. My family's legacy is her only goal in life."

I wasn't about to spare a moment of sympathy for Queen Isadora's heavy royal burden. "And you're her legacy."

"That's how she sees it."

"You said you don't want to be king."

"Even if I did want to, it's not exactly an option for me anymore, is it? I mean, look at me. Imagine what the citizens of the Empire would say if I was crowned absolute ruler tomorrow. Someone dragged out of their own grave who now feeds on life itself like some sort of monstrous leech." Elian raked his fingers through his short hair, his expression anguished for a moment before he composed himself. "That witch has to help me."

"She will," I assured him. I only wish I could have sounded more certain about it, but all bets were off when it came to Valery and what she chose to do. She definitely hadn't struck me as the "helping" type. Maybe for a price, though. A high one.

Jericho and Viktor now approached us. Viktor was scowling, and he didn't say a word to us before he went directly to his motel room and disappeared behind the door.

I sent a questioning look at Jericho.

"Vik hates me," Jericho confirmed with a shrug. "He wanted to come to the meeting, and I said hell no."

"Why would he want to come to the meeting?" The thought was utterly ludicrous to me. "I'm guessing that Valery wouldn't be thrilled about meeting with a Queensguard, even on a good day."

"To put it mildly," Jericho agreed. "But Vik knows that Val's a witch with connections to the black market. The black market means access to contained magic. Contained magic means, potentially, getting his hands on something—a ring, an amulet, whatever—that might shield his identity from the world at large now that he's a traitor to the Empire."

He said all this like it was common knowledge. Maybe to him it was.

"Viktor's Queensgames ads are everywhere right now," Elian said, nodding. "I can see how that might be a problem for him."

Jericho spread his hands. "I told him I'd look into it, but he can't be there today. Or any other day. Val doesn't even know he's here in Cresidia with us, and it's best she never finds out. She'd see any Queensguard as a threat, even one who blew up his entire life to save mine."

He said this lightly, but I saw the pain in his eyes. As if he noticed me noticing, his shields went up, his expression shifting to neutral. He didn't like anyone seeing his vulnerable side. And Jericho Nox was definitely vulnerable when it came to his younger brother.

As reigning champion of the Queensgames, and the youngest Queensguard commander in history, Viktor's face would be immediately recognizable to the vast majority of the Empire. And after he'd betrayed the queen to save his brother's life, recognition from the public meant facing an immediate death sentence. I'd despised him when I learned he'd helped keep the queen's secret about Elian, but I couldn't find the strength to keep hating him after what he'd done to save his brother. It wasn't total redemption, but it was pretty damn close.

Something else occurred to me. "If something like that exists . . . an amulet or whatever so no one recognizes Viktor, maybe Valery can find one for Elian too."

"The black market isn't exactly like a store full of magical trinkets, Drake. These things take time. And a lot of money."

"So, you're saying no?"

"I'm saying . . ." He hissed out a breath. "Fine. I'll add it to the list."

I brightened. "Thank you."

Elian watched our exchange silently, but he finally spoke. "To be honest, it's highly unlikely anyone will recognize me as easily as they'd recognize Viktor," he said.

"You really think so?" I asked skeptically.

He nodded. "My mother had all photos of me removed from public record. It's been sixteen years since I've been seen outside of the palace. Only a carefully selected handful know the truth."

"Including my brother," Jericho said.

Elian nodded. "Including him."

I had to admit that he was right. Even if there were any conspiracy theorists around, they would expect to spot a thirty-three-year-old prince, not someone magically frozen at the age of seventeen. Viktor had a 1,000 percent better chance of being spotted in the wild than Elian did.

"The queen is probably beside herself right now with you and Viktor gone," I said.

"I'm sure she is," Elian replied uneasily.

While I empathized with Elian's precarious situation, the thought that Queen Isadora was probably losing sleep at night over this made me feel all warm and fuzzy inside.

But the sensation faded the moment I thought about Celina. She would also be devastated and confused by the disappearance of both her best friend and her fiancé.

I'm sorry, Celina, I thought. *One day I'll make it up to you, I promise.*

"Drake, can I talk to you for a sec?" Jericho said.

I exchanged a glance with Elian, who nodded.

"I'll wait here," he said.

I joined Jericho twenty feet away. "Did you talk to Valery about controlling the echoes?" I asked. "And about Banyon?"

"Not yet." At my glare, he held up a hand. "Patience, Drake."

"All out of patience."

"Then that's going to be a big problem. Today's all about the prince. After we deal with him, we'll move to the next item on the to-do list."

I hissed out a breath. "I tried to summon an echo for hours last night, and I got absolutely nothing. Very frustrating. But you're right. Elian's problem is the most important, at least for today."

He snorted softly. "You're too generous."

"What did you want to talk to me about?" I asked.

His expression grew deadly serious in an instant. "This: Don't bait her. Don't push her. Don't mess around. I can't magically control her like she can control me. I can't protect you."

I shook my head. "I don't need you to protect me."

"Okay, sure." He rolled his eyes. "How's that hand of yours doing?"

"Fine, thanks." I rubbed the scar as I willed my heart to stop beating so fast. Even I didn't like my tone—bossy and annoyed. Jericho didn't deserve that. "I'm sorry. I know I'm a lot sometimes."

He laughed at that, a low rumble at the back of his throat. "You think so, do you?"

I shrugged. "That's what everybody tells me."

"Yeah, well, I'm not everybody. All I'm saying is, try not to get stabbed again. Okay?" Jericho reached for my hand and ran his thumb over my scar, just like he had last night. And just like last night, the warmth of his touch made me shiver.

I looked up at him. "I'll try my best."

His gaze locked with mine and held. "Good."

⊳⬦⬦⬦⬦⊲

Jericho brought Elian and me to the very center of downtown Cresidia, past throngs of tourists and Queensguards in their very familiar black uniforms with gold trim, and past the city square we'd spent some time in last night. Every guard I saw made my stomach flip, thinking that I was going to be recognized and dragged back to the palace.

We followed the Blackheart through the front doors of the

tallest and shiniest building in Cresidia, which reached high into the sky like an enormous crystal shard. Past the security desk without stopping, and straight to a bank of elevators. Nearby, a huge monitor set into the wall broadcast the latest news. Normally I didn't pay attention to the daily news, but today would be much different.

"After a full year in hiding, a witch directly involved with the assassination of Prime Minister Louis Drake has been found and arrested," the announcer said. "This witch worked with Lord Banyon in an attempt to throw this Empire into a state of chaos and fear."

The camera then focused on a face that was so bruised and swollen that it took me a moment to realize I knew who it was. It was her curly red hair that gave her away.

"Jericho," I managed, grabbing the Blackheart's arm.

He also watched the monitor, his expression grim.

"For three years, impersonating a doctor, Tamara Collins used her dark and evil magic to inflict illness upon her patients," the announcer explained in a voice edged in cold disdain. "The witch has been questioned at length about the warlock terrorist's current location, and now she remains imprisoned for her heinous crimes, awaiting execution."

The footage of Tamara shifted to the announcer's face. "We'll be back with more top stories following this important commercial break."

I was jarred back to reality at the sight of Viktor's face, his rarely seen smile, and a shot of the Queensgames Arena.

"*The glorious Queensgames,*" Viktor said cheerfully, with a background of inspiring music. *"Who will fall, and who will be victorious? Join me there!"*

The elevator opened. Jericho directed me inside and then pushed the top button.

We didn't speak for a long, heavy moment.

"Tamara," I finally said, my voice hoarse.

"Yeah," he replied grimly.

"Where's Mika?" I asked.

"No idea."

The queen was doing this on purpose, of course. Her captured assassin, Jericho, had escaped, and she needed a new symbol. A reminder of how evil magic was, and how much she opposed it for the good of her people.

I hated her. As bright as my love and admiration for the queen had been for my entire life, my hate now burned a thousand times brighter.

I didn't know much about this strange new world I'd stepped into from the safety of the one I thought I knew for seventeen years, but I did know this much with absolute certainty: Tamara was the kindest and most giving person I'd ever met. She didn't have a single shred of darkness within her.

And she most certainly didn't kill my father.

"You know that witch?" Elian asked.

I nodded, my eyes burning with tears. "They're lying about her. She used her earth magic to help patients, not harm them. One of those patients reported her. She got sent to the Queen's Keep, and she was in there even before the assassination."

"And you said Mika? Who's Mika?"

"Tamara's girlfriend," Jericho said. "She was a Queensguard."

"She broke into the Keep to rescue Tamara," I explained. "They finally escaped and . . . and this happened. We have to do something to save her."

Jericho inhaled slowly. "It's too late."

I looked at him with shock. "Too late? She's going to die!"

"You're right; she is."

"She didn't do this!"

"Of course she didn't."

I hissed out a breath. "Then I don't see a problem here."

"Then I'll be the one who sees the problems, Drake. This sucks—I'm not saying it doesn't. But we don't know where Tamara's being held right now. It was nearly impossible to get out of the palace, even with someone on the inside helping us."

I shook my head. "We can get information."

"From where?"

I grappled to come up with a brilliant master plan to break a high-profile prisoner free in record time. My gaze fell on Elian, who was quietly listening to us.

"I wish I could help your friend," the prince said. "I really do. But even when my life was normal, my mother's decisions were always final when it came to magic."

"Except when it served her," I bit out.

He just shook his head, his expression bleak.

My heart wrenched. "There's got to be a way. We can't let this happen. Tamara's innocent!"

"Just as innocent as countless other mages who've been executed over the centuries while Aunt Issy and her ancestors have comfortably been seated on the throne," Jericho replied. "It happens all the time, Drake. It's just not always announced as loudly and officially as this."

I searched his face, trying to glimpse any emotion behind his flat words. "She saved your life. Don't you care what happens to her?"

"Of course I care." The sudden ferocity in his voice took me by surprise. He drew in a shaky breath and shook his head. "But I can't win this one, Drake."

I wasn't giving up that easily. "There has to be something we can do!"

"Not from out here. If we were still there, inside the palace, maybe there'd be a chance. But not out here in the real world."

I hated that I knew he was right. It was hopeless to think I could help Tamara from six hundred miles away after fleeing my old life. My heart pounded very hard and very loud as I watched the numbers swiftly change: forty, then fifty, and we were only halfway to the top.

I turned away from the numbers to the glass wall of the elevator, which gave a sweeping view of the city's skyline. I took the time I had left to focus on my breathing, on gathering my thoughts, but they had scattered in every direction.

The doors to the elevator finally opened. I expected to see a large and well-decorated penthouse suite. Instead, I needed to do a double take at the lush greenery and thatch of thick trees in front of me.

"A rooftop garden," Elian said. "How unexpected."

"Yeah," Jericho replied. "My boss has a bit of a green thumb.

Says that being around nature, while in the middle of the city, gives her a chance to clear her mind."

Frankly, all this natural beauty didn't suit the hard-edged woman I'd met last night. I wasn't sure what I'd expected. A big, executive desk created for a business-minded, black-market boss. Maybe a wall of sharp weapons at the ready. But not this.

We followed the Blackheart out of the elevator and along a winding cobblestone path lined by trees with large, shiny leaves. On either side were tropical flowers—red and orange and purple. I'd never seen such exotic plants in person, never smelled such a heady perfume of life all around, almost like a thick, fragrant fog. Birds chirped and insects buzzed.

Jericho led us along the path, through the thick foliage, which looked like it had been here since the beginning of time. Since it was a rooftop, this tropical forest didn't go on forever. After about thirty feet, the greenery parted to show a circular clearing that featured a round glass table upon a marble-tiled floor.

And there she was.

The witch was waiting for us.

FOUR

Valery calmly watched our approach from her seat at the table.

It seemed I now had my own set of disturbing echoes when it came to the witch—a constant repeating loop of her golden dagger slicing into my hand as she tore the truth out of my throat. Distracted by this, and by the image of Tamara's bruised face, I stumbled over a vine lying across my path. Jericho caught my upper arm to steady me before I could fall.

The witch gave Jericho a pointed look.

"Right, introductions," he said. "Prince Elian, this is Valery. Valery, Prince Elian."

Valery rose from her seat as we drew closer, her attention fixed on the prince. "Your Highness, this is an honor I never would have expected."

"Likewise. Thank you for agreeing to meet with me today," Elian replied. "I know the circumstances are . . . unusual."

Well, that put it mildly, I thought.

"I must admit, I'm fascinated to learn more about your situation." Valery's gaze moved to me. "Josslyn, it's lovely to see you again."

I despise every cell in your evil body and plan to shamelessly use you for any shred of information you can give me, I thought while pushing a cordial smile to my lips.

"It's lovely to be seen," I said aloud.

I'd decided to pretend she was a particularly unpleasant rich woman at one of the many charity balls I'd attended with my father. One I didn't want to piss off in case she closed her checkbook and walked away.

She nodded toward my left hand. "I see that you found a healer."

However, no unpleasant rich woman I'd ever been faced with before had stabbed me.

"I did," I confirmed tightly.

"Who was it?"

Since her dagger-of-truth wasn't currently sticking out of my mangled flesh, I didn't feel particularly compelled to answer her.

I shrugged. "I called the earth-magic hotline and they sent someone right over. Sorry, didn't catch the name."

"Very amusing." Valery's gaze was cool. "Jericho? To whom did you take Josslyn to heal her hand?"

Jericho grimaced, as if Valery's words had power over him and it hurt him to resist answering. Because they did. And it did.

"Daria," he gritted out. "The dancer from Deluxe."

Valery reached for my hand to inspect it; I forced myself to not flinch away from her or show any fear. "It seems that Daria is far more skilled than I originally thought. I'll have to remember that."

"Did you say Deluxe?" Elian asked.

"Yes. Deluxe is my theater," Valery told him. "I acquired it a few years ago."

Jericho hadn't mentioned that. No wonder Daria had been so concerned about Valery finding out. Apparently, the dancer and the Blackheart shared an evil boss.

The prince's expression brightened. "It was one of my favorite places to visit in the city. Mother never approved of Cresidia, even though it's close to our vacation home, but that only made me love it here more. I have many good memories at that theater."

Valery nodded. "You'll have to visit again soon. As my guest."

"I look forward to that."

She gestured toward the other two chairs at the table. "Please, take a seat."

Elian and I sat down, while Jericho remained standing a few feet away, his arms crossed over his chest.

"Now," the witch said, "tell me exactly why you wanted to see me."

Elian didn't hesitate. "Ever since my mother heard rumors that you are able to channel death magic with ease, she's been convinced that you're the only one in the world who can help me." His expression was deadly serious. "But she had no means of contacting you."

"I work very hard to keep my business, and my identity, private."

"Understandable, of course. When she had Jericho in custody, she thought it was the perfect opportunity to find you."

"Indirectly, it seems to have worked. You're here."

I couldn't help but wonder exactly what Jericho had told Valery to explain his escape from the palace if he hadn't mentioned Viktor's involvement or his presence in the city. It was clear to me, despite her—literally—painfully strict control over the Blackheart, that she valued and trusted him, and perhaps didn't need too many details.

Elian nodded. "That you're even willing to speak to me is a great relief. I assure you, I will never reveal your identity or location."

"That goes without saying, Your Highness."

"What would happen if he did?" I asked aloud, and then immediately felt Jericho's sharp glare. I knew he didn't want me to get in Valery's face today, after what happened last night. But there were questions that needed answering, and if no one else asked them, I certainly would. "I mean, it sounds like you have roots here. This garden. Deluxe. A thriving black-market business. A reputation almost as infamous as Lord Banyon's. It's a lot to lose. Yet you're willing to meet Queen Isadora's son face-to-face."

"And willing to meet you as well," she agreed.

"Yes, me as well." I scanned the thick foliage surrounding us. The witch seemed to have a habit of dodging direct questions, but that wouldn't stop me from trying.

"I'm very careful about whom I let into my confidence. It's always a mutually beneficial situation, with an understanding of the importance of confidentiality. And that, Josslyn, is all I'll say on the subject."

The witch might like to speak in riddles, but I knew one thing for sure. If she'd lasted as long as she had, doing what she did, then there were ways she kept others from talking about her. Clearly, she wasn't going to indulge me by revealing her secrets. Couldn't really say I blamed her.

"How many Blackhearts work for you other than Jericho?" I asked. I'd been curious about this for a while. I was sure the threat of death-by-Blackheart was a firm deterrent for loose talk from past clients.

"A few," she replied.

"Where are they now?"

"On assignment elsewhere." To her credit, Valery's tone remained light and cordial. Almost amused by my questions. "Is there anything else you want to know at this very moment, Josslyn?"

One very large question in particular came to mind. I couldn't help but think of the rumors about her—the explanations people gave for her powers. *Immortal goddess of death.* This woman was certainly a witch and a cruel boss who claimed she didn't care if the queen executed other mages. But was she more than that? Were the rumors true?

I chose to hold my tongue on that dangerous line of questioning for now.

"Well, not at this very moment." I suppose anything else could wait until she was finished with Elian.

"I appreciate your interest in my business."

"That makes one of us," Jericho muttered.

"Apologies for interrupting," I said.

"No apology necessary." The witch turned back to Elian and spread her hands. "Let's just say that I have full confidence that you won't reveal my secrets. And we'll leave it at that for now."

Elian nodded. "I understand what it's like to keep an important secret."

"Apparently so. Please, tell me in your own words about what happened to you."

Elian nodded and then began to go over the details about Vander Lazos, the queen's former magical advisor, who'd performed the death magic ritual two weeks after the prince had drowned in Summerside, the location of the royal family's vacation manor, which, as Elian had said earlier, wasn't far from Cresidia. After the resurrection, he remained mostly comatose for more than a decade, only becoming truly lucid over the last year.

I'd witnessed the death magic ritual in an echo. Present at the time were Lazos, the queen, and a bloody and beaten Banyon, who'd refused to help the queen raise their son from the dead because he claimed that such dark magic came with unacceptable risks—for him and for Elian.

"Jericho has already briefed me on what happened in the Queen's Keep," Valery said. "How the queen made it possible for you to feed on prisoners there."

I shuddered at the memory.

The prince's expression shadowed, his gaze filling with pain. "I have no control over myself when the hunger descends."

"Do you feel that hunger now?" Valery asked.

"To be honest, I always feel it—low levels, controllable. Usually. At least, until it isn't." He drew in a shaky breath that almost sounded like a sob. "Why am I so different from Jericho? He was raised from the dead, just as I was. Is it because you're more highly skilled than Vander Lazos?"

"I don't think that warlock had much to do with this outcome," Valery replied. "It could have happened to any mage who attempted to summon the darkest magic."

Elian shook his head. "But he was a powerful warlock, one with a photographic memory! He could recite from ancient books of magic that had been destroyed. And . . . I *killed* him. All of that knowledge is now gone because of me."

It hadn't even occurred to me until now, but it was true. One of the reasons the queen had kept Lazos alive was that he was a walking, talking encyclopedia of magic, thanks to his photographic memory. He read confiscated, forbidden physical books about magic history, journals kept by mages, accounts of elementia across the centuries—and then those books were burned so they wouldn't fall into the wrong hands.

All of that history was now lost forever.

A glint of gold caught my eye as Valery drew out her dagger and placed it in front of her, a jarring reminder of last night. I rubbed the scar on my palm and tried to tamp down my rising panic at the sight of the weapon.

"Vander Lazos didn't have this," Valery explained. "This dagger aids my magic, strengthens it. That and the fact that I've successfully summoned death magic many times is one of many reasons why you are different from Jericho."

"He's strong," Jericho said. "I hate to admit it, but Prince Elian's strength is double what mine is. Maybe even more than that."

"And you haven't aged a day since your resurrection," Valery said, her gaze moving over Elian's tense face. "What else can you tell me about your experiences since your reawakening?"

"I can't die," Elian said, his voice raw. "I tried to, once. And

I thought I succeeded. But I woke up the next day without any sign of my attempt."

My heart ached for him having to deal with this ongoing nightmare. I wouldn't wish it on even my worst enemy.

Well . . .

No, not even Ambrose or the queen.

Valery remained more curious than emotionally moved by the prince's plight. "You are most certainly a mystery, Your Highness."

Disappointment slid through his gaze. "A mystery."

She nodded. "I've never come across anything like you before. It's fascinating. Immortality, superhuman strength, and a dark and ravenous hunger that is temporarily sated only by feeding on the life force of other living beings. All accidentally created by an average-at-best warlock like Vander Lazos, who merely recited a ritual he'd found in an old book."

The witch's flippant response to Elian's pain wasn't sitting well with me.

"Do you know how to help him?" I asked. "Can you, I don't know, use your dagger to draw symbols on his skin like Jericho's?"

"That won't work," Valery said, shaking her head. "This is sixteen years too late."

"You won't even try? I mean, it *could* work."

She leveled her gaze with mine. "It won't work."

"How do you know?" I pressed.

"I just do," Valery said firmly. Then to Elian. "What I believe has happened to you, Your Highness, is an infinitely rare side effect of death magic. A side effect that has, ironically, given you incredible gifts."

"You think these are gifts?" Elian hissed. "I'm compelled to suck the life out of innocent victims whenever the hunger rises. I'm a monster. I want a cure for this. A way to end this hunger and have control over my life again!"

Valery considered this solemnly. "If that's really what you want, then I do believe there's a way I can help you."

The prince nodded eagerly. "Good. How?"

Valery grasped the dagger. "This tool can help to restore a life. And it can also end a life." She paused, waiting for Elian's reaction to this. When no reaction came, she continued. "I believe my dagger can end any life—*any* life, even one as arguably immortal as yours seems to currently be. If you really want to end your hunger before it rises again and bring what you consider a nightmare to an end, then this is the only cure I feel that I am able offer to you."

The prince just stared at her bleakly as the truth of her words sank in.

Valery shook her head. "I'm sorry that this isn't the solution you'd hoped for, Your Highness."

"Me too." Elian didn't look at me or Jericho as he rose from the table. "It seems that I have a great deal to consider. Thank you for your time. Joss, Jericho—I'll wait by the elevator."

He walked away from us, along the pathway and into the thick of the garden, until I couldn't see him anymore.

"No, that can't be it," I said, shaking my head. "There has to be another answer."

"There isn't," Valery replied firmly.

I eyed her with frustration. "You spent, like, five minutes

talking to him. That was all the information you needed to hear to know that the only way you can help him is to stick your magic dagger in his heart?"

Valery spread her hands, her expression serene. "The prince is welcome to continue to look elsewhere for the answers he needs. There might be another solution out there, but from what he told me, from what little I know about this magic, I gave him the best answer I could. I understand that it's a disappointment, but there's nothing I can do about that, is there?"

"That wasn't an answer," I hissed. "That was a flat-out dismissal."

Valery raised a brow. "You think so, do you?"

"I know so."

"Drake," Jericho began. "That's enough for now."

"Hardly." I stood up from my seat, knowing I had to calm down. But every word this woman said, every snide look she gave me, only ignited my outrage. "Why did you even agree to see him?"

"Mostly, to quell my curiosity. Let's just say, anything to do with the darkest magic fascinates me. Especially when it goes so horribly wrong." She cocked her head. "Or horribly right, depending on how you look at it. With his strength and resilience, not to mention his deep ties to the palace, Prince Elian would make a magnificent Blackheart."

I shook my head. "Unbelievable."

"What is?" Valery continued to regard me calmly, but I couldn't help but notice the sliver of annoyance that slid behind her gaze.

"You are. So much power, so much influence . . . yet everything you do is for your own selfish gain. You sit here in your private rooftop garden while other mages—like Tamara—are being imprisoned and executed. Now she's going to die as yet another example of what the queen wants the Empire to fear. You could do something. You could make a difference. But you choose not to. Why? Are you scared, or do you really just not give a shit about anyone but yourself?"

"Drake," Jericho growled. "You seriously need to stop talking now."

"Or what?" I raised my chin. "Your boss will stick her dagger in me again?"

He glared at me. "No. Actually, she'll probably make me do it this time."

Valery watched our exchange. "We're done here. I won't harm you today, Josslyn, out of respect for your father, but I caution you not to speak with me with such disrespect ever again."

"My father was Louis Drake." I leveled my gaze with hers. "And you agreed to help Regis Ambrose kill him. Do you really think you'll ever get my respect, you evil bitch?"

Her gaze turned ice cold. "Jericho, please escort Josslyn out of here immediately."

Before I could say another word, Jericho closed his hand around my upper arm and began directing me away from the witch, along the pathway toward the elevator. Halfway there, I slipped out of his grip. My anger had gotten away from me, and I said things I probably wouldn't have said had I been thinking rationally.

"Jericho—" I began.

"Quiet," he snarled. "I already told you if you pushed her, I wouldn't be able to protect you. But that's all you do. You push and you push."

"I need answers!" I didn't need to be reprimanded right now, especially not by him. "Elian needed her help!"

"Then he came to the wrong place. You don't know her like I do, Drake. You don't know what she does to people who disrespect her like this. What she has *me* do to them. Don't make it come to that, because it will."

A chill sped down my spine at what he suggested. "You wouldn't hurt me."

The look he gave me was pitch black. "I obey her command."

"Fight it."

"I can't."

"You fought her command for two weeks while we were in the Keep."

"That was the loose command of a deadline. Not a direct order to kill." He swore under his breath and studied the ground. "I can't ignore her commands, Drake. It's torture to resist. Feels like someone's got my head in a vise, squeezing tighter and tighter until it explodes. It's even worse after she freshens up my marks, which she did last night."

I finally softened, just a little. I tentatively touched his arm, which was as hard as steel. "You deserve better than this, Jericho."

"No. This is exactly what I deserve, Drake. Every choice I've made has led me here, to this moment." Jericho raised his black-eyed gaze to mine, and there was not a shred of friendliness there anymore. "This was a mistake."

"What was a mistake?"

"You were." He narrowed his eyes. "Letting you come with me and Vik; both of you—you and Elian. It's caused me way too many problems."

I bristled, brushing off my immediate flinch of pain at his words. "You didn't *let* me come with you. I was leaving anyway."

"Right." He straightened his posture and squared his shoulders, glaring down his nose at me. "And now it's time for you to go home. You don't belong here, and if you stay another day, it's going to get you killed."

I searched his face, as hard and merciless as I'd ever seen it. "I'm a witch. How am I supposed to go back knowing that— knowing that there's more in the echoes that I can learn about the queen's secrets? You think it's that easy?"

"It's always easy for people like you. There are plenty of witches who live side by side with regular people, and nobody ever knows the difference. Be one of them. In a few months, you'll thank me. Actually, you'll forget I even existed."

My previous confusion had swiftly turned to anger. "Promise?"

He glowered at me. "Yeah, I promise. You really want to help Tamara? Like I said before, you can't do it from out here. But maybe from inside the palace, you'd have a chance."

"Jericho . . ."

"No. Discussion over, Drake. You can go back on your own, or I'll deliver you to Aunt Issy's doorstep myself. Your choice. But your little vacation into my world is officially over."

FIVE

Jericho took Elian and me back to the motel, as stiff and silent as a tall, brooding statue. Elian had also seemingly lost his ability to speak. He went directly to his room and closed the door behind him. By then, Jericho was already walking away from me.

"Jericho, we need to talk," I called after him.

"Be ready to leave tomorrow," he growled.

"But—"

And that's all I managed to say before the Blackheart disappeared around a corner.

I knew I couldn't stay confined in my motel room, so I went to the beach, staring out at the ocean, watching the waves roll in. And I went over everything that happened today. And yesterday. And every day since the Queen's Gala, when my biggest problem had been what to wear for my first major public appearance since my father's death.

I missed Celina. I missed her so very desperately, even though I knew she'd never understand any of this. She would have woken up in her palace suite to the news that I was gone.

And that Viktor had also left, with seemingly no reason or explanation.

She would have been so confused. And also, even though it wasn't usually in her nature, so incredibly angry.

I tried to summon an echo, but my mind was in too much turmoil to concentrate for long. So, instead, I studied the elements to be found around me—the heat of the sun felt like fire. The sand was earth. The ocean was water. And the warm, salty breeze was air. Elemental magic was all around us, all the time. Mages pulled from what already existed in nature, and then manipulated and used it for good or for evil purposes.

And the queen chose to hide this secret, painting it as a plague on humanity, rather than a part of who we naturally were. Who originally made the decision to portray mages as 100 percent evil? And why would generations to follow go along with it all without any questions?

Elian was the key to changing everything. He was different from the queen. And, even if he wasn't cured, even if he had to deal with his condition indefinitely, he was still the most important evidence to expose his mother's lies, to save mages like Tamara who were held responsible for crimes they didn't commit just by being who they were born to be.

Afternoon turned to evening, and the crowds that had come to get sun on their faces and sand between their toes started to thin out. On my way back to the motel, I walked past a sand-castle someone had built earlier, which had already started to crumble. The absolute certainty I'd felt when I'd left the palace was a lot like that. Swiftly falling apart, ready to be swept away with the tide.

By the time I'd returned to the motel, I'd managed to shake off most of my useless despair and had decided to focus on the one thing I knew I wanted. The truth. I went directly to Elian's room and knocked on the door.

When there was no answer, I tried again. Louder. "Come on, Elian. Open up. Let's figure out what to do next."

Still nothing.

I hissed out a sigh of frustration and moved to the window. The drapes were slightly open, so I peered into the small, empty room and then waited for a minute in silence to see if he'd emerge from the bathroom, but he didn't appear.

"What are you doing?" Viktor said from behind me, making me jump.

I spun around to see that he wore a sweatshirt with the hood covering his hair and a pair of dark sunglasses to help shield his identity. This was day six in Cresidia and he hadn't been recognized yet, so I guess it was working for him.

"Elian's not in his room," I told him.

"Impossible." He moved closer, peeking in the window. Then he swore under his breath. "I left to grab some dinner. I was gone only half an hour at the most."

I shrugged. "Maybe he went for a walk."

"No. I already told the prince to clear anything like that with me. I saw him earlier for a minute, and he seemed upset. What happened during your meeting with the witch?"

"A lot," I told him honestly.

"A lot good, or a lot bad?"

"Let's just say, I'm concerned that Elian isn't safely tucked away in his room with a former Queensguard commander watching over him." My stomach clenched. "What if his hunger's already returned?"

Viktor swore under his breath. "We need to locate him as soon as possible. Find Jericho—he knows this city better than I do."

"You know where he is?"

He nodded. "He messaged me that he's at the fight club in the basement of the Kincadean."

As soon as Viktor gave me directions to the hotel-casino, I set off at a clip. I couldn't worry about what I'd say to Jericho after our ugly exchange earlier. I assumed he hated me now, but that was his problem. I'd pledged to help Elian, and I fully planned to hold true to that promise.

Once I reached the Kincadean, I took a moment to rake my fingers through my long hair and hoped I wouldn't seem too disheveled as I entered the glitzy casino. It was filled with thick crowds of people, all of whom seemed to be dressed in designer clothes and dripping in jewels, while I wore the same casual outfit I'd worn all day.

Inside, I took the elevator down to the basement. The only fight club I'd ever seen had been Rush's, a smoky bar that also had a fighting ring, surrounded by gamblers and heavy drinkers.

This one was much different.

It was quarter-scale replica of the Queensgames Arena, with row upon row of plush red seats for the onlookers. In the center was the ring, raised and encircled with leather ropes. Spotlights set into the ceiling lit up the ring, while keeping the seating area cloaked in shadows. Music throbbed, as loud as a dance club, and the sound pulsed through my body, which made it hard for me to think. Scantily dressed waitstaff carried trays of drinks through the crowd. Each member of the audience looked every bit as affluent as anyone who'd attended the invitation-only Queen's Gala last month.

The audience cheered on the two fighters, shirtless and glistening with sweat, as they circled each other in the ring. They each held a long blade, and when the weapons clashed, the sound rang out above all the other noise, punctuating each blow, each strike. For a moment, I stood there and watched, mesmerized. One fighter finally stumbled, succumbing to his injuries. The other grabbed him from behind before slicing his blade over his opponent's throat.

My stomach twisted as I realized that these sanctioned and fully taxed fights were to the death. It was an outcome so accepted at the Queensgames that I wasn't sure why seeing blood spill bothered me so much.

No, that wasn't true. I knew why. It reminded me of the horror of watching Jericho fall and the life leave his eyes during his fateful match. He'd been dead. Gone. I never would have met him, and I never would have learned the truth about the Empire—about myself—if Valery hadn't chosen to bring him back to life.

The more I learned about magic, about the Empire, about the queen, and about myself, the more I wondered if I'd choose to forget it all and go back to how it used to be.

No, I wouldn't. I couldn't. That wasn't who I was anymore.

The body of the fallen fighter was removed, his blood mopped up, and another fight swiftly began. This time I couldn't allow myself to be distracted. I scanned the crowd, searching for the Blackheart. I began to doubt he was even here, that this had been a huge waste of time, when I finally spotted him.

Jericho was on the other side of the ring, moving with purpose toward an exit at the back of the huge room. I quickly navigated the crowd, dodging a spilled drink, and then the feel of some creepy rich man's hand on my butt. I took a moment to stomp on the jerk's foot before I moved on.

"Jericho!" I called out to him.

He stopped walking, his shoulders tensing. He turned to face me, and he wasn't wearing a smile. "I can't seem to get rid of you, can I?"

Despite my uneasiness about what happened earlier, his dismissive greeting made me want to stomp on his foot too. "Don't worry, I'm not stalking you. Elian's missing."

"Great. Thanks for the update. Good luck finding him."

He turned away from me, but I grabbed his arm. "This is serious, Jericho. You need to help me search for him."

He glowered at me. "Where's Vik?"

"Looking for Elian, of course. He sent me here to find you. To tell you."

"All right, you've told me. Mission accomplished. Bye."

Now I was fuming. I followed the Blackheart right out of the club and along a dimly lit hallway. I scanned the hallway for any eavesdroppers, but we were currently alone. The throbbing sound of the music and the roar the crowd was still loud but not deafening. This was as private a moment as I could hope for, given the venue.

"Jericho, we need to talk."

That earned me a dark look. "Leave me alone, Drake. Don't make me say it again, or I promise you'll regret it."

I could take a hint. Seriously, I could, especially when someone was so relentlessly determined to reject me. But tonight was different.

"I'm not afraid of you," I told him.

"Maybe you should be," he growled.

"Maybe you're right," I replied honestly. "But, at the moment, what I'm afraid of is Elian going full monster and sucking the life out of some innocent people."

"Don't worry too much. There are no innocent people in Cresidia."

Maybe he was right about that, but that didn't change anything for me. I raised my chin. "About what you said earlier? Me leaving tomorrow?"

He waited, his arms crossed over his chest.

"Not happening," I told him.

His jaw tightened. "Is that so."

"That's so," I confirmed.

"Your funeral." He scowled at me. "For what it's worth, your little revelation about your family tree seems to have bought you extra time with Val. She's determined to find another way to get those echoes out of you to make her client happy."

"Her client," I repeated. "You mean Banyon." I was more convinced of my theory with every hour that passed.

He shook his head, his expression darkening. "Her client isn't Banyon. She knows how I feel about that bastard."

"And you really believe that she'd care?" I stopped. I wasn't arguing about this. There wasn't time. "It doesn't matter. Please, Jericho. I need your help to find Elian."

"He isn't my problem. He's yours."

His words were so sharp that I couldn't ignore the pain from them this time. In an instant, my eyes welled up and hot tears slid down my cheeks. I angrily wiped them away and turned from him. "Fine. Whatever. I don't care. I'll find him myself."

I turned away and started to move back toward the club, but he grasped my wrist.

"Stop." He hissed out a breath. "Don't cry. I'm such a dick sometimes."

My eyes widened as I met his gaze. "Wait. What is this? An apology from Jericho Nox?"

"It happens. Occasionally." He hesitated before taking my face gently between his hands, gazing into my eyes intently as if he was trying to memorize my features. I didn't pull away from him. "I'm sorry, Drake."

I nodded. "You're forgiven."

"Good." Something eased in his expression. "Today, with Val . . . watching you confront her like that. It's just that . . ." He hesitated. "Nobody does that and walks away."

"I let my anger get away from me sometimes," I admitted.

He raised his brow. "Sometimes?"

"Fine. More than sometimes." I shook my head. "I can't go back, Jericho."

"Then don't. Stay. We'll figure it out. Okay?"

The painful knot that had formed in my heart during our previous argument finally loosened. It felt as if I could breathe again.

"Okay," I said.

Jericho hadn't moved his hands yet. I pressed back against the wall, my heart now fluttering in my chest. Which was ridiculous. My heart had never fluttered for anyone. Well, anyone except, apparently, Jericho.

Something had shifted between us in moments. Even here, with hundreds of people only steps away, it felt like there was no one else in the universe except me and him.

"Drake . . ." he whispered, leaning closer to me. His lips, so close to mine . . .

Someone entered the hallway and Jericho pushed back from me, his expression clouded now with a deep uncertainty that hadn't been there only a moment ago.

"All right," he said, putting a pocket of distance between us. "Let's go find the prince before he has a chance to cheat on his diet."

Heart thudding, I followed Jericho back to the main casino floor of the Kincadean and forced myself to focus on the problem at hand. I'd been so hung up on finding Jericho, I hadn't thought of what we'd do next. But now—even with the Blackheart's help—I didn't see how I'd be able to find

Elian in a huge, densely populated city like Cresidia.

"This is impossible," I said.

"Giving up so soon?"

I wrung my hands. "He could be anywhere. He might not even be in Cresidia anymore."

"It's definitely a needle-in-a-haystack situation. Or . . . maybe a cursed prince in a haystack would be a better description."

I shot him a look. "This isn't funny."

"I'm not laughing. Vik should have planned for the worst. You'd think with his experience in Queensguarding, he'd be more on top of keeping tabs on a potentially unpredictable prisoner."

"Elian was fine until he saw Valery," I said, my previous anger toward the witch rising again. "She took every last scrap of hope he had left and flushed it down the toilet."

"She's not really a people person."

"No shit."

The Blackheart's expression grew thoughtful. "The question is, where would a currently immortal, life-sucking prince want to spend his evening after finding out he's royally screwed and there are no easy answers to his epic problem?"

I shrugged. "That depends on if he's thinking rationally or not."

"And if he is?"

I tried to put myself in Elian's shoes—someone who'd found out the one person in the Empire he believed could help cure him offered only death as an answer. "If it were me, and all hope was gone and there was nobody to blame or count on, I'd want to feel normal again. If only for one more night."

"And how would you feel normal if you were him?" The Blackheart eyed me. "Sorry, I'm not exactly an expert in how filthy rich people think. But you are. No offense."

"None taken." I considered Elian's limited options, but only one thing made sense to me. "Well . . . he said he remembered going to Deluxe when he came to Cresidia. That he'd loved it there in the past."

"You think that Prince Elian is enjoying dinner, drinks, and a show at Deluxe?" Jericho replied skeptically.

"He's been stuck in a posh version of a prison cell while the queen treats him like a drooling toddler for the last year, and before that he was semiconscious, starving, and constantly in pain—for fifteen years. Dinner, drinks, and a nice view of beautiful dancers wearing sexy, sparkly costumes seems like it would be a fantastic option to me."

Jericho frowned. "You might be right."

My gut told me I was. And my gut rarely lied. "Call Viktor. Tell him."

He shook his head. "No, not yet. My brother's probably beside himself right now. He had one job, and that was to keep an eye on Aunt Issy's baby boy. No gold star for him. Besides, he's still pissed at me that I didn't let him meet Val today." The Blackheart's lips curved to the side. "We'll check it out first. Just you and me."

I nodded. "Let's go."

SIX

"This might be hard to believe," I said out loud, while navigating the crowded sidewalks on our way back to the theater. "But I miss when the memory magic was my biggest problem."

"The good old days," Jericho said, but there was not a hint of humor in his voice. "Any more echoes today?"

"Not yet. I've been trying to summon one, but there's been nothing since the one with Banyon and my father. I wish I'd paid more attention to the details, but seeing my father and the warlock together was too much of a shock."

"I can imagine." He blew out a breath, his brow furrowed. "Look, I know I have my issues with Banyon, but I don't want you to hide anything about him from me. I want to help you figure this mystery out, Drake. I can't let my personal hatred for that guy get in the way."

"That's . . . good to hear. Thank you."

The Blackheart's expression was tense, as if he didn't want to say anything else, but then he shook it off. "I was at that fight club because I was meeting with someone—a warlock who knows a little about memory magic."

I blinked. "Really?"

Jericho nodded. "Val was less than forthcoming when it came to any information that could help you, but the guy I talked to—after I paid him off, of course—was a bit more helpful. He said he'd had a memory box in his possession once. It belonged to a mage from a century ago. He even dipped into a couple of the memories, the proper way. Not the whole box dumped into his head, like in your situation."

I'd stopped walking. Jericho's sleeve was now in my grasp, and I stared up at his face with surprise. "I want to talk to him too. Where is he now?"

"Sorry, but he's not open to further discussion on the subject. The memories he saw were disturbing, apparently. Turned him off experiencing echoes altogether. He ultimately sold the box for a small fortune and never dabbled in the black market again. Nasty little gambling addiction now, which is why he was happy to talk tonight for a nice payoff."

I couldn't believe that Jericho had met with this warlock without me, but given our argument earlier, I wasn't too surprised that he hadn't invited me along. "Fine, okay. What did he say that could help me?"

"According to this warlock, he had total control over the echoes. He could speed them up, slow them down, run them backward . . . kind of like watching recorded footage. And more than that, he said he could see and hear things that the memory creator didn't . . . like, read an address on a letter, or notice a bee landing on a flower. It's not so much a memory as a moment, frozen in time, and you can explore it at will."

I stared at Jericho with shock. What he was describing was nothing like anything I'd experienced yet. "How is that possible?"

He spread his hands. "Magic."

"That doesn't explain anything. Did he say how he was able to do these things while inside an echo?"

"No. He only said that it's possible."

This information did nothing but frustrate me. "This isn't helpful. This warlock's experience isn't the same as mine. Besides, he could have been lying."

He shrugged. "Possibly, but I don't think he was. I'm not saying this is an instruction manual on memory magic, just a push in the right direction."

I considered all of this. "If it is possible, then I need to figure out how to do it for myself."

"There you go. So, basically, the next time you have one, just . . . try to think outside of the box. You're not only an observer, but you can also manipulate the echo to help you find what you're looking for. Does that make sense?"

"I guess so." In my previous echo, Banyon had hinted at a way to make his memories more useful, to gather information from them. If what Jericho was saying was true, then this could be a game changer for me to find the information I needed. "Did Valery point you to this warlock to get more information for me?"

"No."

I waited for him to say more, but he didn't. "So, you found him yourself."

He blinked.

"For me," I added.

"Maybe."

My uncertainty about the information Jericho had given to me now shifted to a bright flash of happiness. "You defied Valery's orders. For me."

"She didn't directly order me not to look for information on that magic."

"Maybe not, but . . . still. Thank you."

Jericho nodded, his attention fixed on the sidewalk ahead of us, and we continued in silence for a few moments.

I hesitated before I spoke again, but I had to say it. "I don't want to have any more secrets between us. And not only about Banyon. About anything." My throat tightened as I said it, but it proved to me just how true it was.

"Everybody's got secrets," he replied quietly.

"Sure, but . . . it's just that, you and me—we've been through a lot together in such a short time."

"Agreed."

"And it's not over yet."

"I know. You still need my help to find the prince."

"That's not what I meant." I tried to wrangle that wandering courage of mine. "You're my friend."

It felt like such a small word to describe how I felt about the Blackheart, but it would do for now.

Jericho gave me a sidelong look. "I don't have friends."

"You have me." I pushed as confident a smile on my lips

as I possibly could. "Sure, I'm a bit messy around the edges, and maybe a little too self-involved—"

"Maybe?"

"Fine, *definitely* too self-involved. But I am your friend, Jericho. Whether you like it or not, I *am*."

He didn't smile back. His brows drew together. "Valery wouldn't be too happy about that."

"Screw Valery."

"No thanks. She's gorgeous, but not really my type."

I rolled my eyes. "You know what I mean."

Finally, I'd earned the edge of a grin, but it faded as quickly as it appeared. "So, no more secrets, huh?"

"Total and complete disclosure," I agreed. "Yes, please."

"Fine. But that deal goes both ways, got it?"

I nodded. "Got it."

We'd reached Deluxe without me even realizing we were still walking, everything Jericho had told me forming brand-new questions in my head. Summoning an echo was one thing, but *controlling* an echo? I'd never considered I could do anything like that.

If it were true, the possibilities were endless. I just wished the echoes would come when I tried to summon them. I'd try again later. And I'd keep trying until it worked.

If some random warlock with a gambling addiction could do it, then why couldn't I?

We entered Deluxe and navigated the foyer leading to the theater. Inside, there was a show in progress. Beautiful dancers.

Feathers. Glitter and sequins. Loud music. I paid no attention to any of it, instead scanning the room, my gaze moving over the patrons at tables drinking and eating, all seemingly without a care in the world.

Were any of them on the list that Banyon showed my father? Were there mages in this audience who didn't even realize they had the power to summon elementia? Or . . . mages who desperately hid who they were for fear of losing a life filled with freedom and status?

And then, finally, I spotted him.

Elian sat at a large booth right in front of the stage. The table was laden with bottles of wine. A beautiful dark-haired girl was seated next to him. After a moment, I realized it was Daria.

For a moment, the angle of their faces made me think of being in the Queen's Keep, of witnessing Elian devouring his victim in a frightening kiss that literally and horrifically sucked the life out of them, leaving behind a desiccated corpse.

Without thinking twice, I closed the distance to his table and wrenched the prince back from Daria. "Elian, no!"

The prince turned, casting a confused look up at me. "Joss? What's wrong?"

I blinked, then looked at Daria, who was touching up her lip gloss with the help of a tiny hand mirror.

"Hi, Jericho," she said brightly. And then with a little less enthusiasm: "Oh, and Josslyn."

"Hey, Daria." Jericho nodded at her. "Made a new friend, I see."

"Oh yes," she said with a smile. "Elian and I have been having lots of fun since he arrived."

"We *were* having a great deal of fun," Elian corrected. "Until we were interrupted."

I gaped at him. "You're . . . okay. Are you really okay?"

Elian fixed me with a cool smile. "Never better."

"You left the motel without saying anything."

"I didn't realize I needed your permission." The prince handed Daria a glass of wine. "Let's make a toast, shall we?"

"To what?" she replied.

"To life," Elian said, raising his glass. "Something that needs to be appreciated fully and completely, every single day, since one never knows when you'll be locked in your room with only weak tea and egg-salad sandwiches."

"I'll, uh . . . drink to that. Sure." Daria clinked her glass with his and watched as Elian drained the wine in a single gulp as she took a single sip.

I realized then that Prince Elian was very, very drunk.

"Elian," I said gently. "I was worried about you."

"That's so kind of you. And entirely unnecessary." Then he frowned. "Oh, you mean . . . *that.* I thought you were worried about my painful disappointment from early this afternoon. But you're worried about my potential behavior now in public. Don't be. My hunger is still under control. My thirst, on the other hand, is bottomless." He signaled to a waiter. "More wine!"

I shared a look with Jericho, annoyed that he looked amused by all of this.

"Do something," I told the Blackheart.

"What do you suggest?" he replied. "Your brother seems to be enjoying an evening out with a new friend after a difficult day."

"In public."

"And?"

"Don't worry, Joss," Elian said dismissively. "Like I said before, nobody knows who I am."

"Who are you?" Daria asked, sliding her fingers through his dark blond hair. "Someone important?"

"Possibly the most important person you've ever had the privilege to personally meet," he told her.

She chuckled at this. "Well, now I'm definitely intrigued. Tell me more."

"I would. If I were to tell anyone in the Empire my many secrets, it would be you, Daria. Do you know how long it's been since I've had the company of a beautiful girl like yourself?"

"No idea."

"An eternity," he said solemnly. "A painful, depressing eternity."

To her credit, she gave him a dazzling smile. "You are a sweet talker."

"It's the truth. Utterly and completely the truth." He studied her for a moment with an unfocused gaze. "Marry me, my love. Give me a reason to want to live another day."

Daria laughed and reached for the fresh bottle that had just been delivered as she flicked an amused look at Jericho before returning her full attention to the prince. "I think you need more wine, Elian."

"I need more of everything," he agreed.

She kissed his cheek. "I have to get ready to go on stage again, but I'll be back later, I promise."

"When you're my wife, you won't ever have to dance for money again," he told her very seriously. "You will be my queen."

Daria laughed lightly at this. "That sounds wonderful."

I pulled Jericho's sleeve to lead him away from the table so we could talk in semiprivate. "Do something," I urged again.

"I'm not doing anything," he replied.

"Aren't you upset? He's all over your girlfriend." I didn't like saying the word, but it had to be said. It had to be acknowledged, since it had weighed on me ever since last night.

"Daria's not my girlfriend. Although, she is most definitely a girl. I know that for an undisputed, scientific fact." Jericho smirked at my dark look. "You're not jealous, are you, Drake?"

I glared at him. "Of course not."

"I thought we'd decided to be truthful with each other."

"Shut up." My cheeks heated up in an instant. Jericho Nox. The only boy in the entire Empire who could make me blush.

His amusement lasted only another moment before it faded. He glanced back toward the prince and groaned. "His Royal Highness is beckoning me."

He moved back to the table, which Daria had just departed from, just as Elian began to pour another glass of wine from the full bottle. "Yes?"

Elian's expression had sobered significantly in the minute we'd stepped away from the table, a stark contrast to his jovial drunkenness. "I need to speak to Valery again."

"I'm not her personal assistant, but I'll see when she can fit you into her busy schedule."

"No, it can't wait. I need to speak to her immediately." He glowered at us each in turn. "Having you both hovering around like annoying, overprotective insects make me think of my mother. Please, sit."

I did as he suggested, with Jericho sliding into the booth next to me.

"Why do you want to see Valery?" Jericho asked carefully.

"I refuse to accept the answer she gave me. There has to be more. Perhaps not the cure I hoped for, but . . . I know there's magic out there—like what Viktor is seeking to shield his identity. There has to be something to ease my hunger, to allow me to function as a normal person again without posing a risk to others. A ring, an amulet, a . . . an elemental tattoo created from enchanted ink. Something. Anything. I don't know. I can't accept that death is the only answer for me. And if there's someone who would know, it's your employer."

"She said she doesn't know," Jericho replied.

Elian slammed his fist down on the table, making me jump. "That's not good enough!"

"Easy, Your Highness. Talking to Valery in the state that you're in is not a good idea. She's big on respect, and I don't think you're in the right state of mind now not to say something you'll regret."

"Summon her here," Elian commanded. "I won't ask again."

Jericho shook his head. "Not going to happen. Not tonight, not like this. Maybe tomorrow I can arrange for another meeting between the two of you, but it's not going to happen tonight. Here's what I will do, though. I'm going to personally take you back to your motel and tuck you in, all nice and cozy. After a nice, long sleep, I'm sure you'll feel much better, despite the inevitable hangover that comes from drinking four bottles of wine."

Elian narrowed his eyes. "You disrespect me."

Jericho rolled his eyes. "Listen, I get that you're dealing with a ton of shit right now, but you seriously need to—"

Elian grabbed Jericho by his throat, his fingers digging in. "You said I'm stronger than you. Shall we put that to the test? Do you want me to make a scene that you'll have to explain to Valery later? She isn't someone who likes the attention focused on her, is she?"

Jericho sputtered, his eyes going wide as he clawed at Elian's grip on him without succeeding in loosening it.

"Elian," I snarled. "Let go of him!"

"I will when he agrees to contact Valery immediately."

"And if he doesn't?"

"Then I'll break his neck. What happens then? If a Blackheart dies after being brought back to life, will he stay dead?"

Jericho finally managed to peel Elian's grip away from his throat. While the dancers took the stage and the music swelled, they were having a miniature version of a Queensgames match—hopefully not to the death—right in the middle of this theater.

There were red and purple marks on Jericho's throat from Elian's grip. The Blackheart's expression held only menace.

"You really want to speak to Val that badly?" he said, his

voice raspy now. "Sure, no problem. Just remember that I warned you."

Jericho gave me a pointed look that told me how much he hated the prince before he moved off, pulling his phone out of his coat pocket.

"That," I said to the prince, "was a big mistake."

Elian said nothing, staring intently at the dance in progress.

"What exactly do you think you're doing right now?" I prompted tensely.

"I don't know." Elian hissed out a breath and shut his eyes tightly. "That isn't me. Not even when I was alive and well did I make pissy demands. I'm a monster now."

I couldn't help but sympathize with my half brother. "No. You're desperate for answers and it's getting to you. I get it."

"Don't try to defend me." His knuckles whitened on his empty wine glass. "I'm undefendable."

"No, you're in pain. And I'm sorry. I wish there was more I could do to help you." I studied his tense expression, his black eyes full of sorrow and regret. "I get that you're driven to find the answers to your problem. But coming at Valery like this, head-on, isn't a good idea. Believe me; I should know."

"What else should I do? Accept my fate?" He drew in a shaky breath. "I lied to you before. I said I didn't want to be king, but I do. It's the only thing that's kept me going all these months, something tangible for me to hold on to. I was raised for it, Joss."

"I know you were, Elian."

There was such anguish on his face, I didn't know what to

say or do to make it better. "There are things I know, things my mother told me . . . As heir, it's my right to know about any burden she carries. She lives constantly under the threat of assassination by Lord Banyon, knowing that if he wanted to get to her, he could. And if she was killed, I would be king. Even now."

I shook my head. "I don't know what you're saying. What did she tell you?"

He reached for the wine bottle, and I didn't stop him from pouring another glass for himself. He took a sip before speaking again, a humorless smile touching his lips. "Family secrets."

A breath caught in my chest. "Like what?"

"I can't tell you. I can only tell my heir on their seventeenth birthday. And if there is no heir—and it's not looking good in that regard, despite my proposal to the lovely Daria—then the secret dies with me. And no one will ever know the truth."

I went very still.

Banyon had believed the queen had a huge secret that could potentially change everything. And now Elian was talking about family secrets, things he'd learned from the queen. Was it possible that this could be what Banyon had been looking for?

Or, more likely, maybe I was reading too much into this. Maybe Elian was talking about something as benign as the location of the family jewels. Either way, he was drunk enough that I wasn't likely to get much sense out of him.

He sent a dark look toward Jericho, now speaking on his phone in the shadows to the left of the stage. "The Blackheart's had it so easy," he said. "He has strength and stamina and a chance at a second life. Why am I the one who's been cursed with this darkness?"

"If you think Jericho's had it easy, you're dead wrong," I told him. I'd dealt with a lot of drunk friends over the last few years—and, in turn, they'd dealt with a drunk me—so I knew I had to be patient with Elian, no matter what he said. Wine loosened the lips, but the truth that spilled out was very subjective. "Actually, he'd be dead right now if Viktor hadn't sacrificed everything in his life to help him escape."

"Yes." Elian ran his index finger over the edge of his glass. "That is what you believe, isn't it?"

"What are you talking about?"

"The Queensguard's sacrifice." Elian's lip curled with distaste. "The Blackheart doesn't entirely trust his younger brother, which is smart of him. I might have said something otherwise, but I didn't feel it was any of my business."

I frowned at him. "Jericho trusts Viktor."

"Maybe on the surface. But there's something there . . . some doubt in his mind. The Blackheart has excellent instincts, I'll give him that. Of course, he's trying to push his doubt down. He doesn't want to accept the truth about his brother."

"What truth? Viktor gave up his entire life to save Jericho. Elian, I don't know what you're talking about, but there's nothing you can say about Viktor that will make me think he's anything but a hero." As I said the words, I realized how much I believed them. I wasn't romantically interested in the ex-Queensguard anymore, like I'd been before the announcement of his engagement to Celina, but it didn't dull my appreciation for the fact that he'd sacrificed his own happiness for that of his estranged brother.

"Oh, yes, he's quite a hero," Elian said with an edge to his words that confused me.

"You don't believe that?"

"I believe that's the lie that Viktor has come to believe. The heroic champion of the Queensgames. Everywhere you look, you see his face. Unlike mine. But I watch those around me. And I'm a very good listener. My mother, for all her security precautions, isn't careful about what she says around me. Or whom she meets with in front of me. You already know that Viktor was part of the inner circle."

Meaning, of course, that Viktor knew Elian was alive, and that he used the Queen's Keep as a feeding ground, since the prisoners there wouldn't be missed by anyone. The other prisoners believed anyone who disappeared had been lucky enough to escape.

"So what? What did you hear?" When Elian didn't answer me, I let out a groan of frustration. "Fine, don't tell me. I don't care. Viktor is a good brother, and now he has to figure out how to survive the rest of his life without being recognized. He'd be executed for being a traitor."

The prince raised one regal eyebrow. "Don't you think it's surprising that he'd sacrifice absolutely everything for a brother he'd already disowned? Surely, there must have been another way to help the Blackheart escape, behind the scenes, rather than to jump straight into the fray. A commander. A champion. Part of the elite and hand-selected secret inner circle as he climbed the social ladder in his swift and steady rise to power. Here's a question for you. What if my mother discovered that this loyal Queensguard who craved more from his life and career was the prisoner's brother? A prisoner with direct ties to a powerful witch whose identity she's been desperate to discover?"

I stared at him. "Wait. Are you saying that Viktor Raden is a spy for the queen?"

When Elian raised his black-eyed gaze to mine, there was no humor I could find there. "Yes, Joss. That's exactly what I'm saying."

SEVEN

Before I could ask more questions, Jericho returned to the table. "She's on her way," he said to Elian, then added, "*Asshole.*"

A shadow fell across Elian's expression. "I apologize for my earlier behavior. Desperation has made me forget my manners."

"Whatever." Jericho eyed him unpleasantly for a moment longer before a flicker of sympathy entered his gaze. "Whatever it's worth, I'm sorry you have to deal with this problem."

"I appreciate that."

"Put your hands on me like that again, though? And you'll have another problem to deal with. You might be stronger and allegedly immortal, but I promise I can still make you hurt really bad."

Elian nodded solemnly. "I have no doubt."

Jericho eyed me with uncertainty. "You're quiet."

"Just doing some thinking," I replied.

I'd just promised not to keep any secrets from the Blackheart, but Elian had dropped this one in my lap like a big, smelly, slimy fish, and I didn't know what to do with it. What the prince had suggested about Viktor made me sick to my stomach. I wanted to deny it, with the certainty I'd had only minutes ago, but something about the accusation felt like it fit.

Viktor. A spy for the queen.

It couldn't be. But—it made a painful kind of sense. A trusted Queensguard—who just happened to be the prisoner's brother. A prisoner with ties to the one mage in the Empire that the queen wanted to find more than any other.

Viktor had given up so much for a brother he'd been estranged from—a reputation, a career, a marriage to the current prime minister's daughter. I still wasn't sure how deep the emotions went between Viktor and Celina, but an agreement had been made and I knew, despite her initial misgivings about an engagement at only eighteen years of age, that Celina was open to the possibility of a future with Viktor.

And now this.

If what Elian had suggested was true, then Viktor hadn't thrown it all away. It would all be waiting back at the palace for his eventual victorious return after a job well done. What would happen to Jericho then? Would he be recaptured? Executed?

I needed to talk to Jericho about this, but not here. Not now.

A mere two songs—and accompanying choreographed dances—later, Valery approached our table, as poised and elegant as she'd been last night at the restaurant. She wore black satin, with pearls at her throat, her lips as red as blood.

She didn't spare me a single glance.

"Good evening, Your Highness," she said evenly. "Jericho tells me that you urgently wanted to speak with me again."

"Yes. Thank you for coming here, but I'm afraid I've had a bit too much to drink. My thoughts are . . . not as clear as I'd like them to be."

"Understandable, of course."

Elian straightened his shoulders and met the witch's gaze directly. "I . . . again, must ask for your help, Valery. I don't want to die—I want to live, so the cure you've presented me with isn't the answer I am searching for. There must be another path for me to take."

"Your mother has already presented another path for you—to feed your hunger when it rises."

He shook his head. "That's not acceptable."

"I'm sorry, but I don't know what you want me to say."

"I want you to help me," he said, and the raw, pained desperation in his voice made me cringe. "Like my mother has always believed you can."

"Your mother was wrong about me," Valery replied, her expression serene.

"So, then what's the truth?" I spoke up, trying to make sense of everything. "I know about the intimidating rumors about you, but they're obviously false."

Valery raised a brow. "Rumors?"

I nodded. "If you really were an immortal goddess of death, you could help him."

I couldn't help but hear Jericho groan.

Sorry, I thought. *But someone has to say it.*

Valery studied me without speaking for several uncomfortable moments.

"If I was an immortal goddess of death," she finally replied, her voice chillingly low, "then, surely, I wouldn't give a damn about lowly mortals who ask lowly favors of me. Would I? Especially not those who don't know their place."

I didn't flinch away from her glare. I'd managed to pick at her shiny exterior just a little, get under that flawless pale skin. I was poking at a tiger—I knew that—but it was a tiger who knew more than she was admitting to.

"All Elian wants is your help," I said.

"Then he came to the wrong place," she hissed. "Because the only person I'm interested in helping is myself."

"You're helping Lord Banyon get his box of memories back," I countered. "So, you do help when you want to."

That earned me a truly venomous glare from the witch.

"Drake . . ." Jericho growled. "Enough."

I recognized a warning when I heard one. But we weren't in a secluded restaurant alcove or private rooftop garden tonight— we were in the middle of a theater surrounded by hundreds of people.

"Where is Banyon?" I pressed. "I'd really like to talk to him. Maybe he can help Elian if you can't."

Valery smiled, a cold and soulless smile that made me hate her more than I already did. "I'll be leaving now."

She turned, but I was so worked up with my frustration for her, my concern for Elian, and my head still in a jumble about the possibility that Viktor could be a spy, that I instinctively grabbed her wrist to stop her.

The moment I made contact a tidal wave of golden smoke

crashed over me. It seemed to come out of absolutely no-where, with no warning, before depositing me into one of Lord Banyon's memories—a memory I definitely did absolutely nothing to summon.

The theater was gone, and my head spun while I grappled to get my bearings. Flames rose up all around me, and I staggered backward, crying out from the burning heat.

I recognized the scene before me. It wasn't my first time visiting the night of this specific memory. The palace fire, sixteen years ago.

Two charred bodies lay across my path and I shuddered as I stumbled around them. I felt nauseous from the horrific sight of the mutilated bodies and the pungent scent of death in the air. A group of Queensguards, their faces covered in soot and their gold-trimmed black uniforms singed, ran past me with their guns drawn.

"Over here," one called as he waved an arm at the others. "Hurry!"

I made myself take a breath to calm down. I remembered what Jericho had said—that I could control the echoes, if I concentrated. I could see more than just what Banyon saw. This, while unexpected and horrible, was my first chance to put that to the test.

I turned and focused on the charred body closest to me, forcing myself to notice something that the warlock wouldn't have noticed. The corpse wore a gold belt buckle. I recognized it as designer, expensive, with the logo of the fashion house etched into its surface.

It wasn't much, but it proved to me that there were details here that I could hone in on if I remained calm and I concentrated.

Good. It was a start.

Leaving the bodies behind me, I swiftly moved to follow the guards. The palace wasn't a single structure—it was at the center of a capsule city, with cobblestone streets and shops and restaurants, taking up a three-mile radius. I knew that the blaze had been centered at the palace itself, a sprawling series of buildings and towers, but contained before it managed to spread everywhere else. Even now I heard the alarms, and trucks filled with water and firefighting supplies sped past me.

The guards moved along the main road that led to the royal residence. The night was lit as brightly as day from the flames. Lord Banyon stood in the center of the street, his back to the guards as he regarded the main palace. His fists clenched at his sides, and fire lit up his arms all the way to his shoulders.

"On your knees!" a guard yelled at him. "Now! Or we'll shoot!"

Banyon didn't move. The fire continued to burn.

"Go ahead and shoot me," he said without a sliver of emotion in his voice.

"The queen wants you captured alive."

"Then she's a damn fool. Because I'm going to burn the eyes right out of her face. Just like this." The warlock turned, slicing through the air with a fiery gesture. The guard's eyes caught fire and he ran, screaming, away from the mage.

I watched all of this unfold with horror.

"Take him down," another guard commanded.

They began to fire their weapons, with more than enough

ammunition between them to swiftly end anyone's life. But Banyon continued to stand, and the fire that surrounded him blazed brighter and hotter. It worked like a shield, I realized in awe, the bullets incinerating before they made contact.

The warlock flicked a hand, lighting up one guard, then another, until they were all ablaze, writhing and screaming in agony on the ground. And then Banyon casually strode past them without a shred of remorse in his dark gaze.

But he wasn't trying to escape the palace city. He headed directly toward the palace itself.

His fire blazed brighter for a moment longer before it extinguished. He frowned and looked down at his hands.

"Not now," he growled. "Damn it. Not now!"

A moment later, someone tackled him to the ground. A lone Queensguard with a knife in his grip. Banyon dodged the fall of the blade, and it sliced against the pavement.

They wrestled on the ground for a moment, until the guard finally managed to press the blade to the warlock's throat. Banyon froze.

"Where's your magic now?" the guard sneered. "Can't keep it going forever, can you?"

"Long enough to do damage," Banyon bit out.

"The queen wants you alive. But I plan to disappoint her."

Blood trickled down the warlock's throat.

Neither of them noticed a figure that approached, slowly, stealthily. It was a teenage girl with dark hair, pale skin, and naked fear upon her face. The fear was the only thing I didn't recognize about Valery.

She watched the warlock and the guard for a moment before continuing on, slipping past them as they were distracted by grappling with each other.

"The queen believes you're the most powerful warlock in the Empire," the guard sneered. "She's wrong, isn't she?"

"Issy's been wrong about many things."

Valery hesitated, and a look of determination chased away her previous fear. She turned, closing the distance between her and the guard in a few short steps.

He looked up at her, scowling. "What are you—?"

She reached forward and touched his cheek. He cried out, the sound of pain and surprise, and then his skin turned dry, ashy, his eyes sinking back into his skull. The knife fell to the ground next to Banyon, and the guard fell to the side. Dead.

A desiccated corpse.

I watched this unfold with shock. It had only taken moments.

Banyon slowly, carefully, pushed up to his feet, wiping the trace of blood from his throat. He eyed Valery warily, but she made no move toward him.

"Do you know how rare your gift is?" he said to her.

"It's not a gift; it's a curse." She stared at her hand, as if it had acted without her permission. "My father called me a demon. He let the guards take me away to be executed. But the fire . . . I managed to escape. You set the fire, didn't you?"

"Yes, I did." His fists were clenched at his sides. "You saved my life."

"If you caused this . . ." She looked around in a circle at the carnage. "How could a single guard take you down?"

He stared at his hands. "I'm weakened. I need to recover my strength." Then he cast a dark glance at the palace. "I planned to find the queen and her favorite commander. And then I was going to kill them both, very slowly."

"Why?"

"Because they've stolen everything from me." He gave her a calculating look. "What do you know of your magic?"

"Nothing. Only that my father blamed me for the crops that wouldn't grow. For the calf that died after I touched it." She drew in a shaky breath. "Only that it frightens me."

"Mages have strived for centuries to do what you can do naturally. You can summon the darkest magic."

"I thought it was earth magic."

"It's not." He gave her a steely look. "How old are you, girl?"

"Sixteen." Valery raised her chin and returned his challenging stare. "You know what this magic is, what it can do. Teach me. Teach me to be strong like you."

He shook his head. "I'm not strong."

"Yes, you are. But if you go after the queen now, you'll die. I've had enough death for one night. Haven't you?"

The warlock stood there for a long moment, surrounded by flames, his shoulders tense, as if contemplating the universe itself. All I could see was pain in every part of him—body, mind, and soul. He'd witnessed his beloved wife's death and his infant daughter stolen from him moments later. And he had then razed the city, leaving countless innocent people dead. There was no joy in him. No satisfaction. No hope. Only pain.

Finally, Banyon turned away from the palace to face the girl, doubt in his eyes fading to certainty.

"Very well, young witch," he said. "I will teach you to be strong."

I expected that the echo would end there, that I would go back to Deluxe as it faded, but when the golden wave hit me this time, it only swept me away to another scene, another memory.

Valery seemed slightly older in this echo, her dark hair long and in a single braid that hung over her shoulder while she carefully turned the last page in a large leather-bound book.

"That was fascinating," she said.

Banyon stood nearby. "Many would find the writings of a warlock from a century ago to be boring."

"Not me. I want more."

"That's the last volume in my collection, unfortunately. At least, for now. I'm always searching for additional rare pieces of magic history. However, I do have something else to share with you today that I think you'll find interesting."

"What?"

"This." He placed the golden dagger that I now recognized all too well next to the closed book.

"It's so beautiful," she said, tentatively drawing her fingertip over the etchings on the blade.

"The legend is that this dagger is thousands of years old and comes from another world, accessible only by magical stone gateways. This particular dagger belonged to a beautiful but deadly immortal goddess named Valoria who lived many lifetimes in many worlds and went by many names. She was a villain or a heroine, depending on who spoke of her. She was the last of her kind, a race of magical beings who watched over the mortal realm. And now this dagger is all that is left of any of them, including her."

"That's certainly a lovely legend," she said. "To go with such a lovely gold weapon."

"It's not a weapon. Nor is it gold, as it appears. It's said to be forged from elementia itself to bring life and death in equal measure to those powerful enough to wield it. That, also, is only legend. What I do know for sure is it infinitely enhances one's access to elementia. I believe it will help you to hone your control over the darkest magic."

"Magic like a goddess, not only a mere witch," she said, entranced by the dagger.

Banyon nodded. "One day, this will belong to you. It seems fitting, for Valoria's legendary dagger to one day be wielded by a powerful witch named Valery."

"Thank you, my lord." Valery met his gaze, and I could see true affection in her eyes. "Where did you get it from?"

His lips curved. "I stole it from my father just before I ran away from home. To be fair, he stole it from his father. And so on for generations."

She laughed at this, as if it were the funniest thing she'd ever heard. "Perhaps he should have seen your act of thievery coming from a mile away."

Banyon began to laugh as well. "Perhaps he did. Perhaps he allowed me to steal it."

Another golden wave moved in to obliterate the scene before me, and then cleared away to reveal another.

Valery stood, her shoulders straight, as a trio of people—a man and two women—circled her. Banyon stood nearby, and the young witch kept casting worried glances at him.

"Well?" Banyon prompted after a few moments passed. "Will you accept Valery into your institution?"

"She's entirely unacceptable," one of the women said, her lip curling with distaste. "Death magic is forbidden."

"In the view of the queen, all magic is forbidden," he countered.

"This girl is far too dangerous, her magic far too unpredictable."

"She wants to learn from the best. I have taught her everything I can."

"Death magic," the man spoke up, his tone cold and unwelcoming, "is a crime against nature. You should know that better than most, Zarek."

"It comes naturally to Valery. This is not elementia distorted to fit a dark ritual. This is as natural as life itself."

"No. Death is the opposite of life. This girl is a danger to the world and, in my opinion, she should be erased from it."

Valery cut a cold look at the man, her eyes narrowing. "Do you want to see just how dangerous I can be?"

"Valery," Banyon said, his voice low with warning.

"They are threatening me."

"They're doing nothing of the sort. You don't need them,

anyway. They don't deserve a student with your level of skill."

The mages scoffed and filed out, casting poisonous glances back over their shoulders. Once they'd left, Valery's tears finally began to fall.

"I'm all alone," she choked out. "No one understands what it's like to be me, what it feels like to have this darkness inside of you that wants to be released."

"Valery . . ."

"Leave me alone!"

She ran from him and he didn't follow.

More golden smoke, another scene appeared.

Banyon stood in his small kitchen alone, reading a handwritten note. His brows knit together and there was pain in his eyes.

ZB—

I chose not to wait until your death to take possession of Valoria's dagger. Perhaps the goddess would have understood me. It seems that I don't fit into any world, so I plan to create my own. You did what you could. I will always be grateful to you for that.

—V

Finally, the last golden wave brought me back to the theater. I was weakened, aching, and felt as if I'd survived a hurricane, weary down to my very bones. The smoke cleared, and I realized that Valery's wrist was no longer in my grasp.

Instead, her hands were around my throat.

"What did you see?" she snarled.

My eyes widened as her grip tightened. At the restaurant yesterday, she'd been so interested in what I'd seen of Banyon's echoes—especially the night of the palace fire. Now I knew why. It contained her past. Her secrets.

"Goddess of death," I whispered.

Her hands were so cold, my body felt the painful freeze of them. The sounds of the theater, the music, the laughter, all began to fade away to nothing.

"Let her go," Jericho snarled. He loomed beside me, and I watched, distantly, as he shoved his boss back from me, hard enough that she released her grip.

I wiped the blood from under my nose. There was a great deal of blood, more than ever before. Just as I made that disturbing realization, my knees went out. I felt Jericho's arms tighten around me as the room dimmed, the music faded completely, and I fell headfirst into darkness.

EIGHT

I opened my eyes, wondering why everyone in the theater had gone utterly silent.

It turned out there was a good reason for it. I wasn't at Deluxe anymore. Instead, I lay in a bed with white sheets that was far more comfortable than what my shabby motel room offered. I pushed myself up onto my elbows and slowly scanned the dark and unfamiliar room until my gaze finally landed on something—or, rather, *someone*—I recognized.

Jericho.

The Blackheart was seated in a chair a few feet from the edge of the bed, his arms crossed over his chest. His eyes were closed, his breathing even.

I watched him sleep, taking this rare opportunity to study him uninterrupted. The small scar on his jaw, his dark hair—as black as ink in the shadows of the room. His head tilted slightly to one side, which gave me a good view of the dagger tattoo he'd gotten when he was fifteen because he thought it would make him look tough in a life that demanded toughness. He hadn't known then how much a dagger would come to symbolize for him only two years later.

"Are you really asleep or are you just pretending?" I whispered.

When he didn't reply, I slipped out of the bed, realizing I now wore black silk pajamas that I didn't recognize. How long had I been unconscious? It reminded me uncomfortably of the night of the Gala, when the memory magic had knocked me out and I'd woken the next day, safely tucked into bed with a worried Celina at my side.

I moved toward a mirror, peering at my reflection and searching for any noticeable damage. I looked fine, all things considered. Even my blue contact lenses were still in place.

What happened with Valery came back to me in a flash. I knew her secret now, and the reason why death magic came so easily to her. It was her default magic to summon. I didn't even know that was possible, but the chilling revelation explained a lot about the witch. Death magic wasn't regular elementia—earth, fire, water, or air.

What had Tamara said about it when she'd sensed the darkest magic inside of Jericho in the Keep?

"There is elementia, pure and natural and ever present like an invisible flowing river, and then there is the magic that lurks in the shadows of what is known, what is accessible to most witches or warlocks. The kind of magic only spoken about in legends, passed from generation to generation."

Maybe even Tamara hadn't known that for some mages, this kind of magic came to them as easily as breathing.

I didn't want to wake Jericho, but I needed to figure out where I was. I pushed open the door to the small bedroom and found myself in a hallway with sleek, dark wood floors. I followed this until it opened up into a large suite with white sofas and chic black-lacquered furniture. This was a luxurious apartment, one of the most beautiful homes I'd ever seen—and as the prime minister's daughter, I'd seen a lot of nice homes. This rivaled even the expansive chambers I'd been given at the royal palace. Floor-to-ceiling windows looked out at the sparkling lights of Cresidia. For a moment, I was hypnotized by the breathtaking view, my bare feet moving over the cool, smooth floor as I gazed at the city through the clear glass barrier.

It was then that I had the eerie sense that someone was silently watching me. I froze, then turned from the window to scan the large living room.

"Hello?" I said aloud. But I was met only with silence.

A table laden with framed photos caught my eye, and more uneasily now, I moved toward it. The pictures included those taken at high-profile charity events, star-studded parties, and theater openings. Valery was in each of them, looking perfect and smiling for the camera, wearing beautiful gowns and flaw-less makeup. In one of the photos, I was surprised to see that she posed with Queen Isadora herself, a smug and knowing smile on Valery's beautiful face.

So, it seemed that the queen had already met the infamous witch without even realizing it. Seeing the queen for the first time since I'd fled the palace, and her control, made my heart pound faster in my chest. I needed this reminder of how much I hated her.

"Drake . . ." Jericho's voice made me turn to see that he stood at the entrance to the room, running his hand through his messy, dark hair. It must have been his presence that I'd sensed before.

I held up the picture. "Your boss knows the queen. At least, well enough to have a picture taken with her."

"Yeah. Sure, whatever." He watched me, his brows furrowed. "So, what? You're just walking around like it's no big deal?"

"What are you talking about? What big deal?" I blinked. "Why do you look so serious?"

"Valery, she . . ." He hesitated, shaking his head. "When she touched you, she did something. Something bad. You went so pale, for a moment . . . I thought you were dead."

I understood what he meant immediately, and a shiver sped through me. "Your boss can kill someone by touching them, like . . . like a . . ."

"Like a goddess of death," he finished tensely. "Yeah. She can."

"You didn't mention that to me before."

"No," he agreed. "I didn't."

A flash of annoyance moved through me. "You should have."

He shook his head. "Part of her power over me is the inability to discuss her magic with anyone who doesn't already know the truth. But now you know."

I hated that she had this kind of power over him. I wished he'd seem to hate it as much, but over the last couple of years, he'd clearly come to accept it.

"I saw her in the echo, Jericho. She knew Banyon. He helped her when she was my age, but then she was rejected—by her own family, then by other mages."

He nodded. "I don't think she meant to hurt you as much as she did. She had Daria come over and . . . do something. It was like Valery had stolen something from inside of you, and Daria—well, she wasn't *healing* you, exactly. It was more like she was restoring what Val took . . . like filling up an empty tank with earth magic. It worked, enough for me to bring you here to Val's penthouse."

What he suggested disturbed me more than I could start to wrap my head around. "I guess I needed a power nap to recover."

Jericho shook his head. "More than a nap. That was three days ago."

I stared at him in shock. "Three days ago?"

"Yeah." He closed the distance between us and swept his gaze over me, from head to borrowed pajamas to foot. "How do you feel right now?"

"Better. Really." My heart skipped a beat at the intense way he was looking at me. "You were that worried about me?"

He didn't have a quick, snarky comeback to that like I thought he would.

"I thought she killed you," he bit out, his voice raw.

"She didn't," I told him firmly, although I shuddered at the realization of how close I'd come to death. "Seriously. You don't have to worry. I'm feeling all right, so you can—"

That was all I got out before he took my face in his hands and kissed me with such unexpected passion that, for a moment, I was sure I was still dreaming. I hadn't kissed him since we were in the Keep, even though I'd wanted to. So much had happened—to him, to me; too many pieces to the puzzle outside the prison, while inside everything had seemed so simple.

This kiss quickly erased any doubt I had. The feel of Jericho's mouth on mine was such a relief that I felt a sob rise in my throat and my eyes burned with tears.

"You scared the hell out of me, Drake," he whispered against my lips. When *I* was the one who didn't have a snappy comeback this time, he frowned. "It would be great if you said something right about now."

"*Something*," I managed. And then, "You kissed me."

Doubt crossed his expression for the briefest of moments before he shook it off. "Is that okay?"

"Definitely okay." I couldn't fight my smile before the expression faltered as quickly as it appeared. "I just thought that . . ."

"What?"

"That . . . after you learned the truth about me . . . that you wouldn't want to do that ever again."

Jericho focused on my mouth for a moment longer before he locked gazes with me. "I don't give a damn who your birth father is. What I think about him . . . well, trust me on this. It's got nothing to do with what I think about you."

His words made something that had gone dark inside of me start to brighten again. I took his hand in mine. "You think about me?"

He snorted softly. "Far too much, to be honest."

"I did say I wanted honesty, didn't I?"

"You did indeed." He slid his thumb over the new scar on my palm. "Now, tell me more about the echo you had just before my boss put you into a coma for three whole days."

I shivered at the thought of it. "Long story short, Valery

saved Banyon's life during the palace fire. His fire magic stopped working, and he couldn't defend himself. A guard was about to kill him on the spot, but she turned the guard into a dry, hollowed-out corpse like . . . like Elian can."

Jericho's expression shadowed. "It's different with the prince. Val has full control over her death magic. Well, except for the other night. You manage to push her buttons, Drake, and make her lose control. I'm thinking those memories in your head don't sit well with her, knowing that there's someone who can peer into the past and learn her closely guarded secrets." He met my gaze and held it. "You can't let her know you saw any of that."

Anger lit up inside of me at the fact that Valery had intimate knowledge about death magic and had cast Elian aside with no real answers to his questions. "She has to know more about how to help Elian. She just doesn't want to. Maybe knowing what he can do and how it's so similar to what she can do hits too close to home for her."

"Maybe. I don't know what Val really wants, to be honest."

"At least I know why she doesn't care what the queen does to other mages. They rejected her, called her unnatural and evil. And her father rejected her out of fear—let her be arrested. Banyon was the only person who accepted and valued her." I fell silent for a moment. "Did you know about her and Banyon?" I asked.

"No. Valery knows I hate him and why I hate him. And she's not in any hurry to fill in the blanks when it comes to her history, anyway."

"He's the reason she is what she is. He's even the reason she has that dagger—she stole it from him."

"Yeah. That sounds like something Val would do."

Prompted by a buzzing sound, Jericho pulled out his phone and frowned down at the screen. "Not again."

"Who is it?" I asked.

"Vik's looking for me," he replied. "He still wants to meet Val to discuss acquiring magic to help shield his identity. He's sick of being cooped up at the motel. I told him I've put my feelers out for something useful, and Val doesn't have to be a part of it, but he keeps poking at me to introduce them. Bad idea. Really bad."

My unsettling conversation with Elian came back to me in full force. Three days—it had been three days since he told me his suspicions about the ex-Queensguard, and I'd been unconscious the whole time.

"Where's Elian right now?" I asked.

"Contemplating his bright future, or lack thereof, in his motel room, last time I checked. Vik thinks it's time for him to return to the palace, but the prince has refused, at least until he knows you're not going to die." Jericho studied my suddenly stricken face. "What's the problem?"

"Did Elian say anything to you about your brother?"

"Like what?" He frowned when I didn't answer right away. "Drake, what is it? You look like you just swallowed a bucket of poison."

"It's bad," I warned him.

"Then I want to hear it even more."

I nodded, trying to gather my thoughts so I could explain this as clearly and concisely as possible. "At the theater, Elian and I were talking when you went to call Valery. The conversation turned to Viktor, and what he did for you, and what a brave and selfless thing that had been." I shook my head. "Elian disagreed. From what he overheard, what he saw at the palace, Elian believes that Viktor is a spy . . . that he helped you escape because the queen told him to."

Jericho stared at me, a deep frown creasing his brow. "Why would the queen have him do something like that?"

"Because she wanted to find Valery. And you know where she is."

Disbelief slid through the Blackheart's dark gaze, and he shook his head. "It's impossible. Sounds like the prince doesn't have proof. Only suspicions. Right?"

"That's true," I replied carefully.

"He's wrong about Vik."

"I hope you're right," I agreed, my heart pounding. "I really do."

"What my brother did for me . . . what he did to help me escape. He gave up everything he ever wanted. For *me*. Nobody makes that kind of sacrifice, do they?"

"Not nobody." I pressed my hand against his chest. His heart was beating very fast. "I don't have a single doubt in my mind that you would have done the same for him."

Pain slid through his black eyes before they hardened and he stepped back from me to make a call, pressing his phone to his ear.

"Vik? Yeah, it's me." A pause. "Are you ready to see Val

now?" Another pause. "Good. Meet me in the city square, twenty minutes. I'll bring you to her."

He ended the call and turned toward the door.

I grabbed his arm, my heart pounding. "Jericho, no. I know you believe in him, but this is a really bad idea."

He shoved the phone into his jacket pocket and began walking out of the room without replying to me. I caught up to him at the elevator, and he gave me a dark look.

"Stay here," he said.

The elevator doors opened, and Jericho got on; the doors closed between us.

And then I quickly went to get ready. After rinsing out my contact lenses and finding my clothes from the other night, I changed out of the silk pajamas in record time. Then I slipped into my shoes and left the penthouse to try to stop the Blackheart from potentially making the worst mistake of his life.

NINE

I knew where the city square was, but I was surprised that Jericho would choose it as a place to meet up with the reigning champion of the Queensgames. It was very public—an intersection of several main streets, flanked by huge hotels, casinos, restaurants, and theaters.

Three days had passed since I'd last been out, and it was night again. A light rain fell, but the weather wasn't keeping anyone inside. Umbrellas of all colors of the rainbow polka-dotted the crowd as people went about their evenings. The square itself was an open area the size of a city block, with benches, food stalls, and a huge fountain that famously shot water into the air every hour on the hour. Street performers milled about—jugglers, mimes, and musicians—entertaining the constant throng of tourists, in search of tips.

The first person I recognized in the square was Elian, who stood at the fountain watching my approach. He held a red umbrella to shield himself from the rain. I quickly closed the distance between us.

Relief filled his eyes. "You're alive."

"I am," I confirmed.

"The Blackheart wouldn't tell me anything, only that you were sleeping."

"Let's just say, I'm currently very well rested. How are you doing?"

"Not well. But I'm still here, waiting for a miracle. Sad to say that none have appeared out of nowhere."

"I'm sorry."

"Me too," he said. "But you're alive, and that's miracle enough for tonight."

From this vantage point, I could see a gigantic advertising screen set onto the side of tall hotel, currently showing a commercial featuring some of the local businesses and upcoming events with a booming voice-over.

Viktor's face appeared on-screen, three stories high, his perfect white teeth set into an alluring smile. "*The countdown is on*," he announced. *"Are you ready to join me for four days of danger and excitement as the battle for the next high champion begins? I'll save you a seat at the Queensgames. See you there!"*

Then I spotted Jericho moving with intention across the square toward someone wearing a dark blue hooded sweatshirt. I set off in his direction and quickly closed the distance between us.

"Think about this first," I warned the Blackheart.

"I told you to stay in the penthouse," he said sharply.

"Obviously, I ignored you."

"Obviously. Stay out of this, Drake."

By then we'd reached Viktor, who gave me a look of concern from under the edge of his hood. "Joss, my brother refused to give too many details about what happened to you the other night, but it was enough to make me worry. I'm glad to see you're fine."

"I appreciate that," I told him, eyeing his makeshift disguise. This was the first time I'd seen him since Elian had put the doubts in my mind. "Jericho, don't do this."

"Do what?"

"Don't take him to Valery."

The Blackheart studied me for a moment. "Is that what you think I'm here for?"

I was confused. "That's what you said on the phone."

Viktor watched us, his arms crossed over his chest. "What's going on? Aren't you taking me to your boss?"

"No," Jericho said, turning to face his brother. "Actually, I have questions about the night you broke me out of the palace. Let's start with this one: Why was it so easy for us to get away?"

I literally bit my tongue to keep myself from adding anything. I thought Jericho had dismissed any questions I'd raised about his brother, that he trusted him without a moment of doubt. But I'd been wrong.

Viktor looked at each of us in turn with confusion. "You think that was easy?"

Jericho spread his hands. "Escaping from a highly guarded prison area in the middle of a highly guarded structure that contained the queen herself? Yeah, it was pretty damn easy, all things considered."

"The most important thing is we escaped, despite several obstacles falling in our way that significantly slowed us down."

Viktor cast a dark look at me, since I'd been the first obstacle.

I shrugged.

"True." Jericho shook his head. "But this . . . doubt. It's stuck around for me like a greasy film. I didn't even know it was doubt until now."

"What doubt?" Viktor asked.

"You left, Vik. Three years ago, you took off and said you never wanted to see me again. That you hated me and didn't give a damn if I lived or died." He rubbed the small scar on his chin. "Still got the proof to show how sharp you made that point to me. After you left, I watched from afar, day by day, week by week, as you made a name for yourself, even beyond your championship."

Jericho's gaze flicked to the screen that now showed the top news of the day presented by a perky announcer who was excitedly talking about Celina and Viktor, whom everyone expected to make their first public appearance together, post-engagement, at the Queensgames.

"You're famous," Jericho continued. "And successful. And, yeah, I'd be dead right now if you hadn't helped me. My list of crimes is long, not even including the attempted assassination of Prime Minister Drake. Any loyal and obedient Queensguard would march a prisoner like me right to his execution without breaking a sweat."

"I'm not any Queensguard," Viktor countered. "And you're not any prisoner."

Elian joined us. "What's going on?" he asked.

"Answers," I told him tightly.

His brows raised. "Finally."

Viktor cast a tense look at all three of us and then said to Jericho, "Let's take this conversation somewhere else. This is too public; anyone could be listening in."

But Jericho didn't move. "This won't take long. All I need you to do is confirm something for me."

"What?"

"That everything you did that night was on the queen's orders. Save your criminal brother, then find out where Valery is so the queen can send a squadron of guards to capture a dangerous, but potentially useful, witch. After that, you get to go back to your perfect life. Am I close to the truth?"

Part of me wanted Viktor to deny this outright, to be furious that Jericho would accuse him of such a heinous act of deception. I wanted him to be a hero who'd done what he had to do to save his brother's life. But Viktor stayed silent, his jaw tight.

"It's true, isn't it?" Jericho snarled. "Every word of it."

Still, Viktor remained silent, his expression unreadable except for the storm in his eyes.

Jericho shook his head. "Instinct told me not to introduce you to Val. If you want a piece of magic to help hide your famous face, there's other places you could get it from if you're willing to dig deep enough into the muck. In your line of work, you'd already know that."

"You don't know what I want," Viktor snarled. "You never have, not even when we were kids. You were always too busy feeling sorry for yourself and obsessing about that warlock, as if killing him would have fixed any of our problems."

Jericho didn't flinch. "No confirmation that you're a spy,

but not a denial either. It's okay. I know the truth. You never could keep secrets from me, Vik. I've heard enough. Feel free to go back to your perfect life now and let Her Majesty know her shiny champion finally failed at something."

Jericho turned away from his brother in dismissal, but Viktor grabbed his shoulder.

"You ungrateful son of a bitch," he snarled.

Jericho cast a dark look at his brother. "Is that what I am?"

"Yeah, you really are."

Viktor hit Jericho in his jaw, and the Blackheart's head whipped backward. Jericho touched the side of his mouth and inspected the trickle of blood on his finger before the corner of his lips quirked up.

"Let the games begin," he muttered.

He shoved Viktor back from him so hard that the Queensguard was literally airborne for a moment, landing hard on his back near the fountain.

"My job comes with a few perks too." Jericho closed the distance quickly and yanked Viktor up by the front of his sweatshirt. "I'm not a warlock, but I'm full of enough magic to kick anybody's ass."

He punched his brother, and Viktor's head spun to the side, a line of blood shooting out of his mouth.

"Jericho, stop!" I told him, finally finding my voice after watching their exchange with my mouth wide open.

"You chose to follow me down here, Drake," he replied tightly. "So now you get to see the show."

A small crowd had gathered, but they weren't alarmed by

the impromptu fight in the middle of the city square. They were cheering and egging Jericho on. I thought they might recognize Viktor, but he still had his hood up, with only part of his face visible.

Jericho's fists clenched at his sides. "Tell me the truth for once in your life. Admit that you agreed to be a spy for the queen."

Viktor wiped the back of his hand against his bloody mouth, his expression tense and soulless. "If I hadn't, you'd be dead right now."

He'd finally admitted it. I'd still hoped I was wrong, even though in my gut I knew I wasn't.

Jericho was silent for a long, painful moment. "You told her I was your brother."

"No. Rush spilled that during his interrogation. Afterward, I was brought in to discuss the matter. The queen wasn't pleased that I hadn't said anything about it until then. I told her that I was ashamed that you were my brother and afraid it would be held against me."

Jericho flinched as if Viktor had hit him again. "So, the truth."

He nodded grimly. "The truth."

"Norris tried to stop us. Wasn't the queen's favorite high commander in on it?"

"No. This was only between me and Her Majesty. I think she thought that Norris would try to talk her out of it."

"So, Aunt Issy put two and two together and realized that she finally had a way to find the witch I worked for, the one with a talent for raising corpses without too many ravenous side effects."

"That's right," Viktor confirmed.

Jericho shot a look at Elian. "Your mother's always looking out for you. I'm almost envious."

"Don't be," Elian whispered, his expression bleak.

"The woman you work for is a stain on humanity, Jericho," Viktor said firmly, wiping his bloody mouth. "She's evil, to the core."

"I could say the same to you."

Viktor flinched. "It's not the same."

"You're right. I only do what Valery tells me to do because she's carved her magic into my skin. You do it for the fame and glory. And the filthy rich bride-to-be, of course."

"I saved your life by doing what I did," Viktor said.

"You should have told me."

"You would have tried to stop me. You would have protected that witch from persecution."

"That witch," Jericho repeated, "is the only reason I'm alive. She saved my life, and now she gives me work so I can survive. I owe her a debt I can never repay."

"There are other ways to survive," Viktor said, his tone softening.

"No, there aren't. You really think I should be thanking you? You should be thanking me. If I'd given you that face-to-face with Val like you wanted, she would have smelled your lies from a mile away. She has this trick she can do with her dagger: When she sinks it into someone, she can pull the truth out of their throats. Any truth. Any throat. Saw her do it again the other night. And she would have done that to you in a heartbeat."

Jericho didn't look at me when he said this, but I shuddered at the reminder.

"More proof that she's evil," Viktor snapped.

"Maybe. All I'm saying is she wouldn't have stopped there. There'd be bloody pieces of you scattered to the four corners of the Empire by now. And I have no doubt she would have made me do the cutting and the scattering as punishment for bringing you here."

Viktor had no reply to that, the brothers staying locked in a stare, both of their fists clenched as if they were preparing for a final battle.

"This isn't over, Jer," Viktor finally said. "My job here isn't done."

"Yes, it is," Jericho replied darkly. "Go—scamper back to the palace with your tail between your legs, Vik, back to that shiny life of yours. I'm sure the queen will forgive Commander Raden for one failed mission. After all, she needs you to make your obligatory appearances at the Queensgames as her resident champion in a few weeks, doesn't she? I have an idea. Let's start tonight."

In one smooth motion, the Blackheart yanked the hood back from his brother's face.

"Look who's making a celebrity appearance in Cresidia tonight!" he called out to the crowd of onlookers. "The reigning Queensgames champion himself!"

Someone screamed. "It's Viktor Raden!"

A moment later, he was mobbed by a couple dozen of his adoring fans.

Jericho shot me and Elian a look. "Time to go."

I didn't have anything to add as we quickly left the square. Viktor watched us leave, the expression bleak on his bruised, cut-up face. The enthusiastic fans surrounding him worked as an effective barrier to stop him from following us.

The rain, which had begun as only a drizzle, began to pour.

"Jericho," I said uneasily. "Are you sure you want to leave it like that with him?"

"Never been more sure about anything in my life," he bit out.

Another commercial for the Queensgames played on the massive screen, a repeat of the one I'd seen before. Viktor's bright smile, his loud and clear invitation to viewers to get their tickets and join him for the four-day tournament. I couldn't help but notice Jericho wince at the sight of his brother so soon after their second, and very likely final, estrangement.

And then the screen flickered as if the digital signal had been lost in a power outage. When it flickered back on, it wasn't broadcasting news or showing a commercial. Instead, the entire screen was taken up by the face of a middle-aged woman with auburn hair.

"Greetings to you all," the woman said evenly. "Tonight, I am addressing the Empire of Regara on behalf of Lord Zarek Banyon."

I froze in place at the sound of that name.

"What in the hell?" Jericho muttered.

The woman continued. "Queen Isadora has chosen to perpetuate a legacy of fear and loathing toward those who have abilities that she refuses to accept or understand. She is a petty, frightened, manipulative woman who, along with her predecessors, has fooled billions with her malignant and destructive lies. Earlier this week, the arrest of Tamara Collins was announced. Tamara is innocent of the assassination of Prime Minster Louis Drake, as is Lord Banyon himself. Elementia is not evil—it never has been and it never will be. And yet the palace continues to build on this centuries-old lie. A lie that has claimed the lives of countless victims." Her eyes narrowed, her jaw tight. "Lord Banyon refuses to stand idly by and allow these lies to continue for another day. Tonight, he demands the immediate release of this innocent witch currently awaiting execution."

The camera panned away from the witch's face to focus on someone else. It was a girl with long, crimson-colored hair seated in a chair, her wrists bound to the armrests. Her pale expression was filled with fear, her eyes glossy with tears.

"Free Tamara Collins immediately," the woman said, her voice strong and pitiless. "Or Celina Ambrose will die."

TEN

The screen went dark and stayed that way for a few seconds before the previous bright and colorful commercials started again. I stared up at them, but all I saw was the naked fear on my best friend's beautiful face.

"Celina," I managed, my voice trembling. The rain came down harder now. My hair was soaked and slicked to my face. It wasn't only fear and helplessness I felt, but rage—a burning, red-hot rage unlike anything I'd ever felt before.

I understood now how Banyon must have felt, the night of the palace fire. I was angry enough by what I'd just seen to burn down anything in my path. I looked at my hands, almost expecting them to be covered in flames. But my hands were only hands. Whatever magic I'd inherited from my birth father—if any at all—hadn't made its appearance today.

"Drake? Look at me." Jericho's tone was suddenly uncertain as I felt his hand press against my cheek.

I raised my gaze to his, not sure if it was rain or tears on my face now. "I left Celina behind," I said shakily. "I didn't say a word, not even goodbye. I just left her behind. And now this."

He shook his head. "It's not your fault."

My head swam with a thousand different thoughts, all over-lapping each other. "Banyon did this."

"Proof that he's not already dead," Jericho replied. "Though, I'm not sure why he wouldn't want to make the announcement himself. Go to all the trouble of hacking the newsfeed, and give the glory to some random witch?"

I realized that the prince was trailing far behind us and craning his neck in the direction of the city square. "Elian?" I called after him.

"I need Viktor to take me back to the palace," he said softly, his brow furrowed.

"Are you serious?"

He nodded and met my gaze. "That witch on the screen . . . she's right. Elementia isn't evil, and Tamara Collins is innocent. Too many have died, and I've done nothing to stop it. And now Lord Banyon is willing to murder an innocent girl to prove a point."

"That's kind of his thing," Jericho said. "Murdering inno-cents, that is."

I took hold of Elian's wrist. "You said something to me before, at Deluxe. About the queen's burden—how you have it too. Something she told you on your seventeenth birthday?"

Pain slid through his gaze. "I shouldn't have said anything to you about that."

"What is it?" I asked, my throat raw. "What is the secret? Please, I need to know."

He shook his head. "It won't help Celina, if that's what you're thinking. It won't do anything except cause irreparable harm. This secret must be kept indefinitely." He frowned. "No, it needs to be forgotten. When my mother dies, I'll be the only one who knows the truth, with no one to tell. I promise, it will die with me, one way or the other."

"Elian—"

"Joss, no." His voice broke. "Just let it go, all right? And let me go back home where I can be kept in a locked room. It's not safe for me to be here any longer."

A large part of me wanted to keep pushing, keep arguing for the truth, but the raw pain and hopelessness in his voice stopped me. I couldn't help but pull him to me in a fierce hug.

"Elian, I'm so sorry," I told him. "I'm sorry we couldn't find an easy solution for you here."

"Me too." He pulled back from my embrace. "Thank you for trying to help me, Joss. It means more to me than I can ever express to you."

"I won't stop, you know. I'll keep searching for an answer."

He nodded grimly, but there was no more hope in his black eyes. "Thank you," he said. And without another word, he turned back in the direction of the square.

I wasn't lying to him. I hadn't completely given up hope on helping my half brother, especially with what I now knew about Valery, but I wasn't sorry that Elian had decided to leave Cresidia. I had other priorities at the moment. Seeing Celina had demoted every one of my previous goals and personal issues.

All of it could wait.

I now cared only about saving Celina's life. While I whole-heartedly agreed that Tamara—and any other witch or warlock currently facing execution—needed to be freed, and that the laws needed to change, and that reparations needed to be made for centuries of crimes by the Empire against mages, my best friend's life had been directly threatened and I refused to stand by and do nothing.

"We're going back to Valery's penthouse," I told Jericho as we continued to put distance between us and the city square.

"Why?" he asked.

"I need to talk to her about my last echo."

He gave me a sidelong glare. "Bad idea, Drake."

"You're right, you know," I said.

"About what?" Jericho asked.

"I can't think of a single reason why Banyon wouldn't have made that announcement himself. Something doesn't feel right about it. He'd want that shining moment, to rub it in the queen's face that he has the prime minister's daughter at his mercy." I shook my head. "From everything I've seen of Banyon's past . . . this doesn't feel like him. It's not something he'd do—kidnap an innocent girl, even a girl with close ties to the queen, and hold her hostage."

Jericho didn't say anything to that for a moment. "I guess we'll have to agree to disagree on what that bastard would or wouldn't do."

I'd been trying to piece together my thoughts since I'd woken up, finding them scattered all over the place. There was a mystery here, beyond whatever secret Elian shared with the queen, that I needed to solve. Everything depended on it.

And it all came back to that night at the Queen's Gala when I first came in contact with this memory magic. No, further back than that—the raid on Banyon's compound two months ago. The details were top secret, of course, but I knew this much: They'd confiscated dozens of pieces of artwork that Banyon had acquired over the years, including Prince Elian's portrait, stolen from the palace itself. The queen had organized a display of these at the Gala as a symbol of impending victory over her greatest enemy.

The gallery had held his confiscated treasures, including the memory box.

When she learned that I'd been infected with magic from a golden box, Queen Isadora had reacted only with sympathy and understanding.

"No one told me there was a piece of magic displayed at the Gala. I never would have allowed it. You never should have been exposed to such a thing. Please forgive me, Josslyn. I swear I will find a way to purge this poison from you fully and completely."

The queen was an accomplished liar, but I didn't think she'd been lying in that moment. She'd had no idea what kind of magic was in the golden box. There were far too many secrets of her past revealed in Banyon's memories.

If the mage who'd created the box had been killed during the raid, that meant only one person knew of the box's existence.

Lord Banyon himself.

"*Where's your client right now, Val?*" Jericho had asked his boss that night at the restaurant.

"*Here in Cresidia,*" she'd told him.

I'd guessed it was Banyon then, and she'd denied it. Or, no. She hadn't denied it. She'd avoided the question, hadn't she? She'd avoided it every time I asked. But the evidence was piling up, and this time, I wouldn't leave without the truth.

We'd reached the witch's building and moved across the tiled floor toward the elevators. On the monitors where I'd previously seen the news of Tamara's arrest, video footage of Celina now played. My heart wrenched. I immediately recognized it as being from her eighteenth birthday party. She'd been so happy that night for someone who'd never enjoyed large parties and being the center of attention. She wore the fuchsia hat covered in crystal stars I'd given to her and was laughing at something. The announcer appeared next to the footage, a grave expression on her face.

"There has not yet been a statement from the queen or the prime minster about the kidnapping of Celina Ambrose. We have also reached out to Celina's fiancé, Commander Viktor Raden, for a comment. One can only speculate that the palace is horrified and outraged by this outright act of war by Lord Banyon and his terrorist faction, who have dedicated their lives to destroying the peace that Queen Isadora fights so bravely to maintain.

"All that has been proven by this heinous act is that no leniency should ever be shown to anyone who would dare do harm to the Empire of Regara. We will continue to report on this breaking news, so stay tuned for any updates through-out the night and however long it takes to bring our beloved First Daughter home safely."

The newsfeed then cut to a Queensgames commercial.

Every time I saw Celina's face, it was like a gut punch, stealing my breath. I forced myself to stay strong and not give in to despair. Despair would do nothing to help Celina.

Reluctantly, and grumbling all the way about this being a bad idea, Jericho took me back to Valery's penthouse again, which was in shadows with only the lights of the city visible through the floor-to-ceiling windows.

"She's not here," he said. "She's probably up in her garden."

I nodded, then went very still. Listening to the silence. Earlier, I'd sensed that someone was watching me. I'd never been all that paranoid, despite having frenemies who enjoyed gossiping about me behind my back. But other than that, it wasn't like me to imagine someone lurking nearby.

Unless someone was *literally* lurking nearby.

This wasn't paranoia. This was instinct.

"I know you're there," I said aloud, my voice echoing in the large, shadowy room. "I know you've been watching me. I know you know who I am and what I'm currently in possession of."

"What the hell are you doing?" Jericho watched me, bemused.

I didn't reply to him. I waited.

But nothing happened. No one other than the Blackheart spoke a word.

"Were you watching the newsfeed earlier?" I persisted,

peering into the shadows. "That was my best friend in the whole world. Celina Ambrose. She's like a sister to me, one of the only people I know I can depend on, no matter what. And that witch is going to kill her. I can't let that happen. If you're here, show yourself. Please. I need your help."

Only silence filled my ears, and the certainty I'd had only minutes ago began to fade away.

But then I heard something. The click of a latch, coming from what I'd thought was just a regular wall.

I turned in the direction of the sound and watched as a hidden door opened, and someone finally emerged from the shadows.

"Josslyn Drake," Lord Zarek Banyon said, his hands clasped behind his back. "We finally meet."

ELEVEN

For all my certainty that Lord Banyon was here, and my immediate, heart-pounding elation that I was right, I'd completely forgotten something incredibly important while putting together the pieces.

Jericho.

There was a long, heavy moment of silence after the warlock spoke before the Blackheart acted. I'd only seen him move with superhuman speed once before, in the Keep, when Lazos had instructed his henchmen to kill Jericho as a test of his abilities, and Jericho had flattened both of them in mere moments.

One moment, Jericho was next to me. The next, he was behind Banyon, his arm clamping down like an iron bar across the warlock's chest, a sharp blade held to his throat.

"I'm going to kill you, you son of a bitch," the Blackheart snarled.

Two horrible outcomes flashed through my imagination in a split second. In one, Jericho slit Banyon's throat and got the vengeance he'd obsessed over for sixteen years. In the other, Banyon dealt with an immediate deadly threat the only way I imagined he would: by burning Jericho to ashes like I'd seen him do in the echoes.

"Jericho, no!" I cried out.

His gaze snapped to mine, and for a moment, all I saw was cold, hard determination. The same look I knew he'd have when he had to follow a mission given to him by Valery that ended in blood.

But whatever he saw in my eyes made him hesitate. Made him doubt. It was as if I'd thrown a glass of cold water in his face and woken him from his unconscious need to act the moment he saw the warlock. But it was only for a moment before the ice behind his black eyes returned.

He was going to do it. And Banyon hadn't yet summoned even a spark of fire in self-defense.

"Jericho, *stop*." It was Valery's voice that cut through the charged silence. Calm, crisp, authoritative. She walked into the middle of the deadly scene, her arms crossed over her chest. "Release Lord Banyon and step away from him. Now, Blackheart. *Now.* Don't make me say it again."

Jericho cringed, as if her words were physically painful— his teeth clenched, the weapon in his hand trembling. Then he finally moved the blade away from the warlock's throat and shoved Banyon forward. Banyon touched his throat, where there was now a thin line of blood from the pressure of the knife.

The warlock said nothing, only giving Valery a pointed glare. She hissed out a sigh. "Jericho."

"What?" the Blackheart growled.

"Look at me."

Slowly, and with much disdain, Jericho met the witch's gaze.

She nodded. "I forbid you from harming Lord Banyon in any way. And I forbid you from killing him. Do you understand me?"

The anguish on Jericho's face as he resisted the obedience magic she'd carved into him made my heart hurt.

"Do you understand me?" she said again, sharper.

"Yes," he hissed after another pained hesitation.

"Good." Valery's gaze moved to Banyon. "I'm sorry this happened, but you promised me you wouldn't reveal your presence here."

"I did, didn't I?" he replied. "But the boy acted as he should. He perceived a threat and he tried to eliminate it. I would expect no less from one of your Blackhearts."

I tore my gaze away from Jericho, whose fists were clenched at his side, glaring at both mages, to find that the warlock regarded me fully.

"You look so much like your mother," he said.

It wasn't the first thing I'd expected him to say to me.

"Eleanor," I replied tightly.

A frown creased his brow, as if I'd surprised him by knowing her name, but then clarity filled his gaze. "You learned about her through my echoes, didn't you?"

It was a bit of a relief that we didn't have to go over this in detail. That everyone was on the same page when it came to the magic stuck in my head.

I nodded. "I've learned a lot through your echoes."

"Apparently so."

It seemed that he had nothing more to say about that, but I saw the questions weighing heavily in the warlock's gaze. I was finally face-to-face with Banyon, with a million questions to ask, and not a single one spilled from my lips. Because none of that mattered to me right now. Only Celina mattered.

"The newsfeed," I said, my throat thick. "Were you watching?"

"No. These last months, I've watch as little of the queen's carefully controlled propaganda as I can." He gestured toward Valery. "Show me what I missed."

Without comment or argument, Valery produced her phone and showed Banyon a replay of the rebel hack of the newsfeed. The warlock watched it silently, his expression grim. Jericho retreated across the room, now only a silent presence. His gaze never left the warlock for a moment.

"Did you know about this?" I asked Banyon tightly when it was over.

He shook his head. "No. But I do know the witch very well. Her name is Agatha and she's a close, personal associate of mine. Has been for years. It seems that she's taken over during my lengthy absence. Using my name for this will only lead to more innocent deaths on both sides."

"Haven't you caused enough innocent deaths in your lifetime to fill a thousand graveyards?" Jericho growled from the shadows.

"Silence," Valery snapped.

Banyon raised his hand. "It's fine. The Blackheart is right. My hands will never be clean of the blood I've spilled. But not like this. There will be no coming back from this act of war."

"I thought you wanted war," I said, my throat raw. "You hate the queen so much, why would you care what this Agatha woman does?"

His brows drew together. "When my compound was raided, there were so many deaths of those who tried to defend me. All gave their lives so I could escape. I've grown weary of this battle, this insurmountable obsession that has given me nothing but pain. I want it to end. I believed that the solution could be found in my memories, but I've come to doubt that these last weeks." Then he hissed out a breath. "I'm wasting precious time here, while it seems as if Agatha works to destroy years of important work I've done."

"What important work have you done?" Jericho asked tightly and without a shred of respect.

"My work," Banyon said evenly, "is to bring about the end of this misguided, evil Empire, once and for all. I have slowly built a strong group of rebels who see past the queen's lies, and mages willing to embrace their magic rather than resist it. There is strength in numbers."

"Millions," I said aloud, thinking back to the echo I'd had of Banyon and my father. "You believe there are millions of mages in the Empire who don't even know what they are. That the queen lies about the numbers, making it seem as if those who can summon elementia are nearly extinct."

The way he looked at me sent a shiver down my spine, as if I'd peered into his personal diary and discovered all of his secrets. But then that accusatory look was gone, and clarity spread across his features.

"Yes, that's right. *Millions*, Josslyn, if not even more than that. And they could all be persuaded to join my fight. But there might be something even more useful to find. After I heard about the memory box, about you, I doubted that anything would come of finding the truth in my past. But maybe it's not too late."

"Unless you've found someone who can extract the magic from Drake, you're shit out of luck," Jericho said darkly. "I think we all know how to quickly get those memories out of Drake, and it doesn't involve a one-in-a-billion air-earth mage."

My heart pounded at what Jericho suggested. Of course, he was right.

"You hate me very much, don't you?" Banyon said to the Blackheart. "Earlier, that was more than a simple act of violence between you and me, someone acting instinctively against a threat. This is personal for you."

"Let's just say, if you even look at Drake the wrong way, I'm going to cut out your beating heart and show it to you before you die."

This threat resulted only in a small smile quirking up the side of Banyon's mouth. "You could try that and see what happens, but I would advise you against it."

Valery sighed. "Jericho won't try anything of the sort. My marks on him are fresh, reapplied only yesterday. He can't resist my command, and I've commanded him not to lay a finger on you."

"Fair enough." He nodded, moving toward the floor-to-ceiling windows, and looked out at the city, his hands clasped behind his back. "I need to leave the city. I need to speak with Agatha. I'll leave first thing tomorrow."

My heart skipped a beat. "I'm coming with you."

Banyon raised a brow.

"Drake . . ." Jericho growled.

"It's okay," I told him.

"It's not okay. None of this is okay. The Lord here is going to get both you and your friend killed in his little behind-the-scenes feud with that power-hungry witch."

"I can handle Agatha," Banyon said evenly. "Now, Valery—"

"I want nothing to do with your rebel agenda, if that's what you're going to say," she cut him off. "I never have, and I never will."

"I know. And I do understand why you feel that way, even if I think you're wrong. I will respect your wishes on the matter." His attention moved to me. "Very well. You will come with me, Josslyn. I still believe there are vitally important answers in the echoes. Perhaps we can find those answers together."

I nodded, as something tight and painful clenching my heart finally eased just a little. "Thank you."

Valery looked at Jericho. "You will go with Lord Banyon as his driver and his bodyguard and report back to me what you learn. Just because I don't want to be a part of his doomed rebel uprising doesn't mean that I wish to be ignorant of information that can and will affect my business."

Driver and bodyguard? My mouth fell open at the audacity of what she was asking him after he'd just tried to kill Banyon on sight.

"Do you understand?" she said pointedly.

Jericho's jaw was so tight, I thought it might shatter. "Yes."

"And do you agree?"

"Yes," he bit out. "Whatever you say, boss."

She smiled thinly at him. "Go now and make arrangements for the journey."

With a final menacing look at the warlock, and not a single glance in my direction, Jericho left the penthouse without another word.

I hated that Valery had the power to control his life. And I had to admit I had mixed feelings about the Blackheart joining us on this journey. His lifelong need for vengeance burned bright, but he'd be a fool to make a move against the warlock. I knew Banyon wouldn't hesitate to burn him to ashes.

I couldn't let that happen.

▷◁◦◦◦◦◦▷◁

It seemed that I would be staying another night as a reluctant guest in Valery's luxurious penthouse. Banyon disappeared into the shadows moments after Jericho left, and Valery curtly let me know she was going up to her rooftop garden.

And then I was alone with my thoughts.

My thoughts weren't currently very good company. My thoughts were very rude and told me that I needed to stop being a damn coward and get more answers. That the night was not going to end like this. Because it couldn't.

I stood all alone in the penthouse for several minutes, my

mind a jumble. Then I walked directly toward the elevator. When it opened for me, I pressed the top button for the roof.

Once there, I followed the pathway that wound through the trees and thick foliage. The rain had finally stopped, the clouds clearing to show the stars and the bright half-moon in the black sky.

At the center of the garden, where we'd sat at the table only a few days ago, Valery tended to some red roses. She briefly glanced at me before turning her attention back to the flowers. "I've always envied those with earth magic. But perhaps that ability would make the creation of such beauty far too easy to hold my interest for very long. Aren't my roses beautiful?"

I stared at her, my fists clenched at my sides. "How can you sound so calm?"

"Is there another way you expect me to be, Josslyn?"

"Banyon was your client."

"Yes, of course he was. And still is. Go get some sleep, Josslyn. By the sound of it, you have a big day ahead of you tomorrow."

"I've been asleep for three days, thanks to you. I'm not that tired." I tried very hard to calm myself, but a fire burned in my heart. "You should have told me about him."

She gave me a cold smile. "I owe you no explanations. You have only made everything infinitely more complicated—for myself, for Jericho, and for your father."

"My father is Louis Drake. The man that you sent Jericho to kill because Regis Ambrose hired you. We went over this already, remember?"

The witch didn't spare me even a glance, utterly focused on her flowers. I wondered if she kept this garden to prove to herself that she didn't kill everything she touched.

"I know you'll never directly admit anything," I said as calmly as I could. "I don't really care. I know the truth."

"So important to you, isn't it? The truth." Her words held a mocking edge. "Trust me on this, the truth rarely provides anything but pain, and it should be taken in very small doses for those with a low tolerance for it." She snipped a rosebud off its thorny stem. "Speaking of painful truths, how is Prince Elian doing?"

As if she cared. I wondered if she'd even mentioned the prince to Banyon. His name hadn't come up downstairs. "He's gone back to the palace."

"I see. I'm sorry I couldn't have helped him."

I wanted to blurt out everything I knew about her, everything I'd seen about her past with Banyon. That death magic was her gift, and that was what set her apart from other mages who only dabbled in it.

But I didn't have a death wish. She'd nearly killed me with a touch at the theater the other night and I had no doubt that she could do it again, and this time without any witnesses and a readily available earth mage to fill me with life-restoring magic.

"I'm sorry too," I said. "There are no easy answers, are there?"

Valery leveled her gaze with mine, seemingly unbalanced by my sudden shift in tone from combativeness to acceptance. "There aren't," she agreed.

I wanted to hate Valery, and most of me did just that. But a small—very small—part of me had slowly started to understand her. Valery was a survivor. An outcast. A woman who had no real home or family. A witch who wore her secrets like a cloak of protection against a world that either wanted to kill her or turn its back on her the moment it knew who and what she really was.

"Jericho wants Lord Banyon dead for what happened to his parents," I said. "Sending him with us is putting his life in danger. He's lucky he's still breathing right now. Banyon is the most powerful warlock in the Empire."

"That is what they say, isn't it?"

What an odd thing for her to say. "It is." I studied her for a moment. "Are they wrong about that?"

"That's not for me to say." She shrugged, her attention fixed on her flowers. "I'm curious if you've ever seen a sign of your own magic. Have you?"

I shook my head. "Never. Not even a glimmer." I stared down at my hands. "I'm not even sure I'm a witch."

"I'm not surprised there's been nothing yet. Between a natural, subconscious repression of elementia, caused by simple fear and ignorance, and the memory magic now blocking it, it would be impossible for you to channel regular elementia."

I eyed her as if she'd started speaking another language. "The memory magic is blocking it?"

She nodded. "Contained magic always blocks natural magic. Usually it's only in small ways, when one uses contained magic in physical form, like a ring or an amulet, but since Lord Banyon's echoes are currently contained inside of you, they work as a thick wall between you and your natural access to elementia. Simple as that."

"Yeah, right," I muttered. "So simple."

Finally, Valery had given me a piece of useful information. Not that it helped me in any way.

I frowned. "About Elian . . . are you sure there's nothing you can suggest to help him? Is he really doomed to be this way forever?"

I watched her, waiting for some sign that she could hold the answers I needed to help the prince.

She shook her head. "I've never seen anything like it before. Not in person. What happened to Prince Elian is like an incurable disease. Death magic has created a dark, bottomless, insatiable pit within him that can never be completely filled. I offered him the only solution I could."

I wished I knew if she was speaking the truth. My gut told me she wasn't.

"Death is not a solution," I said.

"Sometimes it is. Currently, you have more pressing matters to worry about than the prince. Go get some rest, Josslyn, even if you don't think you need it. I'm sure tomorrow will be emotionally draining for you. I know we've had our differences, and that there is certainly no love lost between us, but I do hope you're able to help your friend."

"I hope so too," I said evenly.

I turned toward the pathway that led to the elevator.

"One more thing, Josslyn," Valery said, and I glanced over my shoulder at her. Her expression had tensed. "Tread carefully with Lord Banyon. After all these years, he is a man with very little left to lose."

When a rumored immortal goddess of death gave someone a warning, they'd be a fool not to take it.

TWELVE

The next morning, right on schedule, Jericho arrived, expressionless and grim, and without much to say. Then the most unlikely trio in the history of the Empire left the city of Cresidia together. I sat next to Jericho in the passenger seat of a black sedan. Banyon sat in the back.

"Where are we headed?" Jericho asked, his tone flat.

"Start by heading south," Banyon replied.

"How far are we going?"

"Far."

"Great. I love vagueness."

Banyon eyed him. "Do we have a problem?"

"No. Apparently, I'm just the driver and bodyguard. No problem here."

Jericho didn't even look at me. I'd really wanted to talk to him alone before this, but there hadn't been a chance. As we left the city, I glanced at the warlock over my shoulder to find him watching me.

"Good morning," I said.

"Good morning," he replied.

Okay, this was even more awkward than I ever would have expected, especially after Valery's words of warning last night. Words I'd turned over in my mind instead of sleeping, looking at them from every direction, every angle.

"Tread carefully. . . He is a man with very little left to lose."

I decided it was more of an observation than a warning. Banyon, even at the best of times, and even after I'd had some deep glimpses into his troubled past, wasn't someone I would ever completely trust.

Conversation was limited, to say the least, for the first leg of our journey to a currently undisclosed destination. I stayed in my head, ruminating on everything until I'd worked myself into a lather of doubt and uncertainty.

I hated doubting myself. It was so unlike me—and really wasn't cute at all.

Midafternoon, we took a rest stop so Jericho could refill the car.

"You okay?" I asked him as I got out to stretch my legs.

"Never better." He sent a hateful look toward Banyon, who'd emerged from the back seat, shielding his eyes from the bright sun. "It's all good, Drake."

"What is?"

"The reminder of who I am in the grand scheme of things."

"And who's that?"

His expression darkened. "A nobody who has no control over his life or his future."

"Terrific." I nodded. "I'm going to let you go ahead and feel sorry for yourself over here, while I go get something to eat and figure out how to save my best friend from certain death."

He glared at me. "Yeah, you do that."

I went into the rest stop, pushing away more entirely uncute doubt, and grabbed a sandwich, taking it outside to unpeel the wrapper and eat it slowly.

Banyon approached and I eyed him warily. He eyed me back.

"When did you learn the truth about me?" he asked.

"Oh, you're talking now," I said. "You were so quiet in the car I nearly forgot you were even there."

I hadn't, of course. It was literally impossible to forget that an infamous warlock you'd been taught to fear all your life was practically breathing down your neck.

"I didn't want to say too much in front of the Blackheart," he replied.

"Probably smart," I agreed.

"He despises me."

"He does."

"Is there a reason for this I should know about?"

"I'm sure you have a lot of people who despise you. Jericho's definitely on the list." But I didn't elaborate from there. Jericho's reason for hating Banyon wasn't my story to share, and I couldn't imagine that revealing it would remotely improve things between them. If anything, it would only make it worse.

"Fair enough," Banyon allowed.

My heartbeat sped up. "Please don't kill him."

He raised a brow. "I wasn't planning on it."

"Good." I swallowed down another bite of my less-than-appealing lunch. "Now, to answer your question about when I learned the truth about you, I saw the truth in an echo. The night of the palace fire. I saw what the queen did. What Commander Norris did. And . . . I'm sorry. I'm really sorry that happened to you."

Pain slid behind his gaze. I couldn't help but notice that his eyes were the same slate-blue color that mine used to be. The same slate blue that these contacts emulated well enough.

He nodded. "I'm sorry too."

I was silent for a moment before I had to ask: "When did you learn that I was still alive?"

"Not for far too long."

I didn't speak for a moment as I decided what I wanted to say next. "I know you were working with my father. I saw that too."

"You've seen a lot."

"Only a fraction."

"Of course, but . . ." The warlock cocked his head. "It's strangely encouraging. Can you control the echoes at all?"

I shook my head. "Jericho told me it might be possible. But they've been coming less frequently than they did in the beginning."

"That's also encouraging. I believe it means that you are subconsciously controlling them now, after all this time. So many mages, Josslyn, who don't know their own magic. Who don't believe it's possible, and that's all it takes to cut off their access to elementia."

I laughed, a dry sound at the back of my throat. "So, you're telling me I just need to believe in myself."

"Put extremely simplistically, yes. Yes, that's exactly what I'm saying." His gaze moved toward the Blackheart, who leaned against the hood of the car, his back to us. Waiting. "He's dangerous, Josslyn."

"Who, Jericho?" I almost laughed again. "No doubt."

"I witnessed the two of you together. It's clear that you have feelings for him. However, it's deeply unwise of you to allow yourself to feel anything for a Blackheart."

I blinked. "So, let's get this on the table right away. I'm not looking for a family reunion or friendly, heart-to-heart fatherly advice here. Like I said, I'm sorry about what happened to you. I really, really am. But what I do, and who I like, is my business. Got it?"

Banyon regarded me for a moment of stony silence before he raised his brow. "You do remind me so very much of Eleanor. She never stood for my dominating ways either. I stand by what I said about the Blackheart, though."

"You're certainly welcome to your opinion." I knew we had to get going—I didn't want to waste another minute—but I also knew Banyon wasn't comfortable having a conversation with me in front of Jericho in the car. "Let's change the subject, shall we? You need to know that Elian is in a bad way. He needs a cure for his problem. I'm going to go ahead and assume that someone as connected as you has gotten inside information on him, so I don't have to update you on all the literally gory details about him."

His lips thinned. "Elian is the queen's problem, not mine."

"So that's it?"

"That's it."

"You're even less helpful than Valery, if that's possible." I bit my lip. I couldn't give in to my snark, not with him. Despite all the truths I'd seen in the echoes, I didn't trust this warlock completely. I never would.

I began walking toward the car.

"Josslyn, I need you to know something."

I stopped but didn't turn around. "What?"

"I didn't have Louis killed. It was Regis Ambrose's doing. Valery acted irresponsibly by working with that greedy, power-hungry stain on humanity. I'd like to think if she knew I'd enlisted your father to my side that she wouldn't have taken the job."

Confirmation. Finally.

It didn't fill me with satisfaction. Instead, the knowledge that I was right about Celina's father sat like a lead weight in my stomach.

"I know about Ambrose," I bit out. "But I think you're over-estimating Valery's morals."

"Perhaps I am," he replied. "But I didn't overestimate Louis's. He was a good man. He'd begun to see a glimpse of the truth behind Issy's lies, as painful as it was for him. He was the one who told me about Elian."

I met the warlock's gaze again. "He was a good man," I confirmed. "And if he hadn't died that night, I have no doubt he would have helped you expose the queen's lies about elementia."

Banyon nodded grimly. "He loved you. Never doubt that."

My eyes stung. "I know he did."

With that, we returned to the car and Jericho got us back on the highway.

"Tell me more about Agatha," I said, knowing I needed some preparation for what I was going to walk into. "Why did she act now? What is it about Tamara that makes her the focus of all of this?"

"A good question with a very simple answer," Banyon replied. "Tamara Collins is Agatha's daughter."

I cranked my head around and stared at him in shock. "Wait. What?"

Then Jericho laughed sharply. "Sure. Why not? What's one more dark family secret to add to the mix? Let me take a wild guess: They've been estranged for years, haven't they?"

"That's right," Banyon confirmed.

"Rinse and repeat. I swear, nothing is ever going to surprise me again. Great, so we have a rabid, bloodthirsty mother who's ready to kill for her offspring. Good luck dealing with that."

"I can handle Agatha," the warlock replied thinly.

"I'm sure you can. Just burn her to the ground if she gives you a problem. I know how you prefer to handle problems like these."

"Jericho," I growled. "You're not helping."

"Many people hate me," Banyon said. "But your hate is personal. What do you blame me for, Blackheart?"

"Everything," he bit out.

"Specifically?"

"You really want to know?"

"I really do."

"Okay." Jericho's knuckles whitened on the steering wheel. "The palace fire. You incinerated my parents, right in front of me and my brother. I was only three years old at the time, but I still have nightmares about my mother's last scream almost every night." He drew in a shaky breath. "Drake's told me that it's a more layered issue, what happened for you that night. But I don't give a shit. Those screams are my own echoes. And I don't care what Val says or what she commands me to do—one day I promise I will kill you."

Banyon nodded slowly, then said, under his breath, "I understand the need for vengeance very well."

Jericho didn't look at the warlock; he kept his attention completely on the road. "Yeah. I guess we have something in common."

I didn't know he dreamed about that night. I wanted to say something, but what could I say that would make any difference to him? Nothing. Being forced to be close to Banyon had to be a nightmare for Jericho, and I was so very sorry that there was nothing I could do to help.

We drove all day, until the sun set, and Banyon instructed Jericho to get off the highway. From there, guided by the warlock, we drove along a side road until it led to a large, empty parking lot, seemingly in the middle of nowhere.

"Park over there." Banyon motioned toward an area where the car would be shielded by a line of trees and not easily spotted from the road.

Jericho did as instructed, and we emerged from the car. I cast my surprised gaze over our destination.

"Queensgate Amusement Park," I said out loud.

The huge, rusted, broken sign was missing a *Q* and an *ark*.

"The Queensgate Amusement Park is the secret location of the rebel lair?" Jericho asked, unconvinced.

Despite the lengthy and uncomfortable drive here—both physically and emotionally—our destination had given me an unexpected dose of nostalgia.

I knew this place.

I *loved* this place. Long ago, anyway.

The Queensgate Amusement Park was less than fifty miles west of Ironport, and I'd come here every summer until it closed down five years ago.

News broke that the owner and operator of the park was a witch. She'd been arrested, swiftly executed, and the gates permanently closed on the popular destination. There had been talk of selling the land for new home development, but no buyers had been interested. The fifty acres of property were thought to be cursed by evil magic.

As Jericho and I followed the warlock into the park itself, I realized with shock that the Blackheart held a gun at his side.

"What is that?" I growled at him.

"This? It's a gun."

"That won't be necessary," Banyon told him.

"Maybe, maybe not. In the meantime, it makes me feel better."

Banyon seemed to have nothing further to say, instead walking ahead of us and unwisely putting his back to Jericho, whose attention hadn't left the warlock for a moment.

I knew what he was thinking. One bullet would give him his vengeance.

Jericho flicked a glance at me and must have seen this reflected in my eyes.

"You don't have to worry, Drake," he said.

I shrugged. "I'm still worried."

"I wouldn't make a move, even if Val's latest command wasn't burned into my soul. You want to help your best friend survive the night, and you need the warlock for that. Despite my knee-jerk reaction the moment I saw him last night, I get that."

I studied his tense expression. He tried so hard to keep up an impenetrable facade, but I'd seen through it too many times now to be fooled. I touched his arm.

"I'm so sorry about the nightmares," I said.

A small muscle in his cheek twitched. "I'm not. It's a good reminder."

With that, he turned away from me.

There was no rainstorm tonight. The black sky was lit with the half moon. Beyond the broken sign, which had been a brightly colored neon beacon of happiness back when the park was open and flourishing, was a desolate graveyard of pathways and rides. A roller coaster I remembered fondly stood in the distance, like the fossilized carcass of a gigantic prehistoric creature. Old papers and dried leaves blew past where we stood at the entrance, and the chill in the air made me shiver.

"Are you sure this is the right place?" I asked the warlock.

"No," he replied.

My eyes widened. "What?"

Banyon turned to face me, spreading his hands. "I haven't

been in touch with Agatha in over two months. There is a chance she might have moved locations, but I know she favors this one. She used to work here and knows the layout like the back of her hand."

I peered around at the ominous dark shapes of rides and stalls. For a place that would have once been so cheery and fun during the day, it was nightmare-inducing at night.

Already, I'd started to give in to doubt. To despair.

So not cute.

"So, Celina could be anywhere," I said, my heart pounding loud and fast. "Anywhere at all."

Both Banyon and Jericho had turned to face me, then halted.

"Drake . . ." Jericho's voice held an unexpected edge of panic. "Don't move."

I froze in place. "What's wrong?"

"There's a laser sight focused on your forehead."

"A laser—" I began, but then I saw a red dot appear on Jericho's forehead as well.

"Okay." Jericho held his arms out to his sides and turned around in a circle. "You've got our attention, whoever you are."

A female voice sounded out from the shadows. "Drop the weapon and kick it away from you, Blackheart. And get on the ground, facedown."

I met Jericho's gaze. His had gone hard, cold. Expressionless. I couldn't tell if he was surprised or scared or pissed off. Likely the latter more than anything else.

But he didn't delay the inevitable. He dropped the gun and kicked it away from him, then lay down on the ground, his arms spread out at his sides. Moments later, several figures emerged from the surrounding shadows.

"Search him," the speaker nodded toward Jericho. "He'll have more weapons hidden—coat, boots, thigh, calf. Check everywhere."

Her four large male companions did as she asked.

"Well, well, look who's part of the welcoming committee," Jericho said to her. "I'd say it's been a long time, but it really hasn't been nearly long enough."

"I couldn't agree more," she said.

She turned to me, but I didn't need to see her face to confirm. I'd known from the first moment I'd heard the ex-Queensguard's voice.

It was Mika.

THIRTEEN

"This isn't necessary," said Lord Banyon.

Mika swept her gaze over the warlock, and I could see the recognition in her brown eyes, followed by a moment of hesitation. "Which part?"

"The Blackheart and the girl are with me."

"Your point?"

I had to give it to her—even if she was frightened by the sight of the infamous warlock, she showed no fear.

Banyon regarded her with narrowed eyes. "I don't know you."

"I can't exactly claim the same, can I, Lord Banyon? You're right, though, I'm brand-new around here. We've never met."

"What is your name, young witch?"

She frowned at the question. "Mika. And I'm not a witch." Her focus shifted to me. "You shouldn't be here."

For all the drama of the last couple of minutes, and the automatic fear of having deadly weapons pointed at me, I allowed myself a measure of relief that, at least, Banyon had been right about the location.

"Believe it or not, I'm happy to see you, Mika," I told her.

"The feeling isn't mutual."

I hadn't exactly expected a warm hug. "Where's Celina?"

Mika shook her head, her expression unreadable. "Celina who?"

Nobody ever made it easy, did they? "I need to see her, to make sure she's okay."

"Funny. I feel the same way about Tamara, but no one's escorting me to her prison cell, are they?"

Mika was a hard person to like, aggressive and combative by nature, but I didn't doubt for a moment that her motivation for being here, her motivation for every decision she made, was to save the life of her girlfriend.

But, just by being here, that meant she'd been a part of Celina's abduction, and right now that made her my enemy.

"Take me to Agatha," Banyon said.

A muscle in Mika's cheek twitched, finally betraying her stress. I thought for a moment she might argue with the most powerful warlock in the Empire, whom she surely knew could burn her to a crisp right where she stood. As a former Queensguard, Banyon would have been enemy number one for her. Now she was working with his closest allies. It had to be incredibly confusing and deeply unpleasant for her to be in his presence.

"Fine," she finally said. "Follow me."

At a mere look from Mika, her male compatriots holstered their weapons. Banyon held his hand out to Jericho to assist the Blackheart up from the ground. Unsurprisingly, Jericho ignored it and pushed up to his feet without any help.

We followed Mika along a labyrinth of dark pathways

winding through the park. Despite my good memories of this park, being in the hollowed-out abandoned version of it was an unsettling experience. So much happiness and joy and sunshine had shifted into nothing more than a shadowy ghost town. It felt ominous, with so many buildings and shapes looming up on either side of us, as if there might be actual monsters with sharp teeth ready to jump out and devour us at any moment.

We arrived at a large building set apart from the main grounds. There was a huge sculpture of a dolphin out front, protruding from a massive, dried-up fountain. The sign here read THE ROYAL PRINCE HOTEL. It was an on-site hotel for families to stay at when visiting the park for more than one day. I remembered what it was like in its prime: shining, welcoming, and extravagant, with laughing children running around, followed by their doting parents who'd willingly signed up to wait in lines all day long so their children could have fun.

Ironically, it was here at this park where I'd met Celina for the first time. My father had suggested to Ambrose that he bring his daughter to spend the day with me more than a decade ago. We'd spent the day getting to know each other with the backdrop of waterslides and roller coasters, while being carefully watched over by a squad of guards.

I gazed up at the Ferris wheel in the near distance, which was the riskiest ride that the much-less-adventurous Celina would be convinced to go on. While our fathers talked about politics, or whatever, the two of us had proceeded to get stuck at the top of the Ferris wheel. Celina had a panic attack, and I'd tried to distract her by telling her all about my life in the most animated and amusing way possible. It had worked—I made her laugh so much that tears streamed down her cheeks, and she'd forgotten about her fear until the ride began moving again.

After that, we found ourselves in each other's company more and more, and with each day that passed, our friendship grew. She seemed to genuinely like me, and not just want to be my friend because of my social status, which I had to admit was a rare thing. And I admired her ability to be kind even to those who weren't always kind in return—like yours truly. Our very different personalities helped to balance each other. Someone once told me that she was the string to my kite, keeping me anchored enough to not lose myself completely and fly away.

Right now, I felt lost. I needed my string. I needed my best friend more than I'd ever needed her before. And I knew without a single doubt that she needed me too.

Inside the hotel, as vacant and unwelcoming as every other part of the park, Mika led us to a large dining hall, big enough to have hosted huge weddings or conference banquets. I'd seen Mika speaking on a phone during our walk here, although I hadn't heard anything she'd said. I could make an educated guess on exactly who she'd been talking to, since a familiar face stood in the room waiting for us. The last time I'd seen that face, it had been about thirty feet high and wide on the screen overlooking the Cresidia city square.

Agatha's attention focused completely on Banyon as he approached her.

"Zarek," she said evenly. "I'm very pleased to see you."

"I wish I could say the same," he replied, shaking his head. "What have you done, Agatha?"

Her expression grew pained. "I can explain everything."

"You acted without my guidance. You've put my entire alliance in jeopardy, as well as countless lives. Sit down. Now."

She did, taking a shaky seat at a nearby table.

The warlock flicked his hand toward the men who'd marched us in here. "Leave us." And to Mika: "You too."

Her arms were crossed over her chest. "I'm not going anywhere."

"Mika, it's fine," Agatha told her.

"It's *not* fine. I'm not going anywhere, got it? Whatever the warlock has to say to you, I want to hear it too."

"Who is this girl, Agatha?" Banyon asked, casting a dark look at Mika. "She claims she's not a witch."

"She's not. She's involved with my daughter."

Banyon regarded Mika appraisingly for a few moments. "I understand."

"I doubt that," Mika countered.

Agatha was busy studying me now, with a cutting and unfriendly glare, so I went ahead and returned it with one of my own. Despite her obvious motivations, I felt zero sympathy for the woman who'd kidnapped my best friend and threatened her life in front of the entire Empire.

"Yes?" I prompted with a hiss.

"You're Josslyn Drake," she said without a sliver of kindness.

"Guilty as charged," I replied.

"Is she your prisoner, my lord?"

"No," Banyon replied. "Josslyn is my daughter."

Agatha's gaze snapped to his. "What?"

"What part of that don't you understand?"

"She's . . . your daughter? How is that possible? You never said a word to me about it."

"No, I didn't."

I checked Mika's reaction to this verbal announcement of my epic biological secret, but her expression remained blank. She'd been one of the very few who knew that I currently held Banyon's memory magic in my head, but would have had no idea that I was related to the warlock. After all, the last time I saw her, I didn't even know the truth myself.

"Is that where you've been all this time after the raid, without any message to let me know you were even still alive? Searching for your lost daughter?" Agatha asked. Without waiting for his reply, the witch jabbed her finger toward me. "She could easily be a spy for the queen."

I regarded her with shock. "I'm not a spy. I hate the queen, so trust me, we have that much in common."

"Trust you? I don't think so." She raised a brow. "Why are you here, then? Is that where he's been all this time? Grooming his heir to become our next leader?"

I almost laughed at that. "No, definitely not. I'm here because you kidnapped my best friend and publicly threatened to kill her."

She raised her chin, not an ounce of kindness or empathy in her hard gaze. "Yes, of course, that's right. You and the current First Daughter are closely associated, aren't you?"

"We are," I said without hesitation. "And I know for a fact that Celina is probably scared out of her mind. Take me to see her right now."

Agatha laughed in my face. "I'll say this much, the girl certainly has your air of superiority, Zarek."

Her laugh fell away when she realized that the warlock regarded her with ice in his gaze.

"Be careful, Agatha," he warned. "You know very well how I deal with disrespect, even from you."

The witch took a moment to compose herself.

"Who's the boy?" she asked, turning her attention to Jericho.

It had to be an act, but I couldn't help but admire her ever so slightly for not showing how very frightened she must be right now. The woman may have been a witch, but there was no way she was as powerful as Banyon.

"He's a Blackheart," the warlock said dismissively.

Agatha's eyes widened. "A real Blackheart."

"In the flesh," the Blackheart in question said. "The name's Jericho Nox."

"*Nox*," Banyon replied, turning the name over on his tongue. "An ancient word that means *darkness itself*."

Jericho shrugged. "Chose it myself when I was just a kid since—and this is a fun story—I forgot what my last name was because my parents were murdered when I was just a toddler. My criminal guardian suggested it for me. Said it suited my personality." He gave me a look. "Vik went a different direction, obviously. Much more civilized."

"Obviously," I repeated, stunned. I couldn't believe I had

never, not once, questioned why he and Viktor didn't have the same last name.

He didn't even know his real last name.

Banyon seemed utterly unmoved by this insight into the Black-heart's personal history as he stood over the witch. "Now that the introductions are over, I'm ready for your confession, Agatha."

"I have no confession to make." Defiance flickered in her gaze. "You've been missing for more than two months, Zarek. I'd begun to believe you were dead."

"Have you been searching for me?"

"I've reached out to other factions who've heard nothing. Seen nothing. After your compound was raided, the alliance began to splinter. Both morale and hope have fallen. I took it upon myself to regroup."

"Yes, I saw what you consider regrouping. Your actions were rash and foolish and have jeopardized everything I've spent the better part of two decades building."

"My daughter's life is on the line, my lord."

"A child you'd already mourned, a child who you'd believed was dead for more than year and yet you somehow managed to carry on."

"But she's not dead. She's very much alive. Mika came to me immediately after Tamara's capture and explained that they'd been imprisoned in the Queen's Keep for a year. Mika was able to use her Queensguard security clearance to change the execution orders and send my daughter behind those prison walls—indefinitely trapped, but alive. It took all this time for them to escape."

"A Queensguard?" Banyon cast a look of outrage at Mika, then snapped back to Agatha. "You would be foolish enough to trust *any* Queensguard?"

Agatha didn't flinch. She clenched her fists at her sides. "I trust this *former* Queensguard. I swear I will save Tamara from execution if it's the last thing I do. By any means necessary."

"Brave words, Agatha. As brave as your words on the announcement were, when you invoked my name and made it seem as if this were on my orders."

"I did what I had to do."

"It was wrong."

"Who are you to say what's wrong and what's right anymore?" She rose from her seat. "For years we've patiently waited for you to fulfill your promises. *Years*, my lord!" She slammed her fists down against the table. "But all you've done is make pretty, inspiring speeches to those who already know the truth, that have elicited small acts of rebellion. Over and over and over! Words won't change ignorant hearts and minds. Action will. Blood will. The time has come for both."

Banyon's jaw tensed. "You're making these decisions out of fear, not strategy."

"My daughter will not die. I won't allow it."

The warlock fell silent, clasping his hands behind his back as he began to pace, his brow furrowed. "This isn't the right time, Agatha, and you, more than anyone else, know exactly why that is."

"It doesn't matter," she bit out.

"Nothing matters more. I do understand your pain, but what

you've done—to take that girl, to threaten that girl . . ."

"*That girl* will get the attention of Queen Isadora more than anyone else. It was a bold choice, one made out of desperation, yes, I'll admit it, but I know it'll work."

"You assume that the queen gives a damn about Celina Ambrose's life and would be willing to trade her prized prisoners for it."

"I do. She wouldn't want the bad press that would come from a dead First Daughter."

"Bad press?" He laughed, and it was a dark and chilling sound. "She controls the press. All of it. All the time. You are only giving her more ammunition to demonize our kind to the relentlessly ignorant masses. Celina is beloved by the Empire, a beautiful young woman on the brink of marriage. An innocent. You can claim that you've made this choice strategically, but it's your weakness that's guided you." He hissed out a breath. "Is the girl here?"

The humor disappeared from the witch's face. "I beg you to let me handle this, Zarek."

Banyon's eyes narrowed. "I'll ask once again. Is Celina Ambrose here?"

Agatha took her seat again, her expression defeated. "She is."

The doubts I'd had, that had built up that Celina was possibly being kept at a second location, fell away. The relief I felt nearly buckled my knees.

She was here.

"What does the Blackheart have to do with any of this?" Agatha asked.

"Nothing," Jericho replied before Banyon could speak first. "I'm here representing my employer."

"Valery," she said without hesitation.

"You know her, huh? Small world, isn't it?"

Agatha nodded grimly. "Her ruthless, cold-blooded reputation precedes her. And yours as a Blackheart does as well."

"You're making me blush. Don't worry, I'm just Val's eyes and ears, making sure your witchy shenanigans don't impact her bank account. Try to pretend that I'm not even here."

Part of me desperately wished Jericho wasn't here. Valery knew about his history with Banyon, his lifelong desire for vengeance, and yet she'd ordered him to come with us. She'd ordered him not to harm Banyon.

I may have come to understand the witch slightly better in the last twenty-four hours and empathize—a little bit—with her painful history, but she was an abusive, manipulative woman. This was punishment for Jericho. Or a lesson. Or . . . maybe both.

Instead of a couple weeks locked in a dark room with no food or water, with only his magic-enhanced Blackheart strength to keep him alive—which he'd told me had been his penalty for failing to kill both my father and me the night of last year's Gala—she was forcing him to spend time with the person he hated the most.

"Zarek," Agatha ventured. "I know you're angry, but I ask you to consider this plan . . . not from my point of view, but as a true power play to show the palace that we are done with small acts of rebellion that can easily be ignored or quashed.

Holding Celina and forcing a response from the queen was the sound decision. Frankly"—she raised her chin— "you should be thanking me."

Banyon raised a brow. "Should I?"

"Yes. Tamara isn't any witch; she's the daughter of your closest associate. Your friend." She tensed. "That is, if you still consider me your friend, Zarek. My point is, they chose to make a public display of my daughter on purpose, to get your attention. Perhaps because *your* daughter is no longer at arm's reach from the queen."

What a chilling suggestion. And yet, I couldn't exactly say she was wrong.

If I were the queen and I wanted to get my worst enemy's attention, I would definitely threaten the life of someone important to him. Or important to someone close to him.

I waited for Banyon's response to this. His brows were furrowed as he regarded the witch.

"We've been driving all day to get here. It's late. Provide Josslyn and the Blackheart with accommodations. We'll speak more about this tomorrow."

Agatha regarded him now with disappointment that he hadn't readily agreed to everything she'd just said. "Of course."

And with that, it seemed that the meeting was officially over.

FOURTEEN

I lost track of Jericho in the minutes that followed but found Mika at my side taking me to my temporary room in the abandoned hotel. I let her lead me without argument, soon finding myself in a small room with a king-sized bed, a working bathroom, and cheery, bright wallpaper that seemed as fresh and new as it must have the last time someone stayed here half a decade ago. The electricity worked, and so did the hydro.

Mika was silent the whole way, her expression tight. And then she turned to leave without saying anything else.

"Just like that?" I said to her back.

Her shoulders tensed. "Just like what?"

"You're just going to walk away from me right now?"

"That was the general plan." She turned to face me. "Like I said earlier, you shouldn't be here. But that was before I knew who your father was."

I shook my head. "I didn't know. All my life, I didn't know the truth about him."

"And I'm supposed to believe that?"

"I don't care what you believe, Mika," I replied. "But here's what I believe about you: You're not a murderer. Maybe you did some sketchy stuff when you were a Queensguard. It seems to come with the territory. But you're not a heartless killer."

"I've killed before."

"Not an innocent eighteen-year-old girl."

"Tamara is only twenty-six," Mika countered. "And she's every bit as innocent as you claim Celina is, only the difference is, Celina is the daughter of the prime minister, and Tamara is a witch. One gets a ticket to the royal Gala, the other gets decapitated—maybe, if she's lucky. At least, that would be a quick death. Did you see her on the feed? They'd beaten her half to death. Do you think she resisted arrest? Or do you think they wanted to make it look like she did?"

The ex-Queensguard had successfully silenced any arguments from me.

"I'm so sorry," I whispered. "I really am."

Her harsh expression didn't soften in the slightest. "I bet you are. Everything seems to turn out just fine for you, Joss. You're a privileged princess, no matter who your father is. Some people don't have as many choices or as many chances as you seem to get. You don't know what it's like to be someone like me. Or Tamara."

"I'm starting to get an idea. In case you need me to fill in the blanks for you: Banyon's my birth father. That means I'm a *witch*, Mika. I don't know what my element is—maybe I never will—but it's true. I know it." I stared down at my hands. "I haven't even begun to process what it all means. All my life,

I've believed magic was evil. Not just bad or wrong, but pure, soul-destroying evil. And then I met Tamara, and I started to question what was truth and what were lies. And in the end, or, at least, as of now—which I hope like hell isn't the end of anything—I am so alone and so damn scared."

Mika nodded, drawing in a shaky breath. "If you're scared about what it might mean to be a witch in the Empire of Regara, imagine how Tamara must feel."

I wanted to be mad at her, but I couldn't. The pain on her face was raw now; she wasn't trying to hide it anymore.

"How did it happen?" I asked. "The last time I saw you, you were escaping from the Keep."

Mika's gaze grew faraway. "The funny thing about that prison is that it's pretty much in the middle of nowhere. We made it to Silverside an hour later, the closest town to the Keep. I left Tamara somewhere I thought was safe to get us some food. I was gone only five minutes. Five short minutes." Her expression turned anguished. "When I got back, she was surrounded by Queensguards. I couldn't do anything to help her without getting arrested too. All that time in the Keep, waiting for Lazos to help us escape, and when he finally did, this happened. He's probably laughing at us now."

"Trust me, he's not laughing at you," I said grimly. "Elian killed him that night."

"That son of a bitch deserved death after everything he'd done." Mika shook her head. "If anyone knew the truth about the queen's son . . ."

"What would happen?" I asked, suddenly eager for the

change in subject to something more hopeful than tragic. "If the world knew that Prince Elian was alive, and he'd been resurrected with death magic on the queen's command, what would that mean?"

"I don't know," she replied. "Would anyone believe it? Would anyone really care if the queen's dabbled in magic?"

"Of course they would."

"A lot of people already know, Joss."

"What?"

Mika walked to the window and pulled the pink-and-orange curtains away so she could peer outside into the darkness. "I've found that a whole lot of people, unless they live incredibly sheltered lives, know that not everything is as black and white—good versus evil—as the palace wants them to believe."

"About magic?"

"About everything. About elementia, about witches, hell . . . even about Lord Banyon himself."

I shook my head. "I didn't know."

"Of course not. You're someone who'd never been exposed to a single piece of unnecessary information. Just the curated royal newsfeed, small talk at cocktail parties, carefully planned schooling led by carefully selected tutors. Watched over by security, all day, and all night. Coddled and protected, held up as a shining example to everyone else of what they should aspire to be like."

I scoffed. "That's an exaggeration."

"Maybe from your point of view it is. Not from mine."

I gave some serious consideration to what she'd just said. I couldn't say she was lying. I'd been protected. So had Celina. The fact that my knowledge of elementia had been next to nothing before I met Jericho was stark evidence of that.

"Banyon thinks that the percentage of mages is high, Mika," I finally said. "Really high. Including people on the royal council. That the queen keeps this secret. That she has another secret, one Elian knows too. A secret that could pretty much crack open the whole damn world. Any clue what that could be?"

"Other than what we already know to be true?" She smoothed a hand over her thin braids. "In an empire of billions, there is a big percentage of people who know that they're living a lie, Joss. So, you're asking what I think would happen if the queen's lies were exposed by Prince Elian's continuing existence going live?" Mika spread her hands. "Maybe nothing at all."

"How can you say that?" I exclaimed.

"Because I lived it. Because I helped to enforce it. Nobody likes change, Joss. Everybody much prefers a nice, pleasant, drama-free existence, with a designated warlock villain to fear, and a queen to admire and respect. And the weeks and years go by without major disruptions. It was my job to keep disruptions to a minimum, for far too long. I was well paid. If anyone questioned our superiors, there were repercussions. So, I didn't. At least, not until I did."

"When you met Tamara," I said.

She nodded. "A comfortable life doesn't interest me anymore, not if she can't share it with me." Mika's brown eyes welled with tears, and she turned away from me before any could spill.

"Mika—"

"No, we're done for tonight. I need to go."

And then she was gone, the door closing with a soft click.

But I didn't intend to be left behind, alone in a room. There was too much still to do.

I closed the distance to the door in two steps, just as someone knocked. Clearly, Mika had more to say, and I was ready to hear it.

I opened the door, only to find myself face-to-face with Jericho.

"Good," he said gruffly. "We need to talk."

Without waiting for me to invite him in, he entered, casting his gaze over the hotel room. "This is a way better room than mine. How many vacant rooms are there in this place? Three or four hundred easily, right? You'd think they could spare something bigger than a shoebox for the ruthless, cold-blooded Blackheart. But no. Of course not."

I waited for him to turn to face me before I threw my arms around him and hugged him tightly against me. He tensed, but then I felt his hands press against the small of my back.

He raised a brow. "Maybe I should complain about hotel rooms more often." Then I was treated with a glimpse of a smile. "What do I get if I complain about the food too?"

"I'm glad you're here—"

"I'm glad you're glad."

"—but you need to leave," I finished.

He blinked. "Now you're giving me mixed messages, Drake. But that's nothing new. I know what you're thinking."

"Do you?"

"Yes, you're thinking that I'm going to fight against Valery's command and try to murder Banyon in his sleep tonight, but he's going to wake up and murder me right back."

"Pretty much," I admitted. "Am I right?"

"Can't say the thought hasn't crossed my mind. That I haven't played out a hundred different scenarios in my head today of how I can get my vengeance without getting incinerated."

"And?"

"None ended well. So here I am, in your comfy hotel room, wondering what the plan is."

"Good question. I came here to help Celina escape. But . . ." I chewed my bottom lip. "I don't think it's going to be that easy."

"Escape never is."

"I feel really helpless right now," I admitted. "I don't like feeling like this."

"I have something for you that might help with that. I wanted to give it to you earlier, but I didn't want any witnesses." Jericho reached into his pocket and pulled out the gold memory box before placing it in the palm of my hand. "Here."

I stared down at the box for a few moments in utter shock. "What? Why are you giving me this?"

"Simple. Because you're set on exploring those echoes in your head, and I have a hunch that this box might play a role. Maybe you've just been missing part of the puzzle all this time."

I met his gaze, my eyes wide. "A hunch?"

"Yeah, a hunch." He shrugged. "I get those sometimes."

I realized that I'd never actually held the box in my own hand before this very moment. It was heavy, so much heavier than I expected it to be. "Valery gave this to you?"

"Not exactly," he said slowly.

"You stole it from her?"

He shrugged again. "I'd prefer to say I borrowed it. Indefinitely."

"Jericho, she's going to freak out."

"Val doesn't freak out. She exacts agonizingly painful vengeance on her enemies and others who do her wrong."

I couldn't help but let out a sharp, nervous laugh. "Jericho . . ."

"I'll take it back to her," he said. "But if it works . . . if there's a chance it could help to get you the answers you're looking for, then it's worth it."

I looked up at him, my throat suddenly thick with emotion. "Thank you."

There was that edge of a smile once again. "You're welcome. If you want to give it a try now, I can keep an eye on you and make sure nothing goes wrong. But if you—"

I kissed him, smiling against his lips despite everything. So much had gone wrong over the last month; so much had turned my life upside down and caused me pain and grief and stress. And doubt. But I knew one thing with absolute clarity: I didn't doubt Jericho anymore.

He kissed me back, threading his fingers into my long hair. "Drake . . ." he whispered. "You are full of surprises."

I grinned. "I try. You know, if you hate your room so much, I do have a very big room right here. With a very big bed."

His gaze darkened. "It *is* a very big bed, now that you mention it. Like, massive, really."

"I'm not all that tired, though."

"Me neither. May never sleep again, actually. Very overrated, sleep."

I placed the memory box on the bedside table before sliding my hands over his chest. "We haven't shared a room since the first night in the Queen's Keep."

"Oh, the memories. Shot in the chest. Earth magic. A walled, inescapable prison. A tiny cottage with no lock on the door. And who can forget the pisswater?"

I laughed at the reminder of the Keep's rancid version of homemade wine. "The worst name ever."

He kissed me, and I immediately forgot all about the Queen's Keep.

"We'll fix it all, Drake," Jericho whispered against my lips. "You and me. Nothing can stop us."

"Nothing?"

"Absolutely nothing. Together, Josslyn Drake and Jericho Nox? We're a damn force to be reckoned with."

"Undefeatable champions," I agreed readily, as I pulled Jericho's leather coat off his shoulders. "Forget Viktor. To me, you're the real hero in the family."

The Blackheart tensed. "*Forget Viktor*," he repeated.

Shit. Immediately I regretted my words. "I didn't mean . . . I shouldn't have brought him up."

The room felt colder the moment Jericho pulled away from me. *Damn.*

"My brother lied to me," he bit out. "He betrayed me."

My throat tightened. "I'm so sorry."

A different kind of pain now moved through his gaze. "I'm not."

"What do you mean?"

"The truth about him, Drake. It hurts, but it's worth it not to live in a dung heap of lies. I knew in my gut that something was off about him, about what he did for me. When he walked away three years ago in search of glory, I knew he wasn't ever coming back. It was over, Drake. He made it crystal clear that he wouldn't lift a finger to save me if it would block his path to victory. And now I see I was right."

I couldn't believe what I was hearing. "Then we see things a little differently."

"No surprise there," he replied.

"Viktor *did* save you."

"Only on Aunt Issy's command."

"I think you're underestimating Viktor," I told him. "Maybe not completely, but a little. Yes, he agreed to the queen's terms, but what choice did he have? It allowed him to help you escape. If he hadn't, you'd be dead."

"Would I? Or would the queen have just let me languish in her shiny palace dungeon indefinitely until I finally answered her questions to her satisfaction, or Norris broke the rest of my ribs?"

I cringed at the reminder that he'd been tortured during his interrogation. It would have taken him much longer to recover from his injuries if he wasn't a magically enhanced Blackheart.

"You'll never know for sure. Because Viktor did what he had to do. Honestly? I think he would have helped you escape even if the queen hadn't gotten to him first."

"You're wrong."

I shrugged. "It's none of my business."

"You're right about that, Drake. It's none of your business, and it's not your problem. It's mine." He said this harsher than I expected, and I winced.

"I'm sorry," I said. "I am. But it's how I feel, and we promised to tell each other the truth, remember? Do you want me to doubt every word that comes out of my mouth?"

"No, wouldn't want Josslyn Drake to ever think first before she speaks." A shadow of pain crossed Jericho's expression. "I gave you the box. That's the only reason I came here tonight. We're done here."

With those less-than-charming parting words, the Blackheart left my room.

I didn't follow him.

FIFTEEN

When I woke after tossing and turning all night, regretting my words about Viktor—even though they were *true*— it was midmorning, and I now had two new tools to help me achieve my goals.

The memory box.

And a fresh burst of stubborn outrage.

I made use of the shower in my room and chose to be deeply grateful for the out-of-date toiletry samples positioned on the marble counter.

As I dragged my fingers through my wet hair, I studied my reflection. My temporarily contact-free eyes were a medium-amber color today—not the strange, otherworldly gold they were in the beginning, but not my regular slate-blue either. I inserted the contacts before inspecting the memory box very closely, studying each geometric symbol etched into its surface as I held it up to the light.

And then I closed my eyes and tried to use it to summon an echo. Any echo.

Any echo would do just fine, thanks.

But nothing happened.

I sighed, frustrated, but I knew the problem. I was too distracted at the moment. I'd have to try again later when I was able to better concentrate.

Pulling on my old, dirty clothes was depressing and demotivating, especially with the memory box wedged into the small pocket of my jacket. On my way to find someone to take me to see Celina, I happened upon the hotel's gift shop, which was still fully stocked with a wide range of five-year-old, branded Queensgate Amusement Park fashion. After quickly perusing the selection, I chose a pair of dark blue joggers and an oversize T-shirt with a sparkly gold crown on the front. I also grabbed a zip-up hooded sweatshirt with pockets roomy enough to comfortably carry the small memory box. I put on the new outfit, taking a moment to inspect myself in a nearby full-length mirror.

I looked utterly ridiculous, like an enthusiastic tourist excited for a day of fun and entertainment. But I didn't need a ball gown or the latest fashion; I just needed to be clean and comfortable.

The first person I found was Mika. She eyed me warily as I swiftly closed the distance between us.

"Take me to Celina," I told her. Then added, "Banyon said it's okay for me to see her."

"You're lying."

I glared at her. "Yes, I'm lying. But I want to see her anyway and I'm not going to give you a moment of peace until that happens." My stomach growled. "I also need some breakfast."

She gave me an unimpressed glare back. "Anything else you'd like to demand this morning, Your Highness?"

"That's all for now. I'm not going anywhere, Mika. I need to see my friend and make sure she's okay. Help me. *Please*."

This time I wasn't lying. And all the worry and pain I'd built up since seeing Celina on the massive screen in Cresidia came out in the one word.

Mika didn't have a curt rebuttal to that. All she did was nod. "Fine. You can have ten minutes with her."

I opened my mouth to negotiate for more, but quickly reconsidered. "Thank you."

"Follow me."

I followed her through the hallways, past the dining hall where she indicated for me to grab some food. There were wrapped packages of pastries and other unhealthy fare on a table by the entry. I took a cookie as big as my face from the pile, tearing off a piece of it and chewing it while we walked.

"Are you the one who kidnapped her?" I had to ask the question, as I swallowed down a stale lump.

"No," Mika replied tightly. "But I would have if I'd been asked to. Agatha did it herself with the help of some sort of a magic-infused knockout drug."

I cringed at the thought. Poor Celina. It sounded like the second dose of Dust that she'd been forced to endure; the first had been at the hands of Jericho himself. "How did you find Agatha?"

"Tamara told me where to find her mother. It was her plan that we both come here to see her. It was the last thing she said to me before she was arrested." Mika's jaw tightened. "Tamara introduced me to Agatha when she visited Ironport a couple years ago. I was the reason they had a falling-out and had barely spoken since. Agatha didn't like her daughter spending so much time with a Queensguard. Now I know why. I was the enemy. I didn't even know Tamara was a witch for the first six months we were together, and I sure as hell didn't know her mother worked directly with Lord Banyon. I only found out the truth when she was arrested the first time."

"And you didn't care?"

"At first, I definitely did. I felt lied to and betrayed, until I took a moment and tried to see it from Tamara's point of view. And then I didn't care about anything except seeing her again." She blew out a breath. "Why am I telling you any of this?"

"Because it matters," I said. "And it helps me understand why you're a relentless bitch sometimes."

She laughed at that. "Right back at you."

Silent now, she led me down a series of hallways and up a flight of stairs, until we reached a door. Mika slid a key into the lock and opened it.

"You have a visitor," she announced. Then to me, "I'll wait out here."

I nodded, stepped into the room, and the door closed between us.

The room was decorated in the same bright, summery colors as mine. This was a larger suite, though, with a kitchenette, and a seating area opposite the bed and washroom. Celina stood in front of the sofa, her eyes wide at my approach.

"Joss?" she managed. "Am I dreaming right now?"

Relief hit me like a tidal wave. "More like a nightmare. Celina, I'm so glad to see you."

And then her arms were around me and she was hugging me so tightly that I could barely breathe.

"I'm furious at you!" she cried into my still-damp hair. "You disappeared and I had no idea where you went! Again!"

"I'm so sorry." I pulled back from her, gripping her shoulders so I could get a good look at her. "Have they hurt you?"

"No. Not yet anyway." She drew in a shaky breath. Her gaze fell to my new outfit. "What are you wearing?"

"This?" I turned in a circle. "Very fashionable, I know."

She blinked. "Queensgate Amusement Park."

"Yeah. That's . . . where we are right now."

Her eyes widened. "It is? I haven't been outside. There's a tree blocking my view from the window. We're really at the park?"

"It's abandoned now. But yes." I reached down and squeezed her hands in mine. "I'm so sorry this happened to you, Cel. You must be so scared."

Her eyes shone with tears. "I am."

The next moment we were seated on the sofa. It felt so normal for a moment, just her and me—a mirror image to when I'd reunited with her at the palace only a week and a half ago after disappearing on my misadventure with Jericho.

"Now, talk," I told her sternly. "How did this happen?"

"I was out for a walk," she said, shaking her head. "And it was just like at the boutique that night. I got a face full of pink powder, and the next thing I knew, I woke up here. I had a bit of a head-ache when I woke up, but otherwise, I'm not injured at all. Is this why you disappeared? Nobody answered any of my questions about where you went. Were you kidnapped out of the palace?"

I was about to deny this, but I realized what it looked like. Of course she would assume I was another hostage.

"It's complicated," I told her.

"That's putting it mildly," she agreed. "How do we get out of here, Joss?"

"I don't know yet," I replied honestly. "But I'm working on it."

"Viktor disappeared that night too. He didn't say anything. Nobody told me anything—it's like they were purposely trying to keep me in the dark. But the Blackheart escaped. And Viktor disappeared. You disappeared." Tears streamed down her cheeks. "And then this happened."

I pulled her to me in a tight embrace. "Nothing is going to happen to you, Celina. Do you hear me?"

"You're going to protect me, are you?"

"You know it."

"This isn't the Queen's Gala, Joss. Smiling and nodding isn't going to help me here."

"Smiling and nodding helps in almost every situation. Trust me on that." I pulled back, forcing an easy grin to my face, gently wiping the tears off her cheeks. "I know how scared you must be. But I also know you're stronger than you think you are."

"My father tells me the same thing," she replied.

I tensed at the mention of her father, and she noticed. A frown drew her eyebrows together.

"Something happened at that dinner," she said. "Between you and him. When you left early, before we were even served any food. And that was the last time I saw you. What were you arguing about? He's been weird ever since, and he's drinking so much now, I don't know if he's ever sober."

My best friend looked at me with such intensity, for a moment I wanted to share this truth with her: that her father was a social-climbing, power-seeking scumbag who personally arranged the assassination of the one person standing in his way. And he'd also wanted me killed, just because he thought I was a bad influence on his own daughter.

I considered myself a champion of the truth, but this wasn't a truth I could burden Celina with. Not now. Not here.

"Your father just hates me for some reason; don't ask me why," I said as lightly as possible, as I stood up and started pacing. My hands were in the pockets of my sweatshirt, and I rubbed my thumb absently over the carvings of the memory box.

Celina studied me, still frowning. "Something doesn't feel right. Joss, sit down and tell me what happened to you. Tell me how we're going to get out of here."

I turned to her, imagining what she'd say, what she'd do, if I did just that: told her everything.

That I hadn't been taken as a hostage. That I'd left by my own choice because I knew staying at the palace meant I was the queen's prisoner—a prisoner who'd learned enough of the truth to make me dangerous. That everything Celina knew about the Empire, about magic, about Lord Banyon—even about me—was a massive lie. And that her best friend of over ten years, her chosen sister, was a witch. Although currently I was a witch with no access to my own elementia, if I'd ever even had access to it in the first place.

She'd go through all the stages I went through on my rocky journey to this awakening.

Mostly denial and fear, though. She'd never look at me the same way. And, since she hadn't experienced everything herself, she wouldn't believe me in a million years that magic wasn't evil like we'd always been told.

I knew I wouldn't have believed her either, had our roles been reversed.

"You want to know the strangest thing?" Celina said after silence fell between us for a few moments. "The witch"—she shuddered—"she said her name was Agatha. When I woke up, she was here. She wanted to check on me and make sure I was all right. She apologized for doing what she did, said it was because her daughter is going to be executed. She was crying, Joss. She scares me, but for a moment, just a moment, I felt really bad for her."

"I guess we all do questionable things when life as we know it is ripped out from beneath our feet," I agreed, still playing with the cool metal box in my pocket.

I wondered where Ambrose was right now. How hard he would be working to get his daughter back safely. I didn't doubt that he loved Celina. That was his only saving grace, as far as I was concerned.

He was probably sitting in my father's old study, behind the mahogany desk that had been used by seven different prime ministers, each of their names etched onto a bronze plate attached to its surface to show the legacy of the office.

I'd hid under that desk while playing hide-and-seek with Celina. I remembered it like it was yesterday.

It was the same desk that my father sat at in the echo with Banyon.

And, as I held the image of this desk in my mind, I watched as a ribbon of golden smoke entered the room. At the sight of it, I gripped the box tighter, welcoming an echo. It wasn't exactly an ideal moment for one to arrive, but I couldn't risk losing it, not now, when it was finally happening.

"What are we going to do, Joss?" Celina asked again.

"Hold that thought for just a sec, okay?" I told her just before I was swept away.

The smoke cleared and I found myself again in my father's study, with him behind his desk and annoyance flickering in his gaze.

And me—sixteen-year-old me—having a temper tantrum about my fashion choices.

"It's too short and it's too tight. You're only sixteen years old, Josslyn."

"I know how old I am!"

I realized with surprise that this was the exact same echo as before.

I forced myself to turn my head and search for signs of Banyon. There—the closet door was ajar just a smidge, the faintest hint of movement in the darkness beyond. Clearly, younger Joss had been very distracted not to notice that she'd interrupted a meeting between the prime minister and the most powerful and infamous warlock in the Empire.

I was confused by why I was experiencing this echo again. I'd never repeated one before, but of course it made sense that it was possible to revisit one moment, to turn it over and inspect it, not leaving a single clue behind. After all, the memories had been placed in the box to be studied, like the physical pages in an ancient book that one could return to again and again.

And I had the memory box in my pocket. It couldn't be coincidence that as soon as I got the box, I was able to step into an echo. It seemed to give me more power over summoning the memories.

Thanks to Jericho's gift, I was experiencing this echo again. If I had the box, then perhaps I had control over what I saw and how I saw it.

As the past version of me turned away from my father and left in a huff, I took a chance and followed her out of the room. Out of sight of Lord Banyon. A moment in time, magically captured in this echo, beyond what the warlock had perceived with his own senses, just as Jericho's gambling-addicted warlock had suggested.

I followed myself up the staircase to my room, as younger Joss flung open the doors to my closet and peered inside at the very generous wardrobe that contained many beautiful and appropriate gowns to wear to a formal occasion like the Queen's Gala.

Younger Joss hissed out a sigh, glaring at herself in a full-length mirror, and twisted a long piece of blond hair tightly around her finger.

"You are amazing," she told her reflection. "And you're

gorgeous. Everybody knows it. Everyone's jealous of you. Everybody wants to be you. Especially Helen."

Okay, well, this was embarrassing to witness.

I mean, she wasn't wrong—especially not about Helen. But it was still embarrassing.

"Good luck," I whispered to her as she took her time deciding that, ultimately, she would wear the exact same dress she already had on. It was a small act of rebellion in an otherwise boring life. She didn't know about the tragedy that was going to happen in less than an hour. I wish I could have warned her.

In the end, the dress didn't matter. It never had. But I still wish I would have changed into something different, if only to make my father happy.

My eyes had started to burn with tears of regret as I moved down the stairs and returned to the study. I was incorporeal in these echoes, no substance, since I wasn't really here at all. This wasn't time travel; this was a magically captured moment in time. Still, walking straight through a door was proving to be more unnerving than I thought it would be.

Just then, Banyon opened the door and left, seemingly unconcerned about being seen. He pulled the hood of his jacket up over his head and confidently strode toward a couple guards, who thrust out their hands to him. Banyon placed some money in each of their eager grips.

More Queensguards who were willing to be paid off. Did no one have any integrity anymore?

When Banyon left, the golden smoke began to waft back in.

Wait, no. I wasn't done yet. As my heart pounded, I tried to pretend that this was a video on the newsfeed, recorded and able to be rewatched at my leisure. I also pictured the golden box and imagined running my fingers over the magical etchings on its surface.

I had control here. I couldn't think any differently or this might not work.

Slowly, the smoke receded, and the scene before me began to move backward, to rewind. I didn't let myself celebrate yet—I concentrated until Banyon returned, the door opened, and he entered the study again.

I'd done it. I couldn't believe I'd done it!

This time I quickly joined them.

"She doesn't get such stubbornness from either myself or Evelyne," my father told the warlock. "She must have inherited it from you."

"You think I'm stubborn, Louis?"

"You're the most stubborn person I've ever met in my life. If you weren't, you wouldn't have come here tonight."

"I didn't want to wait another day to show you this."

And there it was. The list of names he drew out of his pocket and presented to my father.

"Is this what I think it is?" my father asked, frowning down at it.

"Just as I've always believed, the queen and her predecessors have perpetuated the claim that mages make up only a minuscule percentage of the population. But it's a lie. This list is only a small sampling of family bloodlines that are touched by magic. You recognize a few names immediately, don't you?"

"I do indeed."

I moved closer, not about to let this moment pass without doing my best to memorize as many names as I possibly could.

"Royal council members," Banyon said. "Members of Parliament, wealthy, personal friends of Issy herself. All potential mages. Issy hides this secret, she protects those who have value to her, while condemning those who don't."

"Names written on a page mean nothing. This isn't inarguable proof."

"That's why I need your help. You're close to her, closer than anyone else. She trusts you. She considers you family after all this time. You can learn more; find more tangible evidence that I'm right about this."

The handwriting was difficult to decipher, especially in the dim lighting. It was the scrawl of someone who had no patience for penmanship. But as my father left the desk and moved to the window, I took the opportunity to scan the list of names.

Their conversation continued—about treason, about fixing what's been broken for centuries. Banyon's hypothesis about the percentage of mages in the Empire, and how the truth can't be rewritten.

I barely heard them anymore, as important as their conversation was to me. It all became a blur. There were names I recognized on this list. Names I could easily put to faces. People who'd socialized with my father and with me, at gatherings here at the official prime minister's residence, and at functions like the Gala. The Queensgames. Theater openings. Charity balls.

These were important and influential names of important and influential people.

But one name, right at the top, stole my breath the moment I saw it. I was sure I'd read it wrong, so I studied it for several long moments, my gaze moving carefully over the sharp tip of the capital *A*. The curve of the lowercase *s* and *e*. I studied it until there was no doubt in my mind of exactly whose name it was.

Ambrose.

"I'm dying," Banyon's words drew me out of my shock. "This disease is incurable, even through magical means."

I finally tore my gaze away from the list.

"How long do you have left?" my father asked.

"Long enough for me to end Issy's reign, one way or the other. Choose your side, Louis. You are either with me, or you're against me. But know this: Nothing—*nothing*—will stop me now."

When the golden smoke moved in this time, it moved so quickly that I didn't even have the opportunity to try to stop it. The echo vanished and then I was back at the Queensgate Amusement Park hotel, facing a girl with the last name Ambrose, who looked at me with alarm.

"Joss, your nose is bleeding," Celina exclaimed.

I wiped my hand under my nose absently, trying to compose myself as quickly as I could.

Ambrose. On Banyon's list.

Celina was from a mage bloodline. As was her father.

Did the queen know that her current prime minister might be a warlock?

"Joss, talk to me! Are you all right?" Celina practically shouted to get my attention. "You just zoned out for a few moments. What's wrong with you?"

Only a few moments? It felt like much longer than that to me.

Again, I couldn't explain anything to her. Not here. I needed more information, more proof. An echo couldn't be shared on the newsfeed or used as evidence.

Could this be the reason Ambrose wanted my father dead? I thought it was for political gain, but if he knew the truth was going to come out about his bloodline . . .

No. The timing didn't line up. He would have had to hire Valery earlier, not the very same day. That meeting between Banyon and my father had been just minutes before we'd left for the Gala.

Louis Drake's fate had already been sealed before he saw the list. But if it hadn't, I know he would have helped Banyon find more proof; he would have used his position so close to the queen to help change the world for the better.

Could I even attempt to follow in his footsteps?

"I need to go," I said.

"Joss, no."

Before she could say another word—questioning or arguing—I pulled her to me in another fierce hug. "I love you, Celina. No matter what happens, you can never, ever, ever doubt that, okay?"

"I love you too," she whispered.

And that was how I reluctantly left her for now, with a million questions and very few answers.

That made two of us.

SIXTEEN

I needed to find Banyon.

But searching for an infamous warlock in an abandoned amusement park proved to be a painful lesson in futility. I wandered through the dried-out carcasses of carnival rides and game booths as I searched near the hotel, but came up empty.

The first people I came upon were Mika and Agatha, who both eyed me without much friendliness as I approached, as if I were barging in on an important conversation.

"Be ready," I heard Agatha say to Mika under her breath.

Mika nodded before turning to face me. "What do you want?"

"Be ready for what?" I asked, then shrugged when I was met with an icy look. "What's happening? Have you heard anything from the palace?"

"That's not your concern," Agatha told me.

"I definitely disagree with you on that," I replied, cutting her my own cold look, then returned my attention to Mika. "You weren't waiting for me outside of Celina's room."

It had been a nice surprise, but an unexpected one. Which, I supposed, was the very definition of the word surprise.

"Something came up," she said.

"Right." I glanced between the two. "What's going on?"

"Nothing of importance," Agatha said smoothly, although there was not a sliver of friendliness in her voice. "And even if there was, I wouldn't tell you. I don't trust you."

If she did, I'd question her intelligence. So, this wasn't exactly news to me. "We have that in common, I guess. Have you seen Banyon around anywhere?"

"No."

"What did you and he decide when it comes to Celina?" I asked, trying to keep my tone casual and not overly demanding. It took quite a bit of effort.

"We haven't discussed it any further," the witch replied. "He's been avoiding me. But I know my plan will work even if he refuses to agree with me. I will get Tamara back, whatever it takes."

Whatever it takes.

Would this witch really kill an innocent girl like she'd threatened if the palace didn't give her what she wanted?

At least from Mika, I saw a glimmer of regret in her eyes that it had come to this. It didn't help to set my mind at ease that Agatha might be bluffing.

What would I do, if it were someone I cared deeply about who'd been wrongly accused of a crime and about to be executed, like Tamara was?

I didn't have to think too hard about that. Jericho *had* been in a similar situation when he'd been arrested and imprisoned at the palace. I'd only known him a couple of weeks by then, and I'd been ready to move mountains to help save him.

I understood why Agatha had chosen this path. But I would never stand idly by and let her hurt Celina. There had to be another way to help Tamara.

The witch wouldn't listen to a word I said on the subject, though. So, I'd have to deal with her later.

"Good talk," I said dismissively. "I'm going to keep looking for Banyon."

I turned away from them, and Mika grabbed my arm to stop me. I frowned and met her gaze, expecting some sort of snide comment. Instead, I was met with an intense expression of uneasiness.

"You need to stay inside the hotel today," she said.

I slipped out of her grasp. "No thanks. Right now, what I need is to find a warlock."

As a former Queensguard, I wasn't surprised that Mika was a control freak. I guess she liked all of Agatha's prisoners and guests under one roof where she could easily keep track of them.

As I moved back toward the hotel, I spotted Jericho standing near the dolphin fountain. Hesitating only a moment, I made a beeline for him.

He swept his gaze over me as I approached. "What a coincidence. I almost wore the exact same outfit today." When I didn't make a snarky comment back about my Queensgate fashion choices, he frowned. "I'm kidding, of course."

"Sure. Okay, whatever." I met his gaze directly. "Last night . . . I—I shouldn't have said anything about your brother. I'm sorry if that hurt you."

Apologies weren't exactly second nature to me, but when they were deserved, like now, I could deliver one with complete sincerity.

Jericho looked away. "I wasn't hurt. Pissed off, annoyed, generally unsettled, yes. Hurt? Not so much."

"So, I'm forgiven?" I asked hopefully.

"Nothing to forgive, Drake."

I didn't believe that for a moment. I still believed what I'd said about Viktor, but sometimes the truth didn't have to be presented without any warning, with all of its razor-sharp edges sticking out.

Lesson learned.

"The box worked," I told him, choosing to change the subject.

I'd regained his full attention. "It did?"

I nodded. "I revisited an echo—the one with my father in it. I was able to read the list this time."

"And?"

"A lot of names I recognized. Including Ambrose." That had been a sharp-edged truth that had definitely left its mark on me.

His eyes widened. "That's . . . a surprise."

"Yeah, it sure is." I twisted my hands nervously, pacing in a short line in front of him. "Doesn't mean the current prime minister is a warlock; it just means, according to Banyon's investigation, that there have been mages in that family bloodline."

"Interesting." He considered this for a moment. "Sounds like maybe Banyon's hunch about the number of potential mages in the Empire is right."

"Maybe," I allowed. Then I took a breath. "Have you seen

Banyon today? I need to talk to him about this. And about Celina."

"No, I haven't seen him yet. But I haven't exactly been looking for him. I'm glad the box is working for you, Drake. That makes all of this worth it." Jericho raised the phone in his hand. "Val's been trying to contact me. I guess she's noticed that the merchandise is missing."

I raised my brow. "*Trying* to contact you?"

"Yeah." He shrugged. "I haven't taken any of her calls or replied to her messages yet. There have been ten so far." He glanced down at his phone as it made a buzzing sound. "Actually, make that eleven."

Valery knew the box was missing. And it wouldn't have taken too long for her to figure out who'd taken it. "Jericho," I said shakily. "Bad idea."

"I've been getting a lot of those lately. But I can't talk to her." He pressed his fingers against his temples. "If I do, I'll be forced to do what she tells me to do."

Great. Another thing to worry about. "So she really did freshen up your marks."

"Yeah." He absently rubbed his forearm. "They're deeper than ever. I feel her magic in me, right down to my bones."

A shiver sped down my spine. "Does it hurt?"

He met my gaze, and there wasn't an edge of humor in his black eyes. "Not yet."

It was like when we were in the Keep. He'd been late on his mission, and he'd started to feel the pain of that magical tether between him and Valery, created with her magic, his blood, and a goddess's stolen ancient dagger.

"You need to take the box back to her," I told him firmly. "That's what she wants, isn't it?"

"The box is useless without the magic in it."

"Not sure she'd feel that way. Jericho . . ."

"No, Drake. Not yet. You said the box is working for you, so you're keeping it for now." He shoved his phone into his jacket pocket, then swept his narrowed gaze over the hotel grounds. "Fine. Let's locate the warlock."

I didn't really care that Mika wanted me to stay in the hotel today. Despite the drama and uncertainty that had gathered like an invisible storm above me, today was a beautiful day—blue sky, bright sun, barely any clouds. It was the kind of day that I would have loved to spend at this park back when life was simple and I thought I had everything figured out.

Life wasn't simple anymore, but I was still determined to figure everything out. Celina safe. Tamara freed. And, one day very soon, Jericho released from his ties to Valery.

And exposing the queen's secrets and lies . . . well, I guess I needed Banyon's help with that.

While we swiftly moved along the pathways searching for the warlock, I couldn't help but take the opportunity to tell Jericho about coming here in the past. How much fun Celina and I had. And how much he would have liked it too.

"You were raised in Ironport," I said. "This park is only an hour's drive away."

"True," Jericho allowed. "But Rush wasn't big on taking me and Vik anywhere that normal kids would consider fun and games. It literally never would have occurred to him. We stayed in our neighborhood, working at his nightclub from the time we could scrub a dish or clean a floor. We were a burden to him."

I cringed at the sad glimpse into Jericho's past. "I knew him for less than an hour, but he seemed like he cared about you. He mourned you when he thought you were dead."

"Yeah, well. It's complicated, Drake. But to answer your question: No, I never came here or to any other amusement park."

"I'm sorry," I told him, my heart hurting.

"I'm not. I mean, do I look like someone who'd ride a phoenix on a carousel?" he asked as we approached the very attraction in question.

I couldn't fight the smile that now tugged at my lips at the mental image he presented. "Actually, you look *exactly* like the type of person who would ride a phoenix on a carousel." With that, I leapt onto the ride, brushing leaves and twigs from the large fantasy bird; the bright orange and yellow paint on its chiseled feathers had faded over the years, but it was still beautiful.

I patted the bird's saddle. "Hop on, Blackheart."

He eyed me skeptically. "Not going to happen, Drake."

"Fine. Be that way." I hopped on instead, closing my eyes and pretending for a blissful moment that I could still hear the music and smell the candy floss and roasted peanuts.

Celina always loved candy floss. She loved it far more than the rides themselves.

I opened my eyes, the reality of our current situation too heavy to ignore for more than a minute. "I need to get Celina out of here," I told him. "I don't trust Agatha for a minute. She's desperate, and desperate people do desperate things."

"I agree completely," he replied.

I looked at him with fresh determination. "When can we get out of here?"

"Tonight, after dark," he replied without missing a beat. He'd clearly been thinking about this even before I'd asked. "They only have about a half-dozen guards, but they'll be easy enough to deal with."

Six armed guards. It sounded like a lot to me. "You're sure about that?"

He gave me a pointed look. "Positive."

"That sounds a little cocky, Blackheart."

"Just cocky enough. Don't worry, Drake. I got this."

"Glad to hear it." I was both grateful and relieved that the Blackheart was on board with this decision, but I knew it wasn't going to be as simple as I wanted it to be. "I still need to talk to Banyon about everything before we leave. Maybe he can make things with Celina way simpler for us than launching a full-blown escape attempt tonight."

Jericho cast a glance around our immediate area, and his eyes narrowed. "Speak of the warlock, and the warlock will appear."

Banyon approached us, his hands clasped behind his back. "Agatha says you were looking for me?"

I quickly dismounted the phoenix and brushed off the front of my very unfashionable jogging pants.

I didn't expect that much from the warlock, all things considered. Banyon had only met me yesterday, despite apparently knowing of my existence for years. I knew he wasn't going to bare his soul or make me any lofty promises. He'd only allowed me to come here with him because he wanted to keep his valuable memory magic in sight.

I wouldn't overestimate my worth to him—he saw me as a walking, talking, flesh-and-blood memory box.

That was his mistake.

"I was," I said, injecting as much strength and confidence into my voice as anyone wearing a sequin-embellished novelty T-shirt could. "I want to you free Celina today."

That came out a bit blunter than I'd meant it to. But it was fine with me. I didn't have much interest or patience for dancing around this particular subject.

"I'm not prepared to do that quite yet," he replied. "I have to agree with Agatha that your friend is very valuable. I've decided that her plan will remain in play for now. It's only been a day, and there's been no response from the palace yet. But I know there will be."

His response wasn't a surprise to me. Not really. Still, I tried to shield my disappointment that nothing ever went as smoothly as I hoped it would.

Fine. We'd go with Jericho's plan. Tonight, after dark. Me, Celina, and Jericho were out of there. I knew there were other ways of helping Tamara that didn't put my best friend at risk.

"Color me curious," Jericho said, "but if there's no response from your old girlfriend, are you planning to kill Celina personally, or get one of your henchmen to do it?"

A breath caught in my chest. And I thought I was blunt.

"I have no plans of killing Celina," Banyon said thinly.

"You make a good point. Killing ends things far too quickly, doesn't it? I should know—I've dealt with a few similar situations for Val, and a little duress goes a long way toward getting what you want." He waved his hand. "A yanked-out tooth here, a severed finger there, a bloody earlobe thrown into the mix . . . proof that you're serious about your demands without the need to permanently stop a pulse. Until that outcome becomes necessary, of course."

"Jericho," I gasped, my heart pounding at the painfully gory picture he painted.

Banyon blinked. "No one is dying here, Blackheart. Not you, not me, and not Celina Ambrose."

"Valery did try to ensure that, didn't she?" Jericho rubbed his forearm, the location of his freshly carved marks. "But I've fought her command before. Not perfectly, but I think it might be possible if I'm motivated enough. And, trust me, warlock, I'm motivated when it comes to you."

Now I glared at him. I thought we'd dealt with this already. What was he doing, provoking the warlock like this?

"You're right," Banyon said evenly. "It is possible."

Jericho frowned. "Wait. What?"

A shadow crossed Banyon's expression, and he regarded the Blackheart without anger or malice. "You shield yourself with this cutting humor, this . . . facade of brashness. But I see your pain just under the surface. I know I caused that pain, and I know you won't believe me and you won't ever accept it, but I'm very sorry about what happened to your parents. If it wasn't for that tragedy, your path would not have led you to work for Valery. You would be free to pursue whatever life you wanted, and with whomever you wanted."

"You're right about one thing," Jericho growled. "Your apology means nothing to me. It's only empty words. Not like Val's. The words Val uses have power, commanding me, getting me to behave or steal or kill or beat someone up. I guess I shouldn't complain too much. I signed up for this. If it wasn't for her, I'd have stayed dead two years ago. So, I guess a life forced to follow that witch's every command is better than total obliteration."

"I thought you said you could fight her command?" Banyon countered.

The fire that had been in Jericho's gaze only a few moments ago began to fade. "I did. But . . . it was different before." He seemed to be debating how to respond, his gaze growing faraway.

If I had access to the Blackheart's echoes, I knew I'd find myself back the night of the Gala, with Jericho perched on a rooftop, waiting for the arrival of the prime minister and his daughter.

His mission—to kill us both. And he'd fought it. Not perfectly, like he'd said. But he had fought it.

"Different how?" Banyon asked.

"That time, the marks weren't fresh. They're fresh right now." Jericho pulled up his sleeve to show the marks on his forearm, raw and red. They made me wince in sympathy. "If my boss tells me to do something, I'm compelled to do it. But I can wait until they fade, if it means I get to kill you."

"Jericho," I snarled.

He didn't look at me. His attention remained fully fixed on the warlock. He was going to get himself killed, and this time it seemed that I couldn't do anything to stop it.

"Valery is a powerful witch with access to the darkest

magic," Banyon agreed, "but she isn't an immortal goddess, even if she fully embraces the rumors that she is. The marks on you are strong; there's no doubt about that. But from what I've seen of you so far, I believe you're stronger. I don't expect you to accept my apology, but please accept my advice to you here today. You can break your bond to Valery, fresh marks or not."

Jericho shook his head. "Only when she's says it's time."

"No. Just like you claimed before, you could kill me right now with the right motivation, and you would have every right to do just that."

A breath caught in my chest. Was he serious?

"Tempting." Jericho's fists clenched at his sides. "But you're wrong. When I resist, it's torture."

"I'm not saying it's easy; I'm only saying that it's possible. There's something on the other side of that pain you feel from resisting her magic. It's *freedom*, Blackheart."

I couldn't believe what he was suggesting—that Jericho could fight his marks. That he didn't have to wait to be released from his contract.

"Wait," I said, my throat tight. "You're really saying that Jericho has the power to choose not to be a Blackheart any longer?"

Banyon regarded me, his expression stony, his slate-blue eyes filled with decades of regret, sorrow, and grim determination.

"Yes, Josslyn," he said. "That's exactly what I'm saying."

SEVENTEEN

Jericho and Banyon eyed each other for a long, tense moment.

"Think about what I've said," Banyon said.

Then he started to move away from us.

I wasn't done yet. "Wait! Where are you going?"

"To consider my next move," he replied, then muttered, "I'm running out of time."

"Are you really dying?" I asked him.

He cast a dark look at me. "What did you say?"

I hadn't mentioned it yet. It wasn't as if we'd had swaths of time to discuss every single one of my revelations about the warlock. He appeared healthy enough to me, but I didn't know anything about his condition.

"You told my father the night of last year's Gala—the night he died—that you were dying. Is that why you're saying you're running out of time?"

His lips thinned. "I've tried to be patient with this unexpected outcome, but I don't particularly like that you have my private memories in your head. Those memories are mine, not yours."

The man had the ability to go from sympathetic to threatening in the span of a heartbeat.

I wouldn't allow myself to be intimidated. Fear wouldn't get me the answers I needed.

"Valery told me to be wary of you," I said, raising my chin. "That you've got nothing left to lose. That you're dangerous. But I'm not seeing any real danger; I'm just hearing a lot of empty talk."

"Is that so," he replied, raising a brow.

"Yeah, that's so. You're right about one thing. I do have your private memories in my head. And every time I experience one, I'm left with a thousand questions."

"Such as?"

"Why haven't you ever made a real stand against the queen herself? I'm not talking about all the crimes you're accused of. I know a lot of the legend behind Lord Banyon is manufactured lies the queen tells to make people hate you. It serves her fear-mongering agenda when it comes to magic."

"Not all lies," he said softly.

"Maybe not," I agreed, with an unsettling twist in my gut at the reminder that my birth father wasn't just a misunderstood hero. He'd done plenty in his life to make him every bit of a villain as the queen was. "But it's been sixteen years since that night at the palace. You planned to kill her, kill Norris—but your power faded. Valery saved you or you would have died. But since then, what? I experienced an echo where you gave a speech to an audience of thousands of mages, promising them that you would bring elementia back. How long ago was that?"

"A long time," he replied tightly.

"Where are those mages now?"

"Scattered across the Empire, living their lives. Surviving and hoping their secrets won't ever be exposed. Not a single one of them powerful enough to make a difference."

Frustration clawed at me. "How do we win the war against the palace without having to kidnap and threaten the innocent daughter of a prime minister?"

I thought my words might ignite something inside of him, but instead, his gaze flattened.

"We don't, Josslyn," he said simply. "All of what you saw in my memories is the past, not the present. Issy won this war a long time ago, and I don't think she even realizes it herself."

The warlock's words twisted into me, and as soft and defeated as they sounded, they only made me angrier.

"How can you say that?" I demanded.

"Because it's the truth."

"You're the most powerful warlock in the world! How can you stand by and watch her continue to spread her lies for years and years and, what? Do nothing?"

He shook his head. "You may have seen some of my memories, but you don't understand anything about me, Josslyn."

"Clearly," I bit out. "I guess I was wrong. I thought you were a badass with the power to light the world on fire, but you're a coward who prefers to hide in the dark."

Outrage flickered in his gaze, but I turned away from him so he couldn't see the tears of disappointment burning my eyes.

But then I realized that, too, was hiding. Hiding from the truth.

Then, suddenly, a thick blanket of golden smoke appeared and flowed over me, spinning me away from the abandoned amusement park before I had the chance to catch my breath.

I hadn't even been touching the memory box this time.

When the scene before me cleared, I found myself in a hospital room, white and sterile, with Banyon lying in a bed. There was a knock on the door a moment before it opened and a man walked in. He wore a white doctor's coat and had a clipboard tucked under his arm. He glanced nervously over his shoulder before closing the door.

"My lord," the man said in a whisper. "You need to leave. There are already rumors spreading that you're being treated here."

He brought a cup of water to Banyon's lips, and the warlock drank deeply from it.

"Treated," he said when he was finished. "But not cured, doctor."

The doctor shook his head. "There is no cure."

Banyon looked down at his hands. "I care less about dying than I do about my magic. I've barely been able to summon more than a spark for weeks now."

"Unfortunately, this is . . . expected," the doctor said gently. "Your disease has advanced. It's so rare; I've only ever seen anything like it in one other patient."

"And that patient . . . ?"

The doctor pressed his lips together. "They lost their access to elementia completely only months before their death."

Banyon didn't seemed shocked by this answer—more that it had confirmed his suspicions. "How long do I have?"

"My best estimate is a year," he said gently. "Perhaps more, perhaps less."

He nodded grimly. "And there's nothing I can do to restore my access to elementia back to its full strength."

"Not that I'm aware of. I'm sorry."

Banyon slumped back in the bed. "No one will ever know the truth as well as I do. What I've seen. What I've learned. There are secrets and truths locked in my memories that I can't even access myself. And now what? They die with me? And Issy wins. Issy always wins. If there was a way to contain my memories, to be able to access them in the time I have left, to find the answers I need before leaving this life once and for all . . ."

The doctor regarded him warily now but said nothing.

A steely determination entered Banyon's gaze. "That's why I chose this hospital. That's why I chose you as my physician. I know you can help me with this last request."

"I don't know what you're talking about."

"Forgive me if I don't play along with your feigned ignorance, Doctor. You are a rare mage that can create memory boxes by summoning both earth and air magic. You have created several in the past, secretly, and for great profit. You will come with me to my compound to create one for me."

The doctor didn't speak for a moment. "The creation of such boxes is not a gentle process. The magic required could kill you."

"Death is inevitable. My memories are my legacy—what I have left of my magic is all but gone. It must be now and it must be you." He pushed up, with effort, to a seated position and leveled his gaze at the doctor. "I'm afraid I won't take no as an answer. Your family, your friends. Everyone you love. You shall put them at great risk if you deny me. So, please, Doctor, say that you'll help me with this, and save us both a great deal of trouble."

For all of his even tone and polite delivery, the deadly threat in the warlock's request was unmistakable.

The doctor regarded this man who had been weak and ill only moments ago, now with the power to destroy his life.

"Yes," he said stiffly. "Of course I'll help you with this, my lord."

The golden smoke swirled around me, erasing the scene I'd witnessed but not the knowledge I'd gained, and when it retreated, I was exactly where I'd been before.

"Drake . . . another echo?" Jericho asked.

"Yes." I wiped the trace of blood away from my nose.

"What did you see this time?" Banyon studied me, cautious and curious at the same time.

"I saw you threatening a doctor's life, friends, and family if he didn't make you a memory box," I replied coolly.

Banyon didn't look the least bit ashamed. "Threats are a necessary tool."

"I understand that," I replied uneasily. "And you're right. If you hadn't said what you had, he might not have gone along with your plan."

"Perhaps he shouldn't have. That doctor was killed during the raid on my compound."

"Would you have killed his family and friends if he'd said no?"

His gaze hardened. "Does it matter anymore?"

"No," I admitted. "I guess it doesn't. What does matter is

that the echo showed me the truth: You are dying. And your magic . . . is it completely gone now?"

The warlock now tied with Jericho for the ability to add the most ice to his glare.

"Forget what you saw," he bit out.

"I can't do that." It didn't matter if he admitted it. I knew the truth. And it meant that he was right—there wasn't much time left to fix this. "I want to help. I want to search the echoes to try to find the queen's big, world-shaking secret—the one you told my father you believe exists—and I know you can guide me to it." I pulled the box from my pocket and Banyon's gaze went to it immediately. "Jericho gave me this; it helps me control what I see."

"No, that's just a container," he said. "It has no control over the memory magic."

"I knew it," Jericho said, shaking his head. "Seriously. Why do I ever doubt myself?"

"No, it *worked*," I insisted. "Before, I had no control, except for summoning one echo, and I wasn't even that specific about it so I'm not sure it even counts. But with this, it's different. Earlier, when I was with Celina, I was able to revisit an echo I'd already seen. I saw the list of mage bloodlines that you showed my father."

"I'm sure you did, but I assure you, the box makes no difference. Valery disagreed with this, but she's no expert when it comes to memory magic. What I think happened, Josslyn, is that you *believed* that the box would help you. And that belief is what gave you control, just as I told you yesterday."

He sounded so sure, but what made him any more of an expert than Valery on the subject? I was the one with the hard-won experience when it came to these echoes. And the box *had* helped me, whether it was magic or belief.

"Sure, fine. Whatever you say. Just tell me what to do—guide me to find the echo you're looking for."

"You're sure, Drake?" Jericho asked. "You just experienced one."

"No time like the present," I told him.

Banyon didn't speak for a moment. "Very well. It was Issy's seventeenth birthday. She was happy that day, with me. With everything. And then her father asked to speak with her. When she returned to me, she was a different person. She told me to go away and never saw me again—not until the night she wanted me to raise Elian from the dead."

"Maybe she just didn't want to be with you anymore," Jericho said. "Because you're an asshole."

"Or maybe," I interjected, glaring at Jericho, "she was worried what would happen if the king found out you were a warlock."

"It was more than that," Banyon said firmly. "I've never doubted that something shifted during that meeting with her father. Something changed her mind about everything, including me. I made the memory box so I could revisit that pivotal moment, to follow Issy into that fateful meeting and hear exactly what was said."

The queen's seventeenth birthday.

I remembered asking Elian about the secret.

"I can't tell you. I can only tell my heir on their seventeenth birthday. And if there is no heir—and it's not looking good in that regard, despite my proposal to the lovely Daria—then the secret dies with me. And no one will ever know the truth."

This was proof that it was the same secret. It had to be.

Jericho's expression remained skeptical, but for me—I trusted my own instincts. They hadn't steered me wrong yet.

I nodded. "All right. Let's find somewhere quiet where I can focus without any interruptions. You can talk me through it, set the scene . . . and I can try to summon that exact memory and see if I can learn more."

"Yes. We can try in a few hours. First, you must recover your strength from the echo you just experienced." Banyon nodded. "In the meantime, I need to speak with Agatha. She's keeping a secret from me, beyond what she's already done."

"I think you're right," I said, pushing off the disappointment that we couldn't get to the echo lesson immediately. To be honest, I did feel a bit weary and in great need of a nap. "I saw her and Mika talking earlier, and it wasn't anything they wanted me to overhear."

With the promise to find me when he was through with the witch, Banyon strode away from us without a backward glance.

Jericho sent a glare after him. "So, you're saying he's dying and powerless, right?"

"I don't know for sure, since he admitted to exactly nothing," I admitted grimly. "But I think so."

"Almost makes the thought of murdering him less fun."

I glared at him. "You're not going to murder him."

"Why not?"

"Because you're not a murderer, that's why."

"Clearly you haven't been paying attention, Drake. Because a murderer is exactly what I am."

"No. Maybe you've killed a few people—"

"More than a few."

I cringed. "Fine. Hundreds."

He scoffed. "Not hundreds. At least, not yet."

"But you were being controlled by Valery. It wasn't really you."

Jericho shrugged. "According to that warlock, Val has no real power over me." He rolled his eyes. "That guy doesn't know what he's talking about. He doesn't know how it feels when I try to resist, especially now when these marks are so fresh." He rubbed his arm, scowling now. "I don't care if he's magic free and dying. I'm still going to kill him."

"No, you're not. You don't kill people indiscriminately."

"Sure. If you say so." He scrubbed a hand through his hair, pacing back and forth. "Okay, here's how this is going to go, now that you've determined that Banyon won't be freeing your friend anytime soon. Tonight, the three of us are out of here. You and Celina go back to your regularly scheduled lives and try to forget this shit show. Then I'll head back to Cresidia and make amends with Val, pay off the memory box, whatever it takes. It's pretty much worthless anyway, according to the warlock. She'll get over it eventually."

I laughed at that until I realized he wasn't kidding. Then I glared at him. "Is this still something you think is going to happen? Me going back to my regularly scheduled life?"

"Yeah, that's exactly what I think is going to happen. Because this?" He held his arms to his sides and turned around in a circle. "This isn't the life you want, Drake."

"Holed up at an abandoned amusement park with a bunch of dangerous outlaws? No, you're absolutely right. That's not the life I want. But I'm thinking there's got to be some sort of a middle ground I can find."

"If it were me, I'd go back," he said, stone cold seriously. "The first chance I got."

"Sure, you would." I was swiftly moving past annoyance and headed right for actual anger. "Because you forget every slight, don't you? Like with Viktor."

"Here we go again," he muttered darkly.

"I think Banyon's right—you accept this life that you claim to hate so much, working for that witch and feeling like you don't have a choice, because you don't want to make a choice."

All bets were off. The truth had to be wielded, sharp edges and all.

"What choice do I have, Drake?"

"Viktor made a choice. Some of his decisions were questionable at best, but he rose up from the life you two had and he made something of himself. You could do the same thing."

He shook his head. "I couldn't have done what he did. I am who I am, Drake. This is who I've always been. My brother's always been different than me in all the right ways."

"You're better than this," I countered.

"You're wrong—I'm not. And Banyon's wrong. I don't have control over my life, and I don't even care anymore. You have Celina; she'll take care of you as you ease back into your champagne-and-caviar lifestyle. I'll drop the both of you at the Ironport city limits. Go back to your life, Drake. This is your chance. Stop fighting the inevitable."

I glared at him. He glared back at me.

I wanted to keep arguing with him, but he'd relentlessly driven home his point.

Instead, I forced myself to stop and take a breath. And think this through without getting defensive and pissy the moment he brought up this subject.

"Maybe you're right," I said slowly.

Jericho's dark brows shot up. "Finally seeing the light, Drake? Better late than never, I guess."

I'd been fooling myself for more than a week now, three days of which I'd been unconscious after a death-magic-wielding witch had nearly killed me. It had been an impulsive decision to leave the palace. I'd felt trapped and unsure what to do. So, I ran away, hoping I'd figure out the answers.

But all I'd found were more questions.

"Maybe I *can* do more from the inside than the outside," I whispered to myself.

"I know you can," Jericho agreed earnestly, but his voice was brittle now. "The queen won't hold any of this against you. Do your part; play your role. Knowing what you know now? I fully believe that you can change the world, Drake."

His words warmed my heart, but tears burned in my eyes. "What about you?"

"Same old, same old. It's okay."

"It's not okay."

"It is," he said firmly.

I swallowed hard. "So, what? I go my way, you go yours . . . and we never see each other again?"

He shrugged. "You never know what the future has in store for us."

"You mean fate."

"Yeah, fate." Jericho took my face between his hands. His lips curved into a smile, but his eyes were haunted. "I think I'm going to miss you, Drake."

"I *know* I'm going to miss you," I managed.

I was leaving. Going back to the palace of my own free will and knowing in my gut that it was the right choice, given my limited options. And I also knew in my gut that I'd probably never see Jericho again.

This was our last day together.

The Blackheart's feigned smile vanished, and a shadow crossed his expression. "Don't wait for Banyon to find you. Go find him. Make him talk you through that birthday echo and see if you can find some good dirt on the queen. But, even without him, I know you can master this pesky magic you've been saddled with. I'll keep looking for that one-in-a-billion mage to remove it, though. If I find one, I'll send word to you. Somehow. I'll find a way."

"Okay," I said. I didn't think I could say more than a single word before I seriously started to cry.

"Okay," he agreed. Then he let go of me and started walking away.

I watched him walk past the dolphin fountain, his shoulders

square, his strides long. There was more I wanted to say to him, but it would have to wait until later. We still had time before we had to say goodbye. This wasn't over yet.

The sound of a gunshot made me jump.

Jericho froze, drawing out his own weapon in the span of a heartbeat. He turned to scan the area, his serious gaze meeting mine. "What the hell was that?"

"I don't know," I replied.

Then I could hear shouting—and the sound of a struggle just out of sight.

"Shit," Jericho snarled. "This isn't good. Get back inside the hotel where it's safe, Drake. And stay there until——"

Another shot sounded out, and Jericho lurched forward before pressing his hand against his chest. Dark red blood spilled between his fingers.

"Jericho!" I cried out.

He fell hard to his knees. I ran to his side, closing the distance between us in an instant, and grabbed hold of his arm.

No, no, no. This memory was too fresh and familiar— Jericho shot in the chest by Tobin before we were shoved into the Queen's Keep. It couldn't be happening again.

"Go, damn it," he snarled at me. "I told you to go!"

I shook my head. "No, you're coming with me. Come on. We need to get help."

Tamara had healed him with earth magic. Maybe her mother had the same skill.

"We need to find Agatha," I told him. "Come on, Jericho, you need to help me. Get on your feet."

But he didn't move. He dropped his gun to the ground—and raised his hand to cup my cheek.

"I need you to know something very important, okay?" He now spoke so quietly that I had to strain to hear him.

"Don't talk. Save your strength," I said firmly, my eyes burning with tears. "Come on. You need to stand up. Now, Blackheart. I'm serious."

He chuckled softly. "Josslyn Drake . . . always arguing with me."

I scanned our immediate surroundings. We were still alone, but I knew it couldn't be for very long. "Fine. What?"

"Just this . . ." He drew in a shaky breath, his pained gaze locked with mine. "I . . . love you, Drake."

"Jericho . . ." I held his gaze, tears streaming down my cheeks.

Before I could say another word, have another thought, the life faded from his eyes.

"No, Jericho. No!" I cried.

He slumped forward, into my arms, and I clutched tightly on to him, sobbing now. This wasn't happening. This couldn't be happening.

And then, suddenly, he was gone, pulled back from me by a uniformed Queensguard. A dozen more appeared behind him.

The Queensguard pressed his fingers against Jericho's throat.

"This one's dead." Then he gestured toward me. "Leave the body here. Grab the girl and move on."

The park was a blur before me as I felt rough hands close around my arms and roughly pull me up to my feet. I was as still as a statue for only a moment longer before I started to fight, punching and scratching whatever surface I made contact with, wanting to kill every single one of these guards with my bare hands. Wishing with all my heart and soul that I could summon fire magic like my birth father to incinerate everyone and everything in a hundred-mile radius and make them all burn.

But I had no fire magic. I had nothing.

Then I heard the distinct sound of helicopters. A sound that grew louder by the second.

I finally managed to get free from my captors, and I staggered closer to where Jericho had fallen.

This wasn't real. He couldn't be dead. Not like this. Not after everything he'd endured, everything he'd survived. To have it come to this—a single bullet to the chest.

And Tamara wasn't here to save him this time.

Before I could take another step, a heavy weight struck the back of my head, and the world went dark.

EIGHTEEN

When I woke up, I found myself on a soft and comfortable bed with silky sheets that smelled like lavender. And for several blissful moments, I couldn't remember what had happened.

But then I did.

I sat up so quickly that the world spun and the dull throb at the back of my head blossomed into a full bouquet of pain. I scanned the room, but it didn't look like the amusement park hotel's decor. This was much finer, far more luxurious, and eerily familiar.

A quick glance down the front of me confirmed that I was still wearing my Queensgate clothes, but the sparkly T-shirt was now stained with blood.

Jericho's blood.

"No," I whispered, shaking my head. "Please, no. It didn't happen. It couldn't have happened."

He was still alive. He had to be. He'd been shot in the chest before we were shoved into the Keep, and he'd survived that injury. As a Blackheart, he healed quicker than normal people did, so it was possible he might not even have needed

Tamara's help at all. He'd survived death at least twice. Why not a third time?

I might be able to believe this if I hadn't literally witnessed the life leave his eyes. He hadn't just been unconscious. Not this time.

Tears streaked down my cheeks as I balled my fists, pressing them against my eyes, and I let out a keening wail from deep inside of me, a sound I hadn't made since I learned that my father had died at the hospital.

"This one's dead. Grab the girl and move on."

The Queensguard's flat statement rang in my ears, over and over. A repeating echo burned into my mind that I could never, would never, forget.

He told me he loved me. His last words were that he loved me.

The door to the room opened without warning, and a familiar figure entered. I raised my tear-filled gaze to see High Commander Norris looming at the entrance.

"The queen has some questions for you," he said, his expression like stone.

Of course, I thought with a pained realization. That's why the decor in this room was familiar to me.

I was at the palace.

The fight had gone out of me, so I didn't protest. I didn't try to make excuses or play the part of the returning socialite. I wiped my face, ran my fingers through my tangled hair, wincing as I touched the wound at the back of my head from where I'd been hit by something very hard. Probably the butt of a Queensguard's gun.

Maybe the same gun that had killed Jericho.

Norris waited, watching me through narrowed eyes, as I got out of bed without a word, and then nodded at him.

He had no commentary for me. No immediate mention of the last time we'd been face-to-face, when he'd tried to stop Jericho's escape. He'd thought I was an innocent bystander, so I'd tried to distract him with what I knew.

"*Do you ever feel guilty about that night?*" I'd asked him.

"*What are you talking about? What night?*"

"*The night you slit my mother's throat. The night you underestimated my father's power just before he burned everything to the ground.*"

I think it may have been the only time I'd ever referred to Banyon as my father. I'd only said it to drive home the point that I knew the truth.

But Norris didn't know that I'd seen that truth for myself.

"Where's Celina?" I asked, my throat raw. "I assume that was a raid to recover her, right? She's safe now?"

"Follow me."

As the high commander escorted me silently out of the room, far smaller and less elaborately decorated that my guest suite had been only a little more than a week ago, I felt in my pocket for the memory box.

It was gone.

Of course it was.

I'd agreed with Jericho that it was the right move to come back to the palace, but not like this, dragged back unconscious and covered in blood.

About to be questioned.

I expected to be taken to the interrogation room, perhaps with an audience and a camera in my face to record my answers to be dissected by those who wanted to determine my guilt.

But it wasn't the interrogation room that Norris led me to. It was the queen's chambers, where she waited for me at the table where we'd had afternoon tea and egg-salad sandwiches with Elian. She was as poised as she'd ever been, her long dark hair pulled back from her face and pinned into perfect place with strategically placed emerald barrettes. She wore a silk-and-satin dress in a matching emerald-green shade. Her pale skin was skillfully contoured with pink blush on her cheekbones and a tasteful amount of eye makeup to enhance her natural beauty.

Queen Isadora stood up, wringing her hands, as she cast her gaze down the front of me.

"She must be given a clean change of clothes immediately," she said, visibly wincing at the sight of the blood on my clothes. "See to it, Commander."

"Of course, Your Majesty."

"Leave us now."

Norris hesitated. "Your Majesty . . ."

"Leave us," she repeated curtly.

"Of course." He bowed, cast a dark look at me, and then left us alone together in the huge sitting room I'd always admired whenever I'd visited the palace with my father.

"Please sit." She gestured toward the chair across from her.

I sat, studying my hands. There was dried blood under my fingernails. Jericho's blood.

"I love you, Drake."

He said he loved me. And then he was gone.

"What a challenging week this has been," the queen finally said after silence stretched between us. "For you. For me. For the Empire."

I couldn't find the words to answer her, so I didn't even try.

"Commander Norris suggested we make this a formal inquiry, but I didn't see a reason for that. I wanted you to be comfortable, Josslyn. I want you to tell me, in your own words, where you've been for the last week."

I knew I had to hide my feelings. To blend in. To say the right thing at the right time. To lie for my own benefit and image. I was usually so good at it. But I didn't have the strength anymore. My head ached, my body felt bruised and broken. And my heart had shattered into a million bloody pieces.

It was over. The queen had won, just like Banyon said. She'd won like she always had and like she always would. And now my very life depended on the mercy of a monster.

"Very well," she said in response to my pained silence, nodding. "Then I'll begin. First, you should know that Zarek Banyon is finally in custody."

My gaze moved to hers. She studied my reaction to this.

"How did you know where to find him?" I forced the words out.

"The witch, Agatha. The one who took Celina hostage. She contacted us late last night to let us know that she was willing to trade both Celina and the warlock for her daughter's release. Clearly, she's very untrustworthy, so a team was sent to investigate, and they found her claim to be true."

Last night. After our arrival and her tense confrontation with Banyon when he'd shown his disapproval of her actions. She'd been so desperate to save Tamara that she'd betrayed him. This had to be what she and Mika had been discussing when I'd interrupted them—the imminent arrival of Queensguards.

Mika had told me to stay inside the hotel.

Now I knew why.

"Where's Agatha now?" I asked, my throat thick.

"Missing."

"And Celina?"

"She's safe. She's traumatized by the ordeal, but thankfully, she's safe."

If nothing else, part of the painful knot in my chest loosened at this news.

"Good," I said.

"She's under the impression that you were also a hostage."

I blinked. "And what's your impression, Your Majesty?"

The queen shook her head. "To be honest, Josslyn, I don't know what I would have thought had I not first spoken with both my son and Commander Raden only this morning."

The painful knot was back and bigger than ever. "And what did they tell you?"

"That you are an innocent girl who fell in love with the wrong boy. And he led you astray. Celina agrees with this analysis, and she promises to stay here with you at the palace, for as long as you need her to."

I exhaled shakily as tears slipped down my cheeks. Both Viktor and Elian had said this to the queen, making me look like a victim rather than someone who'd actively chosen to leave after learning too many painful truths.

The story was helpful to my survival, of course. But that didn't mean I liked it.

The queen poured me a glass of water, sliding it across the table. She had the audacity to look at me with kindness in her eyes as I took a shaky sip.

"So, it's true," she said gently.

I didn't answer her. If I opened my mouth, I knew all that would come out was another ragged sob, so I didn't want to risk it. I couldn't let myself lose what little control I had left.

"I understand more than you realize, Josslyn. I also fell in love with someone extremely unsuitable for me when I was your age. He was so handsome, so charming . . . and so very dangerous." Her gaze grew faraway. "He offered me a chance to see the world from another point of view. I couldn't resist him, even though I tried very hard to do just that."

Was she really doing this? Telling me about her and Banyon like it was some sort of star-crossed love story?

"I don't know what to say," I admitted.

I mean, it was the truth.

"You don't have to say anything, Josslyn. Not until you're ready. But know that I'm here for you, as much as Celina is."

I tried to wrap my mind around the fact that the queen was being 100 percent genuine with me today. This was the woman I'd admired, the one I'd considered like an aunt. A warm, kind, and generous motherly figure, whom I'd known for my entire life.

Because, I realized, this was who she was.

And she was also, at other times, pure evil.

Like two sides of a coin.

In her eyes, I could see her sincerity. She wanted to believe that this was all that had happened to take me away from the palace last week. A girl who'd fallen in love with a criminal who had tried to destroy her life.

It was like a door had been left lightly ajar, enough for me to slip inside before the storm. I'd told Jericho that I'd come back here, to lean on the queen's empathy and forgiveness—and, clearly, her weak spot when it came to me—and try to do more good from the inside of the palace, rather than the next to nothing I could do outside of it. And here I was. Not how I wanted it to be—I never would have chosen this outcome in a million years.

This was my chance. This was now my game to lose.

The question was, what exactly did she know?

Did Norris brief the queen about what I'd said before I'd left? Did she know that I was fully aware that Banyon was my birth father?

She'd mentioned his arrest almost casually, as if it were inevitable. But if she'd had any doubts about my loyalty, I was sure she'd have been more pointed in how she'd told me this.

Or maybe not. I was doubting myself again.

She knew that I was well aware of Elian's issues after seeing the prince kill two people in the Keep. But not that I specifically knew he'd been magically raised from the dead at her command or that he was my half brother.

"I do have one question, Josslyn," the queen said, and I raised my gaze to hers.

"What?"

"This was found on you at the amusement park. Why did you have it?" She placed the memory box on the table in front of her. A breath caught in my chest, but I willed myself to keep my expression neutral.

"Jericho gave it to me," I replied.

"This is what he stole from the Gala."

"Yes."

"The magic from inside of it is still inside you."

I nodded slowly. "He wanted me to have the box in case we found a way to get the magic out of me."

My first lie. I knew it was best to pepper them in, to hide the lies within larger truths.

"I see." The queen peered at the box. "This piece of magic was part of Banyon's collection. Vander told me about contained magic, but I must admit, I've forgotten most of it. I wish he was here right now. He might be useful once again."

"It's too bad," I said as smoothly as I could.

"And Viktor left nearly as soon as he arrived," she continued. "So I didn't have a chance to ask him what his opinion on this piece of magic might be. He's off on his press tour. The Queensgames are now less than three weeks away."

Viktor also didn't know what magic I was "infected" with; he only knew that my eyes were gold beneath the contact lenses. When he'd first seen them, he'd been horrified and had agreed with Jericho that the only way for me to survive would be to rid myself of the magic.

And here we were.

Such a short time ago, in the grand scheme of things. And yet, I felt like a completely different person sitting here today.

However, the queen seemed to believe that I was the same as I'd ever been, which I knew was essential to my ongoing freedom.

"I will have this box kept under lock and key for now," she said, nodding. "It will bring harm to no one ever again."

For a split second, I felt an overwhelming urge to leap across the table and grab the box, to protect it, since it had helped me control the echoes. But I clenched my fists on my lap and willed myself to be still.

The sacrifice had to be made.

Banyon claimed that it wasn't necessary. That all I had to do was believe in myself and I could control the echoes. That the box was only a container, just as Jericho had assumed in the beginning.

Maybe he was right. I'd have to hope that he was.

"Where is Jericho now?" I asked, and the question made my throat hurt. "I mean . . . his—his body?"

She shook her head. "I don't know."

"He was shot in the chest by a guard. He . . . he died." I drew in a ragged breath as the memory crashed into me again. "But . . . I didn't see what happened next."

The queen regarded me solemnly. "There were several casualties at the park. I don't know what happened to the bodies after that. I'm sorry, Josslyn. I know how you must feel. I know what it's like to lose someone that you care deeply for, even if your life will be vastly better off without them in it."

I didn't even try to force myself to agree with her, because if she was able to say this, then she *didn't* understand how I felt, and she never would.

"Thank you." I pushed the two words out with effort.

A small smile touched her lips. "I'm glad we have this chance to speak. And I hope very much that you are grateful to be safely back to your home, since you know that the palace is your home now, Josslyn."

I nodded dutifully, studying the queen's face, her expression. Trying to decipher every word and every meaning I could that might give me an advantage going forward.

"I am grateful," I said aloud.

"You will be by my side at the Queensgames launch party. With Celina too. Just like it was two years ago, when you were both still practically children, rather than the accomplished young women you are today."

The Queensgames launch party. If the royal Gala was an exclusive invitation-only event that billions of people would kill to be at, the launch party was even more exclusive and desirable. A much smaller gathering, held here at the palace, and attended only by the queen's closest friends, her richest acquaintances, and members of the royal council.

The last time, I'd been First Daughter and had reveled in the glamorous press conference attended by dozens of photographers and reporters. My photo had been at the very top of the newsfeed for a whole day afterward.

How utterly trivial it all seemed now.

"I can't wait," I lied, pushing my best attempt at a wistful smile to my lips. "It will feel good to be back to normal again."

"For both of us," she agreed.

There were so many questions I had now, but I held back every single one of them for fear that they'd trigger any of the queen's doubts about me. The woman may be many things, but she wasn't a complete fool. If I said one thing out of line or accused her of any crime against the Empire, then this would all be over for me.

Luckily, I had seventeen years of practice on how to appear poised and as if I didn't have a care in the world.

Banyon wanted to find one specific memory. A memory from thirty-three years ago—the queen's seventeenth birthday, when her father had told her something that had changed her from a girl in love with a warlock, to the cold, calculating heir to the throne.

The same secret that Elian knew and refused to share.

"May I speak to Elian?" I asked her.

"Not today. He's resting. He's had quite an ordeal. I'm just grateful that Commander Raden was there to protect him. Such a disappointment that he never had a face-to-face meeting with that elusive witch. His hopes were so high that his unexpected journey would result in valuable answers. I will have to continue to search for her."

"Yes, it is such a disappointment," I agreed, playing along immediately with the fact that Elian had told his mother nothing about speaking with Valery. Despite the witch's disappointing answer for the prince, it seemed that he would hold true to his promise not to reveal her true identity. And, it would seem,

Viktor had said nothing to give the queen a different impression.

How unexpected, given his official assignment.

The queen's gaze moved over my shoulder. "On the bright side, I have recently met someone I believe could be a valuable resource here at the palace."

"Your Majesty? You asked to see me?"

I turned to see who'd joined us and my mouth fell open at the sight of curly red hair, and pale freckled skin.

It was Tamara.

Our eyes met, and her jaw tensed.

"What is happening?" I managed. "What are you doing here?"

"I asked Dr. Collins to attend to your injury," the queen said. "I was told that you banged your head earlier. Please, Dr. Collins, attend to Josslyn. I'll observe."

Tamara nodded. "Of course."

I sought her gaze again, but she avoided mine, a frown creasing her brow.

"Your Majesty," I said. "Tamara is the reason that Agatha made the deal with you in exchange for Lord Banyon and Celina."

"Yes, that's right. But I had already determined that Dr. Collins's very special skills were enough to save her from execution."

"She wasn't guilty of what you accused her of," I said, then bit my tongue. I had to control my urge to blurt out truths when they didn't serve me.

The queen only shrugged a shoulder. "In any case, I spared her life, and she is very grateful—aren't you, Dr. Collins?"

"Yes, very grateful," Tamara agreed tightly. "It's my honor to serve you, Your Majesty. My mother will understand."

Unbelievable. I needed the immediate reminder that the queen had two sides, but the bad vastly outweighed the good. She'd reneged on the deal so she could have an in-palace doctor who specialized in healing earth magic.

She was a shameless hypocrite. But I already knew that.

"Dr. Collins says that she already knows you, Josslyn," the queen said. "You met inside the Queen's Keep."

"I remember," I said uneasily now.

"She believed your name was Janie."

I forced myself to laugh lightly at this. "I was in search of a cure for my extremely unsavory problem. I wasn't exactly going to be introducing myself to anyone I met as Josslyn Drake, was I?"

"I completely understand," Tamara said evenly. "It's good to see you again, Josslyn."

"Joss," I told her, meeting her eyes. "Please, just Joss."

She nodded. She was close enough to me that I could see the pain and doubt in her gaze, covered by a practiced smile. "Please, Joss, let me heal you."

"All right."

Tamara inspected the wound at the back of my head, which had reduced to a dull ache since leaving my room. "I'm going to use my magic now, Joss."

"Thanks for the warning," I replied, just before I felt a warm and tingling sensation on the back of my scalp. The sensation sharpened unpleasantly, like I expected it to, although it was not nearly as painful as what I'd experienced when Daria healed my hand. Before I knew it, Tamara was done.

I touched the back of my head and there was no damage anymore—and the throbbing pain had disappeared. "Thank you."

"You're welcome."

The queen had risen from her seat to look as well, nodding with appreciation. "Well done, Dr. Collins. You may leave us now."

Tamara didn't linger. When dismissed by the most powerful woman in the Empire, she left immediately.

The queen took her seat again, her expression pensive. "I have tried using earth magic with my son, but it only seemed to make his symptoms worse, not better. However, those witches were not trained doctors. It's something to think about, yes?"

I needed to see Elian. And I needed another chance to talk to Tamara. "Definitely something to think about," I agreed.

"We all have some healing to do as we move on from some necessary losses, but I believe that the future is bright. For all of us."

The queen had said all the right words in the right order. She'd given me my chance to return to my previous life, the life I'd lived for seventeen years, one of privilege, parties, and potential.

The war was over between the queen and Banyon. Banyon was in custody—and as harmless as he'd ever been. Dying, with little-to-no access to his own magic, betrayed by someone he once trusted, despite their many differences.

"After all these years, he is a man with very little left to lose."

Valery's warning echoed in my ears.

All I knew for sure was that he would be no help to me anymore. And with Jericho gone, I was on my own.

The queen had made her case, and she'd made it well. I saw now that she honestly believed that what she did was fully justified to keep a powerful empire of billions safe, happy, and well behaved. She believed that she wasn't a villain, that she was as much of a champion as anyone who'd claimed victory in the Queensgames—flawed, perhaps, but brave and true to her promises.

If Queen Isadora was the hero of this story, then I guess that made me the bad guy. Because now I wanted to destroy her even more than I had before.

NINETEEN

Many might leave the queen's presence full of gratitude that she'd been so understanding of their plight. Even a part of me felt exactly that. And I hated myself for it.

Still, it would have made everything extremely inconvenient if she'd had Commander Norris interrogate me. I'd been a witness to Jericho's questioning, but only what had taken place in a public forum, with the queen present. Behind closed doors, I knew it was a different matter entirely, and the Blackheart had shown the bruises from his brutal methods, just as Tamara had.

In an echo, I'd seen Norris torture Banyon, leaving him bloody and beaten when he'd refused to resurrect Elian. The warlock hadn't summoned fire magic to save himself then, but I knew why. He hadn't quite been broken yet. He still had something to lose—his family. Then, only a couple weeks later, that family was gone.

Nothing left to lose.

I wanted to ask the queen where Banyon was being held. I assumed it was here at the palace, close to the queen so she could keep an eye on her infamous prisoner. Part of me wanted to talk to him again, to see if I could learn anything more or if he could coach me toward finding the queen's birthday secret. Not that I really believed I'd learn anything useful from him. With only a short amount of time left to live, the once powerful warlock had shown me clearly in our single day together that he'd already given up the fight.

I didn't know him. He didn't know me. It seemed that our association would be over as quickly as it had begun. There was no grief inside of me for him, only an endless amount of disappointment. The dark hole that grief had hollowed out inside of me was reserved for Jericho and Jericho only.

Without him, I was totally on my own now. But that would have to be enough.

On my way back to my room, I came across a group of Queensguards gathered around a monitor in the palace press room, a huge room used for hosting press conferences and broadcasting the queen's monthly speeches to the Empire. I drew closer so I could see what had gotten their attention.

Viktor Raden was on the screen, being interviewed by a reporter on the main newsfeed.

"You must be so relieved," the reporter said, her brows together in a show of concern. "Celina is finally safe."

"Relief is . . ." Viktor shook his head. "It's too small a word for what I felt when I heard the news of her rescue."

"You really love her, don't you?"

"With all my heart," he said without missing a beat. "I've already spoken to Celina and she's . . . well, she's the strongest girl I've ever known. I had no doubt that she'd survive this horrific ordeal, but after talking to her, my mind is fully at ease."

"So, can we all still look forward to a wedding soon?"

A smile touched his lips. "Yes, you definitely can."

"Have you set a date for the happy occasion?"

"We have," Viktor replied. "Two months from today, actually."

"How absolutely delightful!" The reporter clasped her hands, beaming a wide smile. "Our beloved First Daughter will make such a beautiful bride for the Empire's glorious high champion."

"She certainly will," Viktor agreed.

The reporter's expression shifted back to one much more serious. "Lord Banyon has finally been captured. Sixteen years after the tragic palace fire, the families of the victims he killed that night will finally see justice done. Do you know when the warlock will be executed?"

"I don't," Viktor's tone now turned deadly serious. "At least, not yet."

"I assume it will be broadcast live for all to witness."

He nodded. "Yes, I'm sure it will be."

"There is a rumor that he has lost his ability to wield deadly magic, which is what made his capture and imprisonment possible without the risk of another tragedy. Can you confirm this?"

"I'm afraid I'm not at liberty to share any specifics on the matter. I'm sure you can understand why."

"Of course." She nodded solemnly. "In the past twenty-four hours, there have been more protests and acts of rebellion by the warlock's followers than there have been in the last decade. It's a difficult time for the Empire."

"I disagree," Viktor said. "There are always those who will

tread on the side of darkness, but this only reminds us how important it is to uphold the light. Lord Banyon's followers can be very loud when they want to be, but they have always been a vocal minority, easily silenced. They present no real threat to the Empire, nor does Zarek Banyon. His days of terrorizing the great Empire of Regara are over now, and every law-abiding citizen can sleep peacefully again without the constant worry of what he might be planning next."

"And just in time, isn't it?" The reporter's smile was back in an instant. She moved between emotions so rapidly, I doubted any of it was more than skin deep. "The Queensgames are approaching. Such an exciting time for us all, and now we have even more of a reason to celebrate, don't we?"

"We certainly do," he agreed. "It will be as great a Games as there ever has been, and I can't wait to be there personally to oversee every exciting match."

With that shift in subject matter, the interview conveniently cut to a commercial for the games, including specific instructions on how to obtain a ticket for the stadium or paid access to a special channel that offered all-day footage of the fighters and the games themselves.

I'd been a Viktor Raden apologist to Jericho, trying to convince him that his brother would have helped him escape even if the queen hadn't enlisted him as her spy. Seeing this, seeing how poised and polished he was on his publicity tour, I wasn't sure I was right about that anymore—despite the belief that he'd said nothing to the queen to reveal Elian's meeting with Valery. There seemed to be no penalty for his failed mission. No, Viktor seemed to have settled back into his role as high champion, admired and respected by all, without the slightest difficulty.

Did he know about Jericho? I'd tried to see some sign of this in his practiced smile, but he shared his brother's ability to remain emotionally unreadable when it served him.

Fame. Fortune. A bright and prosperous future. All Viktor had to do was ignore everything he had learned about the rotten core of the Regarian Empire and its queen.

Was it possible for me to do the same?

A couple of the Queensguards who'd been watching the interview turned to me as if noticing me for the first time.

"Hi," I said to them, and, with effort, pushed a fake smile onto my face. "I need one of you to escort me to Celina Ambrose's suite. Thank you."

That's all it took. I might not be First Daughter anymore, but I was very well known to these guards. Had been all my life. And not one of them knew about my own secrets, my own truth, that would either make them want to arrest me or run away screaming.

I could work with that.

The guard let me into Celina's suite, a series of lavishly decorated rooms fit for a princess. The old me would have been jealous. The new me . . . well, she was still a little jealous. I hadn't totally changed everything about who I was. But I hoped I'd changed in the ways that mattered the most.

"Celina?" I called out. "Are you here?"

I needed to see her. I needed to talk to her. I needed to make sure she was okay.

But it wasn't Celina who entered the room. It was Celina's father.

"Josslyn," Regis Ambrose said evenly, his mouth a straight line. "I heard that you'd returned to the palace."

I froze. I wasn't sure why I hadn't expected to see him. Maybe I'd assumed he'd gone back to Ironport. But of course not. His daughter had been kidnapped by rebels. He would stay near the queen until the matter resolved itself.

"Here I am," I said, forcing calmness into my voice when I felt anything but.

"Yes, here you are," he repeated thinly.

"I want to see Celina."

"I'm sure you do. But she's currently asleep, recovering her strength."

My heart pounded. "Maybe you could wake her up and see if she wants to talk to me."

"No. I don't think I'll do that." He clasped his hands behind his back. "The queen believes in you, Josslyn . . ."

"She does," I agreed.

"But I don't. Let's make this short and sweet, shall we? You are poison. You proved that the night you disappeared with that Blackheart, and you continue to prove it with every venomous word that exits your venomous mouth. I won't have my daughter exposed to your lies for another day."

It was a strange relief to be able to sidestep any feigned niceties with this epic asshole. "Is that so?"

"That is so. Celina thinks you were a hostage like she was."

"I was," I said.

"I sincerely doubt that. I don't exactly know what you were

doing there, but I know there's much more to this story. Don't test me, Josslyn. Not now, not ever again. I promise that you won't like the result. Now, go—get out of my sight."

Ambrose turned away from me.

"I saw Valery," I told him. "Met her. We chatted. Got confirmation that you were the one who paid her to have my father—and me—assassinated. She's not your biggest fan, especially when I told her that you'd already confessed everything to me."

It was a lie, of course, since Valery hadn't confirmed anything of the sort, but I wanted to see his reaction. And I definitely got one. When he turned, the look in his eyes was equal parts horror and outrage.

"If you breathe a single word of this wildly ridiculous hypothesis of yours to anyone," he hissed, "I'll . . ."

"What?" I snapped when his words trailed off. "What will you do?"

"No one will ever believe you. Valery will never publicly say a word against me. To do so would jeopardize her entire operation, which depends on absolute secrecy." Hard ice entered his gaze. "You have no proof. You're just a meaningless, powerless little girl with a bad attitude, living on borrowed time."

While I reveled in the fact that he'd just inadvertently, if indirectly, admitted his guilt to me, I couldn't say he was wrong. Valery would never openly reveal her client list—not to me or anyone else. "Maybe you're right. Maybe I'll have to make peace with the fact that you punish yourself every day for murdering my father so you could steal his job. I've seen how much you've been drinking. Is it the guilt that makes you drink to forget? Or . . . maybe it's because you've heard about Lord Banyon's list."

His eyes narrowed. "What list?" he snapped.

"A list of names that he showed my father the night he died."

Ambrose scoffed. "Louis had no association with the warlock. You're talking nonsense now."

"If you say so." I couldn't be imagining the flicker of fear I saw in his eyes. If he'd thought he was going to intimidate me by confronting me like this, then he'd better think again. He had no idea what I knew. "You know, forget it. Forget I mentioned anything about this."

"Tell me more about this list," he hissed.

"Just that your name was on it. At the top. It was in alphabetical order."

"And?"

I shrugged. "Like you said, it doesn't matter. Nobody will believe me. So don't worry about it."

Ambrose stood there for several silent moments, his expression pained and uncertain. But then he quickly gathered his composure.

"I have been very generous to you since Louis's passing, allowing you to stay at my home. You mustn't ever forget that."

I couldn't help but laugh at that. "Yes, so generous for someone who wanted me dead and buried next to my father."

He shook his head. "You don't want me as an enemy, Josslyn."

"It's way too late for that," I told him.

I took the opportunity to leave before I said any more. I wanted to hold on to my secrets as much as I could and not blurt everything out in anger in an attempt to wound him. Lists of names I only had in my memory weren't proof of anything.

That was the worst thing when it came to Ambrose. I had no tangible proof to use against him. Only my own certainty, my own knowledge, that he was a murderer. No way to make him pay for what he did.

When I returned to my room feeling defeated, I closed the door with trembling hands, my eyes burning. I had to hold it together.

Someone knocked only moments later. Warily, I opened the door, only to see Celina standing on the other side.

"Hi," I managed.

She slipped inside without saying anything, her expression pale and bleak, her eyes red. She searched my face as if it held all the answers she needed.

"I heard you," she said, her voice shaky. "I heard what you said to my father. Every word of it."

No, no, no. My mind flashed back to my short and horrible conversation with Ambrose, my accusations, his staunch refusal to take any direct responsibility or admit his crimes. I already forgot exactly what I'd said, but I knew it was a lot more than I'd planned to say out loud. My outrage and my hate for the man had stomped all over my common sense. Again.

"Celina . . ." I began.

She held up her hand. "No, Joss. For once in your damn life, just listen to me before you start talking, okay?"

I bit my bottom lip. "Fine."

Celina began pacing in short lines, wringing her hands. I expected her to start crying and accuse me of being a horrible person who'd say horrible things about her father. That our friendship was over, and I was dead to her.

Before she spoke again, a hundred different outcomes, each worse than the one before, flashed through my imagination.

Then she met my eyes, her gaze searching mine. "Is it true?"

I blinked. "You're going to have to be more specific."

"All of it. Did my . . . ?" She inhaled sharply. "Did he hire someone to assassinate you and your father at last year's Gala?"

My heart was already torn apart from Jericho dying in my arms—the thought that I had the power to break Celina's heart, as well, was too much for me to bear. To my dismay, hot tears streamed down my cheeks and a sob wrenched free from my throat.

Her eyes widened. "No, don't cry. Please don't cry. Joss, you never cry! What's happening?"

I felt her arms come around me then, and she hugged me to her, when I fully expected her to strike me for accusing her father of such a heinous crime.

She took my face between her hands and forced me to meet her gaze.

"Shit," she whispered. "It's true. Isn't it? Shit, I knew it! I knew something was wrong. All this time, something felt so horribly wrong about all of this. About him, how he's acted ever since that night." She drew in a shuddery breath. "Before she died, my mother warned me that he had a dark streak, that he was ruthless when it came to achieving his goals. And that he wanted to be prime minister more than anything else."

"I don't have proof," I whispered. "Not real proof."

"This is what the two of you were talking about at the dinner before you left. This is what upset you so much."

I nodded.

Celina's expression turned fierce in an instant. "And then you ran away with that horrible criminal."

Just as I was starting to compose myself, the tears began to spill again, even more of a torrential downpour than before.

The hardness in Celina's eyes fell away. "Oh, Joss . . ."

"He's dead," I cried. "At the amusement park . . . they shot him. He's dead!"

All the pain I'd been trying my best to repress during my meeting with the queen, then my unexpected face-off with Ambrose, came flooding back. My knees gave out and I sank to the floor. Celina sat down next to me, holding me tightly and letting my cry until I got control over myself again. It took a while.

"I'm sorry," I whispered.

"No." She shook her head. "Please don't apologize. I didn't know."

"Know what?"

"That . . . that what you felt for him was real."

I just nodded. "It was real. It—it *is* real."

"Then I'm sorry he's gone."

"Me too." The words literally hurt my throat. "I wish I could have told you."

"Of course you couldn't tell me. I would have judged you, like I almost did just now. I wouldn't have understood then, but I want to try now." She grasped my hands as we sat on the floor of my room. "I love you, Joss. You're my best friend in the whole world. I love you and I trust you more than anyone else. I want us to be able to tell each other anything—the good, the bad, and the utterly horrible. Do you hear me?"

Suddenly, Celina was the strong one and I was the one who needed comfort and support. I'd never seen us this way before, but maybe I hadn't been looking closely enough.

I nodded. "I hear you."

"A lot has happened this month."

"You can say that again." There was a haunted look in Celina's eyes suddenly that made me frown. "What is it? What's wrong?"

"I have a secret," she whispered, her eyes filling with tears. "A horrible secret. One I haven't told you yet because . . . because I was afraid you wouldn't understand."

My heart wrenched at seeing the pain on my best friend's beautiful face. "Tell me."

She was silent for a moment, a lock of long crimson hair covering her right eye. She tucked it behind her ear, then looked at me with fresh determination. "Actually, it's easier if I show you."

She pushed up from the ground and held a hand out to me. I took it and let her help me to my feet.

She grabbed a pitcher of water and poured a glass.

"I *am* kind of thirsty," I admitted.

"This isn't for you, Joss. This is for me." She drew in a shaky breath. "Watch carefully."

Celina put the glass of water down on a table and took a seat.

She stared at the water for several intense moments, and then—I could have sworn—the water began to move. Swirling slowly, counterclockwise, and then faster until, to my utter amazement, a small funnel of water began to rise up from the glass, hanging in midair like a tiny, liquid tornado, before it splashed back down into its container.

She turned, her expression bleak, to gauge my reaction to this.

My mouth had fallen open so wide at the sight before me, it took a moment to compose myself.

"You're a witch," I managed.

"I don't know what I am anymore." Celina raked her hands through her red hair and stood up from the chair so quickly that it made a screeching sound. "Over the last year, the strangest things have happened to me around water. Just weird and unsettling moments when it . . . it felt like it was calling to me. Like I could feel it deep in my being." She pressed a hand against her chest. "I can't explain it, but it's true. I tried to ignore it, but it was like an itch that needed to be scratched. Always there, always whispering to me in my head. I thought I was going mad. But one day I decided to listen to it, to open myself to the frightening possibility it presented. And . . . well, this is all I can do. It's not much at all, but it's . . . it's also too much."

The list. The list with the name Ambrose on it.

Magical bloodlines.

"Water is your element to summon," I said, awed by everything she'd just told me.

Her breath hitched. "I don't even know what that means."

"I do. Don't worry, Celina. I can help you."

She shook her head. "No one can know this. No one does, not my father, not . . . not Viktor. No one but you. I needed you to see this, to know that I trust you, no matter what. I trust only you with my secret, Joss."

Celina regarded me now, the fear naked on her face as if she were preparing herself to be rejected and cast away.

"You can trust me," I told her firmly. "We sure have a lot to talk about, you and me."

When I hugged her, she let out a sigh of relief so deep and powerful that I literally thought I felt it in my soul.

TWENTY

Over the next few days, I told Celina everything. *Everything*, but in small, digestible chunks so as not to overwhelm her. Starting on the night of the Queen's Gala when I'd randomly walked in on a robbery, to Jericho bringing our shopping trip to a staggering and frightening halt, to visiting Jericho's estranged guardian Rush at his fight club to get his dubious advice, to our time in the Queen's Keep and meeting Vander Lazos, former magical advisor to Queen Isadora herself.

Then, ultimately, Jericho's revelation about the night he was sent to assassinate my father and me, and how his fight against Valery's command had left me unharmed and my father with a nonfatal wound.

About Prince Elian, resurrected from death, allowed to hunt for prey in the confines of the walled prison.

And I told her about the memory magic and how it had given me a more layered opinion of Lord Banyon . . .

My biological father.

And my biological father's list of names.

Yeah. Had to admit even to myself, it was a lot.

To Celina's credit, she never flinched—not even when it came to the Banyon-is-my-birth-father stuff. Well, maybe she flinched a little when it came to that particular revelation, but she never told me to stop talking or accused me of wildly elaborating or lying. She listened, asked questions to clarify what she didn't understand, and never judged me for the decisions I'd made during this strange journey of discovery I'd been on that had changed my life forever.

This was *our* secret now.

It was like I was seeing my best friend with new eyes. I'd always thought she was fragile, in need of the support of someone who could help her with her confidence and self-esteem. But now I realized that wasn't quite right. Celina may have been an introvert to my extrovert, but she was definitely not weak in the slightest. My best friend was the strongest, smartest, and most open-minded person I'd ever known.

She sat with me while I tried to summon fresh echoes in my search for the big secret, but I was having trouble finding even a single one.

"It's the box," I told her, frustrated. "I need the memory box."

"You said it wasn't necessary."

I shook my head. "Banyon must have been wrong. I had it with me at the hotel when I was with you. That was my last echo, and I was able to control it. I need that control right now."

"I don't know what to tell you." Celina shook her head. "This is all new to me."

"I know; I'm sorry."

"Don't be sorry. Just stop making excuses for yourself and keep trying."

I snorted. "Yes, ma'am."

I would have loved to talk to Tamara about all of this, but, despite her new status at the palace as the queen's personal earth-magic physician, she was inaccessible to those outside of Her Majesty's inner circle. Since I was desperately trying to fit in and not ruffle any more proverbial feathers, especially after my heated face-to-face with Ambrose, I hadn't pushed to see her. Yet.

For now, I needed to be patient. Too bad that patience was my own personal brand of torture.

I needed to talk to Elian. I assumed it would be possible, but days after my arrival it hadn't happened yet. It was worrying, to say the least, not to have any idea how the prince was faring after his brief visit to Cresidia and having his small grasp on hope for the future yanked out of his grip by the one person he thought might have the power to help him.

I hadn't given up on finding a cure for him, but the longer it took, the more likely it was that his hunger would fully return. If it hadn't already.

My wardrobe held at the prime minister's residence was shipped to the palace, and I had my hair styled and freshly high-lighted, my skin and fingernails polished and pampered. The queen sent her beauty team to me every morning to apply my makeup and plan my outfit for the day.

My regular classes resumed the day after I returned to the

palace, along with Celina's—a year more advanced than mine due to our one-year age difference—and a very grumpy tutor attempted to catch me up on everything I'd missed over the last month. I did my best to pay attention to every subject, and to answer every question. I tolerated this "return to normal" since I needed it to appear as if that's what I wanted more than anything else.

I'd gone over and over what the queen had said to me, trying to find the malice in her words, the threat behind her tales of the past, of what she might do to me now. But I came up empty. Queen Isadora was a liar, a hypocrite, and a murderer, but it seemed like she genuinely liked me as much as she said she did.

This meant one very important and useful thing to me: She didn't see me as a threat. After a few days of trying to be my old self, I realized why.

I wasn't a threat. At all. To her, I was a seventeen-year-old girl who'd lived a pampered, privileged, and sheltered life. A girl who could get knocked unconscious from a bump on the back of her head. A girl who'd been exposed to magic, but one who had no power and no real plan on what to do next. A girl at the mercy of those who really wielded the power in this empire.

And if I couldn't summon and experience another echo, then I had no chance to learn the secret only she and Elian knew. Without that, and with Banyon locked up and powerless, I had nothing.

I asked myself "what would Jericho do?" in nearly every situation I found myself in. From dinner with the queen, to enduring High Commander Norris's accusatory glares when we passed in the palace hallways, to the cold greetings I was given by Ambrose when we were unable to totally ignore each other's existence.

The Blackheart would likely deal with nine out of ten problems by sticking a sharp blade into it until it stopped moving. So, quite honestly, that wasn't very helpful at all.

I missed him so much.

I missed his snarky comments, his stoic presence, his argumentative nature, his annoyed glares, and his heated looks. I missed knowing I could trust him, that he had my back. That he gave a damn about whether I lived or died. I missed his face. I missed his strength. I missed how mind-blowingly amazing it felt when I kissed him.

I missed . . . *him*. And I would never, ever, ever forget him.

Three weeks passed without learning anything new. Without Jericho.

It was the day of the Queensgames launch party when I swore I saw the Blackheart walking toward me down the hallway, his gaze fixed on mine. All I saw was someone familiarly tall and handsome. Broad shoulders, dark hair, and a square jaw.

My breath caught.

But it wasn't him. It was Viktor, in his black-and-gold Queensguard commander uniform.

"Joss," he greeted me. "I just got back from my tour. Celina told me you were here."

I tried to fight past my disappointment and heartbreak to find my voice.

"I'm here," I agreed.

"The queen asked me to personally escort you to her chambers." He lowered his voice despite there being no one within listening distance to us. "The prince has asked to see you."

The thought that Elian was finally willing to talk to me again was a relief, but I didn't budge an inch from where I stood.

Viktor frowned at me. "Is there a problem?"

He couldn't be serious.

I let out a hollow-sounding laugh. "How can you just stand there and act like nothing's happened?"

He hissed out a breath. "We didn't leave on a good note. I know that. But it's over. I made my choice, not that I actually had a choice. If I hadn't agreed to the queen's terms, Jericho would have been executed. But I know he'll never see it like that. My brother's always been as stubborn as a damn mule. He gets it in his head that I'm an opportunist, only out for glory no matter who or what I need to trample on my way there. Maybe all of that is true. And maybe I'm not ashamed of it."

I just stared at him. What the hell was he talking about?

"Viktor . . ." I began, but he wasn't finished yet.

"That scar on his chin?" he said. "He probably said I gave him that on purpose, but it was an accident. He grabbed my arm. I happened to be holding a broken bottle at the time. It happened. As soon as I saw the blood, I came to my senses." His expression darkened with regret. "I never would have cut him on purpose."

I shook my head. "Viktor . . . stop."

He scrubbed a hand through his hair. "He'll never forgive me, but it doesn't matter. I did what I had to do. I don't know. Maybe a quick execution would have been better for him than working for that witch for the rest of his life. But that's his choice, not mine. Right?"

"Don't you know what happened?" I asked him, my voice breaking.

Viktor seemed to pull himself out of the grip of his own unpleasant memories to focus on me again. "What are you talking about? What happened?"

"At the Queensgate Amusement Park . . . Celina's rescue . . ."

"What about it?"

"Jericho was shot by a guard." I pressed my hand against my chest, my eyes burning. "Here. He . . . he was killed."

Viktor blinked. "No. That's impossible."

I shook my head. "I was there. Right there with him. A guard checked his pulse, and . . . he didn't have one. Viktor, he died in my arms."

He didn't speak for a moment, his brows drawn tightly together. "I know there were casualties, but I didn't know about . . ." He inhaled sharply and seemed to struggle to compose himself. "I've been gone all this time, doing ridiculous, meaningless interviews, one after another. I knew I couldn't refuse a single one to appease the queen for my failure. Elian asked me to say nothing about what happened in Cresidia. And I've been working on my speech for the party tonight . . . but I didn't . . . No, this—what you're telling me—it can't be right. He's not dead."

Despite his refusal to accept what I was telling him, the tone of his voice had changed. I heard raw pain there. And when he raised his gaze to mine, his eyes were glossy.

"I'm sorry, Viktor," I managed. "I . . . I know you two had problems, like any siblings do. Well, maybe your problems were bigger than most siblings. But you need to know that Jericho loved you, despite your differences. He said only good things about you, that you were strong and smart and driven to succeed. He was so damn proud of you, even if he never admitted it to you out loud."

Viktor searched my face as if hoping that I would admit I was only messing with him. Finally, the heavy truth settled in.

Jericho was gone. We'd both lost someone we loved.

"How could he have been proud of me?" he whispered, as if it would hurt too much to speak any louder. "If I'm not proud of myself?"

"I guess it doesn't work that way." I swallowed hard. "Listen . . . I know you told the queen that I only left the night of the escape because I was in love with him. Thank you for lying for me."

He searched my face. "It wasn't completely a lie, though, was it?"

I wiped a tear off my cheek. "Not completely."

"Didn't think so." Viktor nodded, his expression grim. Then he shook his head as if trying to compose himself. He rubbed his eyes and straightened his shoulders. "The queen is waiting. Come with me."

Viktor led me through the hallways toward the inner circle. I wanted to say more to him, but I didn't know what. He might have loved his brother, might have taken the mission from the queen mostly to save Jericho's life, but I still didn't trust him like I trusted Celina. He already knew too much about me as it was. I'd have to leave it there for now.

It wasn't long at all before we reached our destination, and he opened the door for me. Viktor didn't linger for another moment, turning on his boot heels and walking away.

I took a moment to try to center myself and push my grief for Jericho away as much as I could. I needed to be "on" with the queen today. I couldn't arouse her suspicions—not now, not when I was about to see Elian for the first time in weeks. Besides, I could use this opportunity for my own gain too. Because after the failures of the last three weeks, I'd made an important decision. I needed the memory box back as soon as possible.

How was I going to convince her to give it to me without it looking suspicious? No idea. But I'd figure out a good enough story. She knew the stolen magic was still inside me, but not what it was. The fact that she hadn't made this more of an issue showed me how comfortable she was with magic in the first place. She knew it wasn't as evil as she'd always claimed. Just inconvenient.

Liar. Hypocrite.

I had to keep reminding myself of what I'd seen her do. The lies she'd told. The cruel and unnecessary laws she created and upheld, and how she continued to keep Tamara at the palace. The kindness she always expressed to me personally had made the water very muddy when it had previously been crystal clear.

Perhaps I'd even hint at the truth—that the magic could give some deeper insight on Banyon. News had gone dark on the warlock over the last week. No escape attempts that I'd heard of. No execution scheduled. The lack of information had made me more nervous with every day that passed. And I hated being nervous. It was so unlike me.

All I knew was that I hadn't had a single, solitary echo since the last time the box had been in my possession at the amusement park. Something had shifted inside me, making the magic inaccessible to me when I needed it the most.

And this was my chance to do something about it. I would refuse to leave her suite without the box in hand, no matter what I had to say or do to ensure it.

"Josslyn, please come in," the queen's voice beckoned to me. Then she spoke to someone else. "Look who's here to see you, my darling."

And there he was, seated at the very table where we first truly met, where I'd realized there was a rather strong personality behind the vacant act he put on.

Prince Elian glanced over at me and met my gaze. He was painfully pale, with dark circles under his black eyes. He looked like he hadn't slept in days. "Hello, Joss."

"Your Highness," I said, dropping into a shallow curtsy. "It's so good to finally see you again."

"I'm sorry I've been keeping such a low profile lately, even for me."

"No need to apologize."

The queen regarded her son with love and patience. "He's done incredibly well lately, despite his disappointments. He's improved so much in the last month alone, it's like I finally have my son back after all these years."

"Is that true?" I asked aloud. "Do you feel like things are better for you now?"

"Yes, of course," he told me. "All is well."

If the queen didn't recognize that as a flat-out lie, then I couldn't really help her.

"Tell her," the queen urged. "Tell Josslyn that you're very grateful to her for keeping you safe during your trip."

"So grateful," Elian agreed dully, without meeting my gaze.

The queen spoke again after silence fell between us. "I was very cross with him, and so very worried, but I knew if he was with you and Viktor, then he would be all right. And he is. Safe and sound and back where he belongs."

"I'm sorry to have worried you, Mother," Elian said.

She cupped his cheek. "All is forgiven, my darling. Now, I have important business to attend to prior to the party tonight, so please take some time to reacquaint yourselves. There's tea and egg-salad sandwiches for you both to enjoy."

The queen turned to leave the room, and I forced myself to say something before she was gone. "Your Majesty, a word. Very quickly, if you please."

"Yes?" she replied. "What is it, my dear?"

Confidence, that's what I needed. If I sounded the least bit uncertain or tentative, she would know immediately that something was awry.

"The golden box . . . you know, the one that I had on me when I arrived here . . ." I began.

"The memory box," she said, nodding.

A breath caught in my chest. I was sure that someone had just pulled the floor out from beneath my feet. "The . . . memory box?"

She nodded. "Lord Banyon has been questioned at length on what exactly that little item was amongst his other stolen belongings."

"And he told you it was a . . ." *Force it out, Joss,* I told myself. *Stay calm. Don't freak out.* "A . . . memory box?"

"Yes." She flicked her hand dismissively. "Apparently, it's a way of magically containing one's memories so they can be reexperienced."

Oh, yes. I knew what a memory box was all too well. I just didn't think that she did.

If Banyon was answering questions under duress, that had to mean he was weaker than I already believed.

"Is that it?" I forced out. "Huh. That explains so much." I pressed my hands to my head. "I've had these flashes of images—very blurry, very indistinct images—but I haven't understood what any of it meant. All I know is that this evil magic makes my nose bleed."

"If it helps, it sounds as if this piece of magic is relatively benign, all things considered. Zarek says that he contained the memories of his wedding day so he could relive it." She hissed out a breath. "How very trite of him."

"So very trite," I agreed readily. Perhaps I was wrong about Banyon. He hadn't told the whole truth, so maybe he still had a little fight left within him. "So . . . it's just that? One day? One memory?"

"Thankfully, yes. As for the box itself"—she flicked her hand dismissively—"I had it destroyed the day you arrived instead of merely locked away in a safe."

My throat closed up so much I could barely speak. "So, it's gone."

"Yes, it's gone."

"Good," I forced out. "I wanted to check, so I wouldn't have to keep worrying about it."

"Zarek made it clear that this inconvenient magic will eventually dissipate from you, so it's not something you must deal with forever. Nothing more needs to be said on the matter, as far as I'm concerned." She smiled kindly. "I'll see you at the party, Josslyn."

"Yes, Your Majesty," I agreed quickly. "See you there."

"Don't stay too long. My son needs his rest."

"Of course."

With that, Queen Isadora left me and Elian in her chambers alone.

The prince had gone to sit at the table, glaring at the plates of food there.

I sat down heavily across from him, my mind a storm, rehashing what she'd just told me. Banyon had been covering for me, covering for himself. He'd done what I had been trying to do—sprinkle the truth in a stew of lies to make it more believable.

Only his wedding day. The queen would never feel threatened by that memory, only annoyed.

"What was that all about?" Elian asked. "What memory box?"

I cared about Elian, just like I cared about Viktor. But I would continue to keep my secrets in my own very tight inner circle for now, consisting of only my best friend.

"Don't worry about it," I said. "Now tell me, how are you feeling? Really?"

"How do I look?" he asked.

"Not great," I admitted.

"There you go."

"I know the queen mentioned that she might have Tamara try to heal you."

"She did try. A few times now." He leveled his black-eyed gaze with mine. "It only made me hungrier. That witch is terrified of me."

I cringed. "Should she be?"

"Yes. Everyone should be. I'm getting close, Joss. So close. More quickly than ever before this time." He shakily took a bite of a sandwich before throwing it back on the plate, disgusted. "I hate egg-salad sandwiches," he muttered.

"What happens when the hunger . . . ?" How could I even put it? "When you, like . . . ?"

"Lose my damn mind?" he finished for me. "Lose any semblance of control I have over my own life and start to suck the life out of helpless victims?"

I grimaced at the picture he presented. "Basically."

"For starters, I'll be put in a holding cell that was made especially for me—with three-foot steel walls. Later, I'll be sedated and taken to the Keep. By then, I'm not exactly mentally present anymore. But who knows? Maybe my mother has another plan in mind, considering how poorly my last trip to that prison went."

My heart ached for him. "I'm so sorry. I know you've given up, but I haven't."

He searched my face. "It's been three weeks, Joss. Have you discovered some sort of magical cure for me?"

"Not yet," I admitted.

Elian nodded grimly. "You know what the worst thing is, and I hate to even say this out loud, but . . . Lord Banyon. He's here, locked up. Waiting for his execution. Questioned at length about everything. And he hasn't, not once, asked to see me. It's like he doesn't care. He's never cared that I'm his son." He swore darkly under his breath. "I hate feeling sorry for myself. It's so pathetic."

"You're right; it is," I replied.

He glared at me. "Thanks."

I shrugged. "Just speaking the truth here, Elian. Look, I don't know why you're suffering like this, but what I do know is what Banyon told Jericho. That it is possible to fight against the magic inside of him. I know it's not the same for you. But there was something magically controlling Jericho, and when he put his mind to it, he could push back against it."

"Lucky him. It's different for me."

I wasn't about to share the news of the Blackheart's death with Elian. It would only sideline this conversation, and I'd already shared enough grief with Viktor for one afternoon. "Here's what I know about you, Elian. You were raised from the dead sixteen years ago. And you were mindless for most of it. But you're not now. You have a mind; you have a force of will. And you have a tangible goal—to beat this. To get control over yourself and whatever this darkness is inside of you. You could embrace this darkness, but you haven't."

"I can't," he gritted out. "And I never will."

"Good. It means that you're better than your mother. You're not someone who will justify evil acts for the greater good." I paused, considering my next words. "You know the big secret, whatever it is. The secret you share with the queen. I know you feel powerless right now, but that secret is power, Elian. You need to tell me what it is. We need to share it with the world."

"Sure." He laughed darkly at this. "Maybe I'll show up to the press conference this evening, give a little speech to update everyone on where I've been for the last decade and a half. And then . . . just go ahead and destroy the world with a few more words."

"There are other ways," I argued.

"No there aren't, Joss. I told you, that secret will die with me. It would be better that it does."

Frustration tightened in my chest. I'd had such hope for the prince, but I saw now that talking to him was a waste of my time. "Why did you even ask to see me today? Just to share some sandwiches and misery with me?"

There was something broken in his eyes when he looked at me. "I need you to contact Valery. Tell her that I'm ready for her cure. It's time."

I shook my head. "Elian, no."

He stood up, tears shining in his eyes. "Don't make this harder than it has to be. Please, Joss. Please help me end this, once and for all."

With that, he left me in the room alone.

I tried to gather myself as much as I could before I left the queen's chambers and the highly secured inner circle of the palace, my mind in free fall. I desperately wished that an echo would hit me, sweep me away and show me all the answers I needed to make everything okay again.

But nothing was okay. Nothing had ever been okay, I just never realized it as fully as I did now.

Not so long ago, all I'd wanted was to rid myself of this magic before anyone knew I'd been tainted by it. Now all I wanted was to be able to control it, to find the answers I needed to . . . to what?

What could I change with only the truths I could see in the privacy of my own mind? It was like knowing the truth about Ambrose, but also knowing he would never answer for his crimes.

A month ago, I'd left the palace with vengeance as my fuel, wanting to go out into the world and find the answers I needed to make this sick feeling inside of me go away. Had I wanted to change the world for the better? What a lovely, selfless thought that was, and I'd convinced myself of it. But who was I kidding? I wasn't selfless. I'd always been desperately selfish. I was sure that my first words were to ask for something to make me feel better, more comfortable, and happier. Sure, I might not have felt like I totally fit in among my casual friends or with Celina, but I didn't color too far outside the lines.

All my life, I'd never questioned what I'd been told about

magic, and I'd been wondering why that was. I couldn't go back in my own memories and see things objectively. I saw through the lens of my own self-image, the one that built me up like a hero of my own story, just like how the queen saw herself in her personal recollection of her past.

But I was no hero. I was no villain. I was just . . . me. And the only power I had here was to save my own ass, to survive another day and hope that it might be a bit better than the last.

Pathetic.

The queen had her victory. Banyon was her prisoner—her fiercest enemy was now dying and powerless. She was ready to celebrate tonight, at a party full of the very people who helped her rule an empire of billions.

And half of those people's names were on Banyon's list.

The thought wafted into my mind, slipping past a crowded room of negative thoughts and despair.

The list.

Magical bloodlines, proving that there was a higher percentage of mages than anyone had ever believed. A few thousand mages scattered across the empire could be contained, defeated, imprisoned, executed. But if there were millions . . .

The answer might not just be in the memory magic. The answer could be attending the party tonight. If even I'd seen the light of truth these last weeks, after a lifetime of believing magic to be evil, then I couldn't be the only one. I thought about what Mika said—most people already knew that magic wasn't that bad. She thought it meant hopelessness. What if it meant possibility?

What I needed more than anything else were more allies. More people I could trust. Even if we could spark just a small whisper of the truth circulating through the Empire, it could catch fire.

Louis Drake may have been the queen's personally chosen prime minister for two decades, but he wasn't a bad man who would simply stand by and let innocent people perish. Maybe he didn't know the truth for far too long, but when he did, he was ready to learn more.

If he hadn't died a year ago, what might have changed?

I'd never know the answer to that, and the thought broke my heart. It also gave me the strength to go forward into this party knowing I had to talk to as many people on the list as I could. I had to figure out who might be on my side.

A few hours later, the stylists arrived right on schedule, and they helped me get ready for a party I now wanted to attend more than ever before. I sat in front of the mirror, my blue contact lenses in place, as they skillfully applied my makeup and styled my hair in long, soft golden waves.

And I inhaled slowly and exhaled even more slowly.

Show me a memory, I thought, speaking to the magic within me. *Please. Show me what I need to see to give me hope that all is not lost.*

I received the same result I'd gotten for weeks now when I attempted this exercise several times a day.

Nothing happened.

Maybe what Banyon told the queen was true. Maybe the magic had already left me, just as I was starting to accept it as a priceless gift rather than a dark curse.

The stylists finally departed, leaving me dressed in a beautiful dark blue satin gown, silver high-heels, and sapphire-studded jewelry at my neck and wrists. The girl in the mirror looked perfectly polished and utterly photo ready, as she waited for her best friend so they could arrive at the party together.

I used the time I had left to mentally prepare myself, to call on the old Joss who excelled at parties and small talk, loving every minute of it. I needed her tonight more than ever before as I straddled the thin line between survival and rebellion.

Finally, I was drawn out of my thoughts by a knock on my door. Still distracted, I opened it up, fully expecting it to be Celina.

But it wasn't Celina.

My visitor was tall and handsome, with dark hair, broad shoulders, and a square jaw. He wore a black-and-gold Queensguard uniform.

But it wasn't Viktor this time.

"It looks like your return to normal life is going very well, Drake," Jericho said dryly, sweeping his black-eyed gaze over me from head to toe. "Congratulations on that."

TWENTY-ONE

The Blackheart moved past me into the suite and swept his gaze around his new surroundings.

"Nice room, not that I'm surprised," he said. He waited for a moment, then glanced over at me. "Nothing to say to me?"

I just stared at him, certain I'd wake up from this dream at any moment. And I didn't want to, not yet. I liked this dream very much.

"You're dead," I told him with a shake of my head. "So, you're not really here."

"I'm not dead. Not at the moment, anyway." Jericho hissed out a breath, studying me now. "And I most definitely *am* here."

My heart thudded and my vision swam. "I think I'm going to pass out."

"You're not the fainting type, Drake."

I struggled to breathe, sucking in a mouthful of air as I tried to process what was happening. "How is this possible? You . . . you died. Right in front of me. Three weeks ago! And you're here? Just like that?"

He raked his hand through his dark hair, his expression now pained. "I'll explain real quick, okay?"

"Real quick," I agreed. "Please, as quickly as possible."

"You're right, I did die. That bullet took me out. I felt it . . . the life draining from me." He shook his head. "The last thing I saw was your face, your eyes. And then there was nothing. A big black hole for what felt like a long damn time. Then I started to feel something again, and it hurt really bad. I opened my eyes, and that hurt too. Mika was there; she was dragging my body out of sight of the guards. They were distracted, loading up the helicopter with your friend, and . . . you. I saw you. Unconscious. One of the guards was carrying you over his shoulder. For a second, I thought they'd killed you too."

I touched the back of my head with trembling fingers, where the wound had been before Tamara had healed me. "They knocked me out."

Jericho nodded, his black eyes haunted. "I tried to get to you, but I wasn't able to move yet. My body was dealing with . . . well, being dead. Again." He scratched his forearm. "It was the marks Val gave me before we left Cresidia. They were fresh, all that juicy magic swirling around just under my skin. I figure if she hadn't freshened me up when she did, I might only be a bad memory now."

The marks. The same ones that had brought him back from the dead after the Queensgames, a sword through his chest. They'd worked again, two years later. But my gratitude toward this miracle, courtesy of Valery, was shadowed almost immediately by the memory of weeks of utter silence.

"Why didn't you contact me? Let me know you were okay?" I said, angry now.

Jericho's lips quirked at my irate tone. "Well, firstly, it's not exactly that easy getting a message to someone here at the palace. And, secondly, I didn't just snap back, good as new. I could barely move for a week. I've been recovering and it's been rough. Only started to feel like myself again a few days ago, or I would have been here sooner."

I searched his face, still trying to reconcile the fact that this was really happening, and it wasn't just a dream. "You're alive. You're really alive."

"I really am," he agreed.

"And . . . you came here, you broke into the very same palace you escaped from a month ago, and . . . stole a Queensguard uniform just to see me?"

He grimaced. "Not exactly, although that does sound much more romantic, doesn't it? Mika's here too. Since she saved my ass at the park, I promised to help her find Tamara and get her the hell out of here while the party's going on as a distraction. Don't ask me where Agatha is; she's in the wind. Probably with the other rebels demanding Banyon's release. Mika said she regretted giving him up the moment the Queensguards stormed the park, knew she'd made the wrong decision out of desperation, and it wouldn't do a damn thing to save Tamara in the end. Anyway, I wasn't even going to check on you, but I . . . couldn't seem to stop myself."

I stared at him, suddenly outraged at the suggestion. "Why weren't you going to check on me?"

He shrugged. "I didn't want to get in the way of your reintegration." His gaze moved down the front of me. "Back to your shiny, glittery, normal life."

"Yes, so normal." My outrage faded as soon as it arrived.

It couldn't fight against my utter gratitude and relief that the Blackheart was alive. "Do you remember what you said to me at the park? After you'd been shot?"

Jericho cleared his throat and looked away. "It's all a bit blurry, to be honest. Why? Was it something memorable?"

"You could say that." I took a step closer to him, tentatively reaching out a hand to touch his chest. It was solid, real. He was real. And so was his steady heartbeat.

He eyed me warily. "Drake?"

"Just checking to make sure you're not a ghost," I told him.

"Definitely not a ghost." He placed his hand on top of mine. "And . . . I do remember the last thing I said to you."

"You do?"

"Yeah. It was something I've never said to anyone else. Ever." Jericho met my gaze full on. "I love you, Drake. I've loved you for longer than you even realize. Longer than *I* even realized."

A tear slipped down my cheek. "Jericho . . ."

He shook his head. "Don't worry—you don't have to say it back. But I'm holding to that 'truth' thing you said you wanted between us. No lies. No bullshit."

He began to pull away, but I grabbed a handful of his stolen uniform.

"The truth," I repeated, and then I smiled for the first time in what felt like forever. "I love you too. I love you, Jericho."

Something shifted in his dark eyes then—some hold on his stoic shield that protected him from the world finally broke. He cupped my face between his hands and gazed deeply into my eyes.

"I really, really hoped you were going to say it back," he told me. "I missed you, Drake."

"I missed you too."

And then he kissed me, a kiss that was hard and deep and endless. He gathered me into his arms and pulled me tightly against him. It was everything I'd dreamed of in the weeks he'd been gone, believing I'd never see him again. But he was here. He was alive. And he loved me.

Jericho Nox loved me.

"You're very accident-prone, you know that?" I told him softly against his lips. "You really need to be more careful."

He smiled. "You know all the right things to say, Drake."

"I'm very happy that you're not dead."

"Me too."

I kissed him this time. It was so amazing to finally be able to kiss him, not wondering when he would shut down or pull away, scared to let someone get too close to him.

"Drake . . ." he whispered

I raised an eyebrow. "Are you ever going to call me Joss? Everybody calls me Joss."

His lips quirked. "I'm not everybody."

"True," I agreed.

He slid his thumb over my bottom lip. "I messed up your makeup. Sorry about that."

"It's okay. It was totally worth it," I told him with a grin.

Jericho's jaw tightened and he eyed the door. "Mika's waiting for me. As much as I'd like to keep you from going to that party, I'm guessing there's no way around it."

"Not really," I admitted reluctantly. "Tamara's here in the palace, so you and Mika can get to her. She's alive and been given special privileges by the queen because of her earth magic. She wasn't going to be executed, after all."

"Aunt Issy knows valuable magic when she sees it. Mika will be relieved to hear that."

"Yeah, but she still needs to get out of here as soon as possible," I said. "Quick recap for you, first. Elian's given up hope, and his hunger's coming back with a vengeance. Tamara tried to heal him, but it didn't work. Only made the hunger worse, he says. He won't tell me what the big secret is and is now determined to die with it being unknown. He wants me to contact Valery to make an appointment with her dagger."

"Got it." He nodded grimly. "Any more useful echoes?"

"None since the amusement park. And the queen destroyed the memory box." I shook my head. "I think it's over, Jericho. All I have is the list; I can remember some of the names from it. If I can find those people, those families, some of them will be at the party tonight . . . if I can talk to them. Get them to start asking questions, making some noise."

He looked at me skeptically. "That's your plan? Pitch a 'let's stand up for the truth' and make some noise? Weak, Drake."

I glared at him. "I'm open to suggestions on a better plan."

"Have you seen Banyon?"

I shook my head. "He's locked up somewhere; I don't know where. Inaccessible. Heavily guarded. Why? Were you planning on helping him escape tonight too?"

He scoffed. "Hardly. I've made my peace with not carving out his heart, but that doesn't mean I'm ready to donate a kidney for him. That big secret's in your head, Drake. The queen's seventeenth birthday, right? You can't give up on finding it."

"I'm not giving up."

"That's what it sounds like to me." At my sharp look, he shrugged. "Maybe Banyon was right. You don't need the box; you never did. You're the biological daughter of the most badass warlock in history. And even without him, you're a badass who does what she needs to do to get what she wants. Right?"

"Maybe I used to be. I don't think I can do it, Jericho."

"What is that?" He scrunched his nose as if smelling something bad. "Doubt? Josslyn Drake is doubting herself? That's so unlike her."

I thought about it for a moment. "Very true."

"You don't need a damn magic box. You are the damn magic box."

I couldn't help but smile at that. "You say the sweetest things to me."

He chuckled. "Try your best to keep a low profile at the party tonight, okay? I'm going to be busy for a while with Mika. After that, I'll find you again. And we'll . . . continue this conversation."

"Only this conversation?"

His gaze darkened. "No, not only."

The smile stayed on my face. "I'll be waiting."

Jericho kissed me again and then slipped out of my room as if he had never been there in the first place. But he had. He was alive, and he would be back later.

And, despite all of my problems today, tomorrow, and in the

future, that made me happier than I'd felt in an eternity.

It was only a few minutes later that Celina arrived, wearing a stunning emerald-green gown. She'd shown me a drawing of it earlier this week, by the same designer as the one who'd been commissioned to create her wedding gown.

"You're glowing," she said, eyeing me suspiciously. "And your lipstick is smeared."

I ran to the mirror to quickly fix it. "How strange."

When I was done, she hooked her arm through mine. "Come on, we're going to be late. You can tell me who you were just kissing on our way to the party. And don't leave anything out. My imagination is going wild right now."

I didn't tell her everything. But I told her enough. I carefully watched her out of the corner of my eye as she initially seemed to resist my tale of Jericho, back from the dead. But then she relaxed into the story.

"How do you think it's going to work between you two?" she asked quietly as we made our way through the palace hallways, headed for the banquet hall.

"It's complicated," I agreed.

"Me and Viktor are complicated. You and Jericho are . . . I don't even know what the right word is." She squeezed my hand. "I guess nothing worthwhile is easy, right?"

"Seems that way," I agreed.

"Viktor told me that Jericho is his older brother," she said, her voice tight. "You didn't tell me that."

"I didn't feel that it was my secret to share." I waited, my breath held. Then I prompted. "And . . . ?"

"And . . . my head nearly exploded. But then, it all started to finally make sense." She laughed lightly. "I'm guessing that a double date is probably not going to happen anytime soon."

I couldn't help but laugh as well. "Hey, you never know."

"True enough."

I was already counting down the minutes until the party was over, or at least until a time when I could slip away without anyone noticing. That would be after the private dinner and the queen's speech, which would be followed by a video showcasing some of the highlights of past Queensgames to the three hundred guests. Viktor would then make his short and inspirational speech as outgoing high champion.

Then, in the palace press room, where reporters and photographers waited, the queen and Viktor would take part in a broadcasted question-and-answer session for an hour or so.

Not me. This had nothing to do with me, thankfully. For the first time at any party I'd ever attended, I would be dodging all photo opportunities.

It had been two years since the last Queensgames launch party, but I remembered it well, especially how jealous my friends had been and how they'd demanded that I share every single detail with them upon my return to Ironport. I'm sure they said nasty things behind my back about how I didn't deserve such VIP treatment, even though I was First Daughter then. Maybe they were right.

I wondered if the queen would have treated me with such care over the years if I'd been Louis and Evelyne Drake's biological daughter, or if it was solely due to my blood ties to a man she once loved. How does a love that once burned so bright turn to hate?

I sincerely hoped I'd never personally find out the answer to that question.

Celina and I entered the banquet hall, a massive room filled with round tables laden with white roses and yellow lilies in crystal vases, centered on silk and lace tablecloths, with golden plates and cutlery shining under three separate crystal chandeliers. An orchestra played in the corner while the guests, each one of them dressed more elegantly than the last, moved around, embracing their acquaintances and chatting politely amongst themselves.

I scanned their faces, trying to put surnames to everyone my gaze fell upon. There was Mildred Carlson, the widow of Conrad Carlson, a member of Parliament who'd served with my father for many years. She also studied the room, a fan of wrinkles extending from the corners of her eyes.

She'd never liked me. Maybe I was too loud, too much of a troublemaker. Or maybe her granddaughter Helen had told her lies about me. Or truths. It could go either way, really.

I hated Helen.

At least *she* wasn't here tonight. Still, "Carlson" was definitely a name on the list.

My gaze next fell upon another surname on the list, a man who held a glass of red wine tightly in his hand and had not an ounce of kindness in his bloodshot eyes as he glared at me.

Regis Ambrose.

Celina groaned. "Looks like my father's already drunk," she whispered to me.

"I'm sorry," I replied.

"Me too. The queen isn't happy with him. He's paranoid, thinking that she knows the truth about what he did. He hasn't slept in days."

I wanted to say *good*, but I knew, as much as Celina understood my plight, that Ambrose was still her father, and she was still his daughter.

Jericho said he'd made his peace with Banyon, no longer seeking bloody vengeance for the deaths of his parents. I hadn't made any peace of my own yet. But by the looks of it, Ambrose might be heading directly toward his own demise, fueled by his own choices and guilt.

His cold gaze shifted away from me toward someone else, and his eyes widened. I watched as fear moved across his expression before he turned, wine sloshing over the edge of his glass, and quickly took his seat at the head table.

I glanced over toward where he'd been looking, only to see a familiar face.

Valery was here. Our eyes met and she smiled and nodded toward me, but I was too surprised to see her to return the greeting. She wore red, a bright crimson gown that stood out like a splash of blood in the center of the ballroom.

Before I could close the distance between us and ask any questions, the queen entered the hall, and, with all eyes on her, she approached the head table to take a seat at the center, with me on one side of her and Ambrose and Celina on the other.

"My dear, you look absolutely stunning," she told me.

"Thank you, Your Majesty. You do as well, of course."

In a stark contrast to Valery, the queen wore white—a full-length gown with a train made of delicate, intricate lace.

"I'm so pleased you could be here with me tonight," she told me.

"Me too," I lied.

Without further ado, the dinner portion of the evening began, along with the sound of polite conversation, forks and knives scraping against their golden plates covered in mouthwatering recipes created by the queen's favorite chef, and the music of the orchestra.

Behind the head table, which would also serve as the speech podium, I took some time to study the other guests—at least half of them were familiar faces I'd been introduced to over the years at parties much like this one, while I'd been at my father's side.

Of these faces, there were at least a dozen whose names I remembered from Banyon's list beyond Carlson and Ambrose. Among these powerful members of the queen's circle of friends and acquaintances, there had to be a few with rebel leanings. People who would rise up against her when the time was right. Mages who were hiding their magic for fear of repercussions to themselves and their families.

Did they know that there could be millions of us? It would still be a minority in an empire of two billion, but it was better than nothing. I had to believe that. I *did* believe that.

I tried to interpret each expression, searching for some sign, some clue I could latch on to that would help me figure out who my allies might be, going forward.

I kept coming back to the crimson-clad Valery, seated at a

table in the direct center of the room. She kept pleasant conversation with her tablemates, but her gaze remained fixed on Ambrose.

Ambrose's forehead was slick with perspiration, and he was on his sixth glass of wine by then, at least.

"Who's that woman, at the center table?" I asked the queen. "The beautiful dark-haired lady in the red gown?"

The queen peered off in that direction. "Oh, that's Alana Kincade. Lovely, charming woman, from a very wealthy family in North Regara. They practically own half of Cresidia."

Alana Kincade. I remembered the framed photo Valery had of her and the queen in her penthouse. Of course she'd use a pseudonym.

"Do you know her very well?" I asked.

"Not well at all, I'm afraid. But she's recently made a hefty donation to the Queenstrust, and I wanted to reward such generosity with an invitation to my most prestigious event." The queen leaned toward me, almost conspiratorially. "I have a big surprise planned for my guests a little later. One that no one will forget anytime soon."

I used to like surprises. I didn't like them anymore.

"Oh?" I took a sip of wine and swallowed it down. "What is it?"

"If I told you, that wouldn't be much of a surprise, would it?"

"Good point," I allowed uneasily.

She patted my hand approvingly, skin against skin. I had a sudden flashback to my first vivid echo, the one I'd had when I'd touched Norris at Rush's club, of when he'd tortured Banyon.

It didn't work every time, but—sometimes, contact helped

to summon an echo. Someone who'd been with Banyon when he'd created the memory in the first place. Vander Lazos had even been able to help direct my echo to help me see the truth of Elian's resurrection.

Contact.

I'd thought I needed the memory box. But I didn't have it now—and if it had been destroyed, I never would. I had to stop relying on it if I ever wanted to find the truth.

Banyon had told me that all I needed was belief—in myself, in my magic, in my abilities. Maybe he was right.

Maybe the piece I'd been missing was myself. Or, more specifically, the belief I had in myself. My doubt was what had been blocking me for weeks now.

So, I forced myself to release any remaining doubt, once and for all, gripped the queen's soft, manicured hand, as well as my own confidence, and summoned the memory I needed to see.

TWENTY-TWO

The golden smoke wound its way around me, taking my consciousness out of the banquet hall, and spinning me away to another time, another place. I found myself standing on a grassy hillside, overlooking a wide crystal-blue sea.

It worked. I could barely believe it, but it worked!

With me were two other people. Banyon and the queen, both only teenagers, no older than I was. They stood, holding hands, looking out at the water.

"We'll take a boat," Banyon said. "We'll explore, just you and me. You've got to wonder what's on the other side of that ocean, don't you, Issy?"

"I know what's on the other side," she replied. "Nothing that interests me. This is my home, Zarek."

"I know. You can't blame me for trying." He grinned. "The Empire's big enough, I guess. I was just trying to think of a good birthday present for you."

Birthday. My breath caught and held at the sound of the word.

Banyon's smile faltered when she didn't say anything. "You seem like you're a million miles away today."

She bit her bottom lip and turned away from him, running her hand absently over her flat belly. "I have a secret."

"Oh? What is it?"

"I . . . I don't know exactly how to tell you." She laughed, but it sounded nervous. "My father is going to kill me, but I'm not unhappy about it. I think it must be fate."

"Fate, is it? Now I have to know."

She opened her mouth as if to speak, but then doubt crossed her expression. "No, not today. I'll tell you tomorrow, I promise."

"Very well," he replied. "I'll look forward to that."

She was pregnant. That had to be it. And teenaged Banyon had no idea.

"You know, I do have another present, just in case you didn't immediately agree to travel the world with me," he told her. "Look at me."

She turned, only to find him lowering himself to one knee. He raked a hand through his light brown hair and grinned up at her. Something sparkled on the outstretched palm of his hand. It was a gold ring.

"Marry me, Issy," he said.

Her eyes widened. "Zarek! What are you doing?"

"I'm asking you to marry me."

"You don't know what you're saying." She scanned the area, her face paling. "My father doesn't know you even followed me here to Summerside."

He didn't seem put off by her reaction, as his lips curved to one side. "Maybe today is the perfect day to introduce me to him. Maybe I should ask his permission before I give you this ring. That's probably the right thing to do when dealing with a royal princess, now that I think about it. But you know I'm not so good with following the rules."

"Do you know what he'd do if he found out what you are?" she whispered.

He rose to his feet and took her hands in his. "A warlock?"

She flinched. "Don't say that out loud."

"A warlock who's in love with you. Madly, passionately in love with you, Issy. And we were meant to be together. You and me, we're going to change the world."

Isadora stared at him as if shocked by his words, but then a slow smile spread across her face. "You're mad—do you know that?"

"Maybe a little." He laughed and pulled her against him, kissing her passionately. "Mad about you, from the first moment we met, even if I'm just a lowly warlock."

"One day when I'm queen, perhaps I'll make you a lord. Such old-fashioned official titles have been all but abandoned over the last century, but it has a ring of respectability to it, doesn't it?"

"*Lord Banyon*," he tried, then grinned. "I do like the sound of that. Now, let's forget your father for one moment, okay?"

"Forget about him? He could be watching us right now."

"Let him. The world belongs to us, Issy."

"Mad, definitely mad," she said again, shaking her head, but she was laughing now, as he turned her around in a circle.

"Tell me you love me, Issy," he said.

"I love you," she replied without hesitation.

"Forever?"

"Forever," she agreed.

A wave of golden smoke moved in and moved out, revealing another scene. The sun was lower in the sky, but Zarek and Isadora wore the same clothes as before, so I assumed it was the same day.

"Wait here," she said, her voice hushed. "This should only take a minute."

"I'm counting down the seconds." Zarek grasped her chin, leaning forward to give her a quick peck on the lips. "Then I'm taking you for something to eat, something sweet. Something your father wouldn't approve of. And then I'm asking you that question again, and I'll ask it every day until you say yes."

"Like it's that easy for me?"

He shrugged. "You'll be queen one day. Everything is easy for you, Issy."

She raised a brow. "Change the world, huh?"

"Only for the better."

"I'll be right back, Lord Banyon." She gave him a wink, then slipped through the gates of a large home I recognized as the royal vacation home, the same one I knew that Elian had been at when he'd drowned in the same blue ocean they'd been looking at earlier.

Banyon watched Isadora swiftly approach the house and disappear inside. He turned and waved at a couple guards standing nearby, who watched him with narrowed gazes.

"Good afternoon," he said. "Just going to wait for the princess here. It's her birthday today, you know. By the way, she's in love in me, and the feeling's mutual."

They had nothing to say in reply to that.

I twisted my hands and waited, along with Banyon, until, perhaps ten minutes later, Isadora exited the house and walked slowly back to him.

"Well?" he said.

"You need to leave," she said, without any lightness in her voice. She didn't meet his eyes directly.

He blinked. "Leave?"

"You shouldn't have come here."

"I . . . don't know what you're talking about. What happened? Did the king say something to upset you?"

"Not at all. He just made me realize that this, you and me—it's not going to happen. I should have told you that there's someone else, somebody I like more, who's much more appropriate for me."

A shadow crossed Zarek's expression. "Who?"

"Gregor. My boyfriend. My . . . fiancé, actually."

Annoyance flashed through his gaze. "I don't even know who the hell Gregor is or what the hell you're talking about, Issy!"

"It was fun while it lasted." She shrugged a shoulder. "But I'm done now. I'm seventeen; I need to be taking my responsibilities at the palace more seriously."

"You said you loved me!"

"I lied." She raised her chin. "We're done, Zarek. That's final. Don't come back here or I'll be forced to tell my father what you are."

His eyes widened. "You wouldn't do that."

"I would. And I will. Goodbye, Zarek."

She turned away from him.

"Issy, wait!" he called after her.

She gestured toward the guards, who moved in without hesitating. They grabbed Zarek's arms and started to drag him away from the gate.

"Don't resist," she told him over her shoulder. "I don't want you dead. I only want you out of my sight forever."

As the guards dragged him away, he let them without summoning even a spark of magic in defense. The pain and confusion in his gaze made me wince.

And a ribbon of golden smoke moved in, winding through the scene before me.

"No, stop," I told it, holding up my hand. "I'm not done yet."

I didn't let any doubt creep into my voice or my mind. I didn't need the memory box for this to work. I had control over these echoes now. I wouldn't allow myself to believe otherwise, not anymore. I'd wasted far too much time doubting my own abilities.

As if obeying my command, the smoke stopped, then immediately began to recede. My heart pounded as I concentrated on moving the scene backward, instinctively using my hand as if to rewind the swift and painful breakup I'd just witnessed. I watched as Isadora retraced her steps to the house, Zarek waiting, pacing. I rewound the echo until I reached the right spot. Then I released my invisible control over the memory magic and let it play out again, starting from where he kissed her softly, briefly, for what he didn't realize would be the last time.

"Then I'm taking you for something to eat, something sweet," he told her. "Something your father wouldn't approve of. And then I'm asking you that question again, and I'll ask it every day until you say yes."

"Like it's that easy for me?"

"You'll be queen one day. Everything is easy for you, Issy."

"Change the world, huh?"

"Only for the better."

"I'll be right back, Lord Banyon."

This time I trailed after her as she walked away, toward the house, leaving Zarek at the gates. I watched as she slid her hands over her stomach, her expression filled with hope, as a genuine smile played at her lips.

I followed her into the house, not allowing myself to give in to the doubt that had already begun to creep in: that I was so far away from Banyon's experience of this moment. I wouldn't doubt. I wouldn't question. I simply allowed myself to observe, taking in as much of the scene as I could.

I followed the seventeen-year-old Isadora along a marble-tiled hallway, up a winding stairwell, past beautiful portraits and priceless pieces of artwork—a few of which I recognized from the display of Banyon's stolen treasures at the Queen's Gala. Finally, she reached a large sitting room, lined with wooden shelves that stretched to the high ceiling. On these shelves, to my surprise, were books made of paper. Thousands of them.

I didn't let myself get distracted by this rare sight of the physical objects that had since been reduced to digital-only content. Jericho told me it was easier for the queen to revise or rewrite a digital book, as opposed to paper ones, so she could control history and information consumed by the general public.

"Isadora, come sit with me." It was the deep voice of King Dannis, the queen's father. He had a thick black beard and bushy eyebrows. He sat in a large leather armchair, holding a lit pipe in one hand.

Isadora sat in a chair opposite him, her back straight, placing her hands on her knees. "You wanted to see me, Father?"

"I did. Tell me, is your warlock boyfriend waiting for you outside?" he asked.

Her eyes widened a fraction before she appeared to compose herself. "I don't know what you're talking about."

"Let's not play games. Not today. The boy you think you've been secretly seeing for months now, I know that his name is Zarek Banyon. I know that he can summon fire magic. And I know that you imagine yourself in love with him."

She twisted her hands. "Father, it's not what you think."

"So, you're not carrying his child right now, as we speak?" At her look of abject horror, he waved a hand. "You will marry Gregor, the boy I'd already chosen as your future husband. He's vastly more appropriate. Your marriage will take place next month. No one needs to know the child is anyone's but his."

"Father, no." Her voice was hoarse now.

"The subject is closed. That is, if you want to keep the child within you, for I can make another choice when it comes to that if you continue to push me."

Her eyes glistened, and she appeared to be fighting an inner storm. "I accept your decision, Father."

"Good." The king grasped the arms of his chair and gave her a steady look. "Now, on to other important subjects. It's time, Isadora. You're seventeen. And you will now learn the truth, a truth I've known since my own seventeenth birthday. When you learn this truth, you will understand why it must be this way. Are you ready?"

She composed herself, even running a hand over her dark hair as if to neaten it. It did nothing to mask the doubt in her eyes at going from one dramatic subject to the next in the span of a few heartbeats. "Of course I'm ready. I've been waiting all my life to learn the royal secret."

"You cannot tell anyone but your heir on their seventeenth birthday. Do you understand this?"

"Yes, Father. I understand."

I realized I was holding my breath as I waited for him to speak again.

The king stood up and began pacing the room. "Zarek Banyon is a warlock. You know what we do to warlocks."

I frowned. Back to Banyon again?

Isadora nodded, her expression pained. "Yes."

"It is the way it has been for centuries now. Magic is evil, a blight upon humanity."

"I know."

"And you believe it."

"Yes, Father."

"Those who are tainted by magic are born evil."

"Yes." Her voice quavered. "I believe that."

"And yet you would still allow yourself to become involved with someone like Zarek Banyon." His gaze hardened. "Perhaps you're weak willed, Isadora."

"No, Father. I'm not. I'm strong, like you. Zarek . . ." She inhaled sharply. "He's different."

"He's not. All magic is evil. There are no exceptions to this rule. However, only the smallest of percentages of mages are currently a true threat to the Empire. Centuries ago, this was not the way. A war began, between those who could channel powerful magic, and those who could not. So many died needless deaths. For a time, there was the risk of total annihilation, the literal end of the world, here in the Empire and beyond." He gestured at the shelves. "There are books here that document those days. They are very dangerous books, Isadora, that tell dangerous truths. Books that can't be found anywhere else since their very existence poses a threat to the Empire."

She listened, utterly silently now. As did I.

"Our family's rightful and ultimate power was given to us by the universe itself, so we can rule over all, and this power needs to be constantly maintained. It has taken generations to erase all evidence of the truth, Isadora—the horrible truth. And it is this: Magic stains the soul of every living being who walks the face of this earth. Every one of us is infected by this inescapable evil. Every one of us wakes each morning with the potential to lose ourselves in it. And that is why we must fight back against it."

I wasn't sure I heard him right.

Isadora frowned, shaking her head, just as confused as me. "Everyone? No, that's impossible. Mages are arrested and executed when discovered. They are a small minority, a rare affliction. A mutation."

"*Everyone*," he repeated. "Magic is a disease that we are all afflicted with, a disease with no cure, only an ongoing treatment.

And the best treatment, the treatment that has worked with the most success over time, is ignorance. If one is led to believe that they are not born with this darkness within them, they will not be tempted to explore the depths of their own potential depravity. Therefore, they will pose no threat to the Empire, or to their own souls. Over the centuries, this horrible truth has thankfully been forgotten, and any magical abilities rendered dormant, except in the rarest of cases. Like the warlock who has fooled you into believing he cares for you."

"Everyone in the world is born with magic within them? Even you and me?" she repeated, still shaking her head as if to deny this.

"Yes," he replied grimly. "Magic is everywhere, Isadora. Magic is life itself."

"And magic is evil."

"Yes."

She raised wide eyes to him. "But we're not evil."

"Only through living correctly can we be saved from the darkness. We are strong, Isadora. But others . . . they are weak. If this truth was ever fully revealed, it would result in anarchy. Chaos. The end of the world. And, yes, we must sacrifice a few in executions for the sake of the many, because fear is a powerful tool for a king, the most powerful tool of all. You will learn to use it wisely and well when you become queen. I will give you books to study so you will understand. Handwritten journals of your ancestors who carried the burden of this secret with them. Do you understand what I've told you here today and why it's so important that you keep this secret as I have?"

"Yes," she whispered. "Because if I don't, it will destroy the world."

"Exactly. Now go and tell the boy that you will never see him again."

Her gaze shot to his. "But—"

"Tell him, or he will be executed today, and I will make you watch." Her look of horror didn't make him flinch in the slightest. "Choose well, daughter. I too was in love with someone inappropriate on my seventeenth birthday. I told her what I'd learned and she paid a very high price for my mistake. It was a harsh but necessary lesson. There is no going back to the girl you were yesterday. Today, you begin your preparations to take over my throne. This is your birthright as my heir. The Empire is all that matters. Legacy is all that matters. At any cost."

I watched as a hardness slowly spread across Isadora's face, and she nodded slowly. "At any cost," she repeated.

When the golden smoke moved in this time, I didn't try to stop it. I didn't try to rewind the scene before me or explore it any further. I was too stunned. Of everything I'd imagined the secret to be, this was definitely not it.

In moments, I'd returned to the banquet hall, the queen's hand in mine. She searched my face, frowning. Even though it had felt like I'd been gone for a significant amount of time, for her it was only a few moments.

"Your nose is bleeding," the queen said with concern, quickly handing me a napkin. "Are you all right?"

I dabbed at my nose absentmindedly as I stared at the queen with shock.

Not thousands who were mages, unaware of what they really were. Not millions, like Banyon believed.

Everyone. Everywhere.

For a moment, I honestly thought I was going to be sick. Right there at the head table.

"Where were you just now?" the queen said under her breath, her brows drawn together. "It was as if, for a minute, you were in a trance."

I shook my head, reaching for the glass in front of me and taking a shaky sip of water. "It's nothing."

I needed time to process this, what it meant. How could all these years have passed and no one but the heir to the throne know this secret? How much had been suppressed, how many killed, how many books and journals destroyed, to keep the world from knowing the truth?

"The more I think about it," the queen said, "the more I wonder if Zarek was telling the truth about the magic within you. The . . . memory box. Did you see something disturbing, Josslyn?"

I shook my head, trying my best to summon my calm-and-collected self, the one with all the necessary social graces.

I felt her hand on mine, drawing my attention to her again.

"You look quite unwell, my dear," she said with concern.

"I'm fine," I assured her.

Fine, I thought, *for someone whose world just imploded for the second time this month. Or . . . was it the third?*

This was the secret Elian now kept, that he didn't want to

share. I understood why, and why he thought it would destroy the world.

I disagreed with him on that, but I understood why he'd feel that way.

The truth wasn't world destroying. It was world *changing*. The second had a future, albeit uncertain—the first did not. I guess I was an optimist.

So much made sense now that had never made sense before.

The queen searched my face for several moments, her expression tense, before she gestured toward Commander Norris, who lingered at the edge of the ballroom. "Escort Josslyn to Dr. Collins's current location immediately," she said. "That will take care of this."

"I don't need a doctor," I told her.

"I will have to insist." She leaned closer. "The magic is clearly causing you distress. I was afraid of this. Go with the commander and consult with Dr. Collins. In a few minutes, all will be right with the world again."

It wasn't ideal, but I decided to go with this without further argument. The queen thought I had a headache, brought on by an unpleasant reaction to the memory magic. She wasn't far off, but there was nothing Tamara could do about it.

Talking to Tamara about what I'd seen might help me sort through the details and figure out my next move.

Grudgingly, I stood up and began to follow Norris out of the banquet hall.

Celina sent a curious glance toward me from the other side of the head table, and I could only give her a pained shrug before I followed Norris out of the room, quickly heading along an unfamiliar hallway.

I didn't like being this close to the commander. He'd been a presence in my life for as long as I could remember, and I'd always liked him well enough. Now that I knew what he'd done, how easily and remorselessly he'd killed an innocent and defenseless woman at the queen's command, those memories were irrevocably tainted.

Did he know the truth?

No. If the queen hadn't shared what she'd asked Viktor to do, she wouldn't share the big secret. She'd kept it, all this time. The former king had believed, heart and soul, that magic was evil, and therefore everyone was born evil, only able to redeem themselves by sheer ignorance or absolute restraint.

But the queen was different. She'd had a magic advisor and raised her own son from the dead with magic. She wasn't a true believer like her father was.

That made her even worse, in my opinion.

It wasn't long at all before we came to a steel door, with two guards stationed in front of it. Norris nodded at them, and they opened it up. I saw Elian inside, sitting at a small white table in a large dark room, his hands clasped tightly in front of him. He raised his black-eyed gaze to mine, his expression flat and strangely soulless.

"What's he doing here?" I asked, confused. "Is Tamara trying to help him again?"

"Something like that," Norris muttered. He gestured at the guards, who roughly took hold of my arms.

I looked at them with alarm. "Wait . . . what are you doing?"

Before I could fully register what was happening, they shoved me into the room with the prince, closing the door in my face.

A moment later, I heard the lock click heavily into place, and I realized what was happening—why the queen had asked Norris to bring me here.

She sensed that I knew something I shouldn't know.

And I'd just been offered up as a meal for her son.

TWENTY-THREE

That doubt I'd worked so hard to push away was back with a vengeance.

Elian watched me through his pitch-black eyes, and it felt all too much like a lethal predator watching its helpless prey just before it moved in for the kill.

"Joss?" A voice from the shadowy corner of the room, thin and reedy.

I turned to see Tamara sitting there, hugging her knees to her chest, in an attempt to make herself as small as possible.

Keeping one eye on Elian, I moved toward her as calmly as I could.

"Talk," I managed. "What happened here?"

"The queen wanted me to try again, even though she knows very well that my magic does nothing to help him." Her fearful gaze darted toward the prince. "Every time, I feel something pulling at me . . . something trying to devour my magic when I'm attempting to heal him. It's frightening. That's when I push away, but it's only made it worse."

"Did the queen tell you everything about Elian?" I asked.

"No. But I can feel the death magic inside of him."

"Like Jericho's."

She shook her head. "No, not like Jericho's. This is . . . deeper, infused with every cell of the prince's body. I told you Jericho's magic was like ink absorbed by a sponge. Permanent, but not originally a part of who he is. With the prince, this dark magic feels like it *is* him."

I chewed my bottom lip, nodding. What she said, as disturbing as it was, started to make sense to me.

Elian was like Valery.

Valery must have sensed this—that Elian was born with the same ability as she was.

"I think he was born with the ability to channel death magic," I said aloud. Finally, things were clicking into place for me when it came to Elian's unusual ailment. "And then he was raised from the dead. Death magic on top of death magic—it seems it's created a void inside of him. A dark, nasty, bottomless death-void that constantly needs life to fill it."

Elian hadn't moved yet, although he continued to silently study me and Tamara as we spoke.

"Do you think I'm right?" I asked her. "You're the expert."

"I don't think you're wrong," she replied. "I'd heard stories of death magic coming naturally, but that's all I thought they were. Stories. I didn't believe it was possible—for a mage to be so different from others of our kind."

Others of our kind.

She had no idea how many of our kind there were.

The weight of my new knowledge sat like a huge, jagged

boulder in my chest, and I sent a wary glance toward Elian again. I hadn't told the queen what I knew, or the extent of the memory magic within me, but . . . somehow, she'd sensed it.

She knew that I knew far too much. And that finally had made her see me as a threat.

Now she wanted to solve three problems in one locked room: Get rid of a witch with rebel ties who hadn't proven as useful as the queen had originally hoped. Get rid of someone who'd come to learn too many royal secrets for her own good. Lastly, find a way to satisfy her cursed son's hunger for another month or two. At least now I officially knew where I stood with Her Majesty. She might have honestly liked me as much as she'd always claimed, but I was expendable, especially now that my birth father was in custody, powerless, and at her mercy.

I focused on Elian again. "I know the royal secret you carry, and it's . . . well, it's a big one. But you're not alone anymore."

His eyes narrowed by a fraction. "I *am* alone," he whispered, "and I'm very hungry. I—I'm sorry, but I can't control this for much longer."

His voice was so hollow and soulless that it sent a violent shiver coursing down my spine.

He's going to kill us, I thought with a cold sense of certainty.

No. I couldn't give in to doubt—not here, not now, not ever again.

But doubt was a persistent little bitch. And she'd brought along her even-less-attractive friend "despair" as her party guest.

"Well, Elian, I have good news and bad news for you," I

told him, keeping my voice as strong as I could, despite the dire situation.

He didn't say anything, so I continued.

"The good news is that Valery is here, at the launch party. And I'm guessing she probably has that very special magic dagger with her. I mean, if I had a dagger like that, I'd take it with me everywhere I went."

Relief entered his gaze, and he managed a shallow nod.

"The bad news," I continued, "is we're locked in here, with at least two armed guards outside, and I'm willing to bet the queen only expects you to leave this room alive. So, unless you can hold on to that appetite of yours indefinitely, we're all screwed."

I shared a heavy look with Tamara.

"We are screwed," she confirmed.

"Not helpful." I glared at her. "Can't you do anything? You're a witch."

"So are you," she countered.

"Yeah, well, I have a big chunk of contained memory magic standing in between me and any potential elementia, so unfortunately, I'm going to be exactly zero help at the moment."

Tamara shook her head. "I've only used my magic to help others, not to harm. I'm sorry."

"Don't be sorry—just help me figure out how to fix this mess. You know more about death magic than I do."

"That's not saying much, is it?"

I turned to fully face the prince. "Elian, I need you to be strong right now."

He was shaking his head. "I'm losing it, Joss. You're not safe here."

"That's what your mother is hoping for. But you can't let her win. The secret—the royal secret. I see how much of a burden it is for you, but I believe you can change everything. You're different from her; you care that you've hurt people who don't deserve it. I don't believe you would ever agree to rule the Empire with fear as your sharpest weapon, keeping the truth from everyone indefinitely."

"What do you think you know?" he asked, his voice low.

"That everyone in the world is born with the potential to summon elementia. That elementia is more than just magic—it's life itself. But we've all forgotten the truth. It's been erased from history by your predecessors, and the lie was maintained by your mother. And once people forget what they're capable of, or they're afraid of something, they don't even try to be anything more than what they are. They've been conditioned to believe they're powerless, so they *are* powerless. Am I close?"

Elian's black eyes widened. "Very close."

"Your mother believed the lie that this could destroy the world, but I disagree. It would destroy your family's legacy when it comes to your hold on absolute, undeniable power . . . yes, it sure the hell would. And I know that's a lot to give up, and everything will be very chaotic and hugely complicated for a long time as people figure out what the future should look like. But they'll figure it out."

"How do you know that?"

I shrugged. "I just do. I also know that you can fight this. That you shouldn't just give up. You're not a monster. You're not powerless. You're someone with an incurable disease. And diseases can be treated."

"You make it sound so simple," he muttered, his brow deeply creased with a frown.

"What if it is that simple?" I countered, quickly thinking it through and casting a look at Tamara. "You've been trying to heal him, but that's impossible. This void inside of him that a double dose of death magic carved out . . . maybe it can't be fixed, not permanently . . ."

I remembered the night at Deluxe, when Valery had almost killed me.

"*She had Daria come over and . . . do something*," Jericho had explained when I woke up three days later. "*It was like Valery had stolen something from inside of you, and Daria—well, she wasn't healing you, exactly. It was more like she was restoring what Val took . . . like filling up an empty tank with earth magic.*"

"The void needs to be filled," I told Tamara. "And when it empties, it needs to be refilled. Do you understand?"

She frowned deeply, her expression pensive, but then she nodded. "Yes, I think so."

"Everyone has their own taste," Elian said absently, and all remaining emotion had vanished from his voice, leaving it flat and cold and very scary. "Earth, air, water, fire . . . I know what element each person holds within them. Some are sweet, some salty, and some are spicy."

"Sounds like an interesting buffet," I managed uneasily, backing away from him as he began to approach me. "Tamara?"

But then the prince was right in front of me, his hands gripping my shoulders. His fingers pressed so deeply into my flesh that I knew there would be bruises left behind.

His black eyes met mine.

"I can already taste your magic, so close to the surface compared to all the others," Elian rasped. "I taste air, light and flowing. I taste earth, sweet and fresh."

My magic, he'd said.

"No," I managed. "That's the layer of memory magic that's stuck in me. Banyon's memory magic. I want to tell you all about it, Elian—everything I've seen. Everything I've learned. Just take a breath and listen to me, okay?"

But the prince was now beyond the ability to listen or rationalize his actions. He was gone, replaced by the beast I'd first met in the Queen's Keep, a creature driven only by his insatiable hunger.

A hunger for the magic that lies within all of us.

And, currently, the magic that lay within *me*.

Elian drew even closer to me, his mouth open, his face now appearing frighteningly corpse-like, angular and hollow. A scream caught in my throat, and I started to feel a painful pulling sensation from deep within my being. I watched with horror as a thin, wispy line of golden smoke exited my mouth and entered his.

I couldn't speak. I couldn't move. I could only watch him inhale my magic, strand by strand, his eyes as black as death. The room seemed to darken more than it already was, and I had to fight to stay conscious. Distantly, I noticed Tamara trying to pull at Elian's arm, pull him away from me, but it was in vain.

"*Magic is life*," King Dannis had told the teenaged Isadora.

And Elian was taking my magic. Devouring my life.

I heard a heavy, metallic crashing sound, the sound of a steel door being wrenched off its hinges. A moment later, Jericho appeared, his expression fierce, his gaze dark and fixed on the prince.

"I don't think so," he growled, grabbing Elian by his throat and shoving him hard across the room until the prince slammed into the wall.

I sank down to my knees, the world still a dark and distant echo, and watched as Jericho drew a knife out from beneath the black overcoat of his stolen Queensguard uniform. The Blackheart braced his forearm against the prince's chest, the sharp blade against his throat.

"No!" I managed to cry out.

"Not now, Drake," Jericho told me. "I need to fulfill my promise to Lazos and finally kill this beast."

"You can't do that!"

"Oh, but I can. And I think he's going to let me. Aren't you, Your Highness?"

"Do it," Elian managed. "Please, stop me from hurting anyone else."

"Done."

"Jericho, stop." I pushed up to my feet. "I think Tamara can help him."

"Hey, Tamara." The Blackheart acknowledged the witch without moving his focus away from Elian for an instant. "Good to see you again. Mika's not far behind me, so you guys can get the hell out of here and not look back. Don't worry about the guards. I took care of them with a little Dust, so they'll be in dreamland for a while. You're welcome."

The witch's pale expression held only determination now, the fear gone from her gaze. Her fists clenched at her sides. "Step aside and let me try to help Prince Elian."

"Why would you want to do something like that?" he asked.

"Because I'm a doctor and that's what I do."

A thin line of blood trickled down Elian's throat as Jericho considered this, his jaw so tense it looked like it might shatter.

"What do you think, Your Highness?" he bit out. "You nearly killed Drake just now—why would I give you the chance to finish the job?"

"I have a fraction of my control back now," Elian replied tightly. "Enough to hold on for a few more minutes."

"If you're lying to me, I will make you hurt. And if you can bleed, you can die. This might not be Val's dagger, but it will still do a whole lot of damage. I don't care how strong you are—you will lose. Understand?"

"I understand."

I watched from my weakened puddle-like position on the floor as Jericho reluctantly withdrew his blade from Elian's throat and took a step back.

"Do what you have to do," he gruffly told Tamara. "And do it quickly."

She nodded, took a deep breath, and approached the prince, who eyed her warily.

"Do you know how to heal me now?" he asked, and I heard a heartbreaking sliver of hope in his words.

"No," Tamara replied. "Joss is right. I don't think there's any true healing for the disease you have. But there might be a treatment. Elementia is a renewable resource, bottomless, endless. I am not going to try to heal you with my earth magic this time. I'm going to . . . offer it to you freely. You don't have to take it forcibly from me; you only have to accept it."

Elian searched her face, frowning, and then he gave her a shallow nod. "I understand."

"Good." Tamara sent a worried look at me, but then I saw the doubt leave her gaze, replaced by determination. She returned her attention to the prince, placing her hands on either side of his face. "Don't take," she reminded him. "Only accept. If you're currently in control of your hunger like you say you are, then this should be possible."

And then she closed her eyes and her hands began to glow with golden light. Elian closed his eyes as well and let out a shuddery sigh.

Jericho came to my side, sweeping my hair back from my face, his expression pained. "Drake, are you okay? Did he hurt you?"

"I don't know," I whispered. "I think I'm okay. I'm still breathing."

"Always a good sign. I guess I got here just in time." He held out his hand to me and helped me to my feet while Tamara and Elian continued their experimental transfer of magic.

"I don't know about that," I told him. With trembling fingers, I removed my contact lenses. "Are my eyes still gold?"

He gently took my face between his hands, gazing down at me with a frown. "No. Definitely blue now."

My stomach clenched at the confirmation. "Shit. The memory magic . . ."

"It made for a tasty meal for the prince," he finished.

I nodded. "I think it's gone."

The Blackheart grimaced. "That used to be the goal for you. Not so much anymore, huh?"

"Not so much," I agreed, my throat thick.

Elian had taken what he needed from me, fed on my magic, but only the first layer held within me before Jericho stopped him. The contained magic. Magic with a beginning and an end, that could be kept inside a golden box and sampled by someone who wanted to revisit their memories.

It was gone. Banyon's memories, the echoes of his past. All of them.

They were gone.

And I didn't know how I really felt about that. At the moment, it felt a lot like grief. Like I'd lost something I'd barely begun to appreciate.

I chanced a look at Elian to see he and Tamara were still locked in their treatment session. The golden light from her hands had formed tendrils of magic that moved over the prince's face, penetrating his mouth, his nostrils, his eyes with earth magic.

"Enough," Elian finally whispered, pushing her hands away from him. "I think that's enough for now."

Tamara took a shaky step back from him, wiping her brow with the back of her hand.

Slowly, Elian opened his black eyes again. We all waited, breathless, to hear what he would say.

"I feel better," he said, his words shaky. "Better than I've felt in a very long time. Thank you."

Tamara let out a sigh of relief. "It worked." She looked at me. "I think he'll need this sort of treatment regularly, before he feels any hunger. It's preventative."

"Like having a big salad before you go to a feast," I agreed, giddy with our success. At Jericho's look, I shrugged. "That analogy works for me, okay?"

"Good enough for me," he agreed. "The prince is on a permanent, controlled diet, so he doesn't binge eat."

"Basically," Tamara confirmed.

Her gaze moved to the opening in the room where the door once had been. I had to assume that Jericho had torn it off its hinges with help from his Blackheart superstrength.

Mika stood there, also wearing a Queensguard uniform, her wide gaze fixed on Tamara.

"You're alive," she managed.

Tamara's eyes welled with tears. "Jericho was telling the truth. You're really here. What are you doing here?"

"Rescuing you. Or . . . trying to." Mika swept her gaze over the room, taking in each of us before landing on Prince Elian. She grimaced, but otherwise ignored him.

"Mika. Do me a favor?" I asked her.

"First time for everything," she replied.

I had to laugh at that. Not much, but a little. "Get Tamara out of here and don't look back."

"Done and done," she agreed.

"One more thing?" said Jericho.

Mika looked at him. "What?"

"Try not to get captured again five minutes from now. That would be awesome."

"Right back at you. I guess we're even now, Blackheart." Mika gave him a grin before she embraced Tamara very tightly. "I was so worried about you."

"Worried enough to help my mother kidnap Celina Ambrose and nearly get herself killed in the process?" Tamara countered.

"Yes, *that* worried." The tremble in Mika's voice betrayed her frayed emotions.

"I missed you," Tamara said, holding Mika's face between her hands and gazing into her girlfriend's eyes. "I missed you."

"I missed you more," Mika replied fiercely. "Now, let's get the hell out of here."

Tamara turned to embrace me, and I held on tightly for several moments. Considering we'd both almost died only minutes ago, it felt like we'd forged a deep bond.

"Thank you," I told her. "For everything."

"Take care of yourself," she replied.

"You too. And, like Jericho said, don't get yourself captured again, okay?"

She laughed. "I'm going to try much harder this time."

"Good luck, you two." Mika gave me a nod as she took Tamara's hand. And then they were gone.

"You know," Jericho began, "I feel like I said something about you keeping a low profile tonight."

"Parties can be so unpredictable," I replied with a shrug.

"Clearly."

When he turned toward the opening to the room, a Queensguard now stood there, blocking him. A very familiar Queensguard.

Jericho's form went rigid. "Viktor."

"You're alive." Viktor's voice was no more than a whisper.

"I am. And . . . I'd really like to stay that way if given the option."

"Jer . . . I'm . . ." Viktor took a moment to compose himself, straightening his shoulders and raising his chin. "You shouldn't have come back here. You must know that by now, don't you?"

"And yet," Jericho said, spreading his hands, "I can't seem to stay away. Something about this palace calls to me like nothing else."

"First name Josslyn, last name Drake?" Viktor guessed, giving me a dirty look.

A shadow moved across Jericho's face. "Is this going to be a problem right now, you and me?"

Viktor said nothing for several moments, holding his older brother's tense gaze with one of his own. Finally, he holstered his gun.

"No problem. Get out of here while you still can."

Jericho hesitated. "Really?"

"Do I have to say it twice?"

"No. Once is more than enough. Thanks, Vik."

The brothers held each other's gazes, and it felt as if they had a heavy, unspoken conversation between them.

"Are . . . we going to hug it out?" Jericho asked, raising his brows.

"Maybe some other time," Viktor replied, and the barest

edge of a grin touched his lips. Then his gaze shifted to Elian.

"Your Highness, let me take you back to your chambers."

Elian nodded. "Very well."

I grabbed the prince's arm as he moved past me, and he met my eyes.

"The royal secret," I whispered. "You could change everything if you wanted to. You could right so many wrongs."

Elian's lips thinned, a frown drawing his brows together. "It's not as easy as you make it sound."

"It's the easiest thing in the world."

His expression turned grim, and he left with Viktor without saying another word.

"Win some, lose some," Jericho said. "So, the prince's tank is full; life is good again. For a few minutes, at least. What now, Drake?"

My first impulse was to escape from here again, right on Tamara and Mika's heels. Maybe join them in forming a rebel faction to pick up the fight where Lord Banyon had faltered after all these years. Even without Elian's help, we could start to share the royal secret with as many people who would listen to us.

But that would have to wait for just a bit.

"I need to go back to the party—" I began.

"No," he cut me off.

I blinked. "You didn't let me finish. I need to get a message to Celina. I can't disappear on her again."

"Bad idea."

"I also need to locate potential allies, which was my original plan."

"It's a bad idea." At my look of determination, he groaned. "But, fine. Let's go be rebels."

TWENTY-FOUR

Jericho may not have been happy about my decision, but he grudgingly accompanied me along a series of hallways leading back to the party, grumbling all the way. The uniform he wore helped him move about freely, without drawing any suspicions as he walked a few paces behind me like a proper palace guard.

In the banquet hall, the dinner plates had been cleared away, the lights dimmed, and the queen had taken her position behind the podium to give her speech.

Of course, I didn't take my previous seat at the head table next to the woman who'd just tried to murder me. Instead, I stayed at the back of the room, out of sight of the head table, with Jericho now at my side.

He swore under his breath. "Valery's here?"

I gave him a surprised look. "I thought you already knew that?"

"Hardly. I haven't seen her since my most recent death."

"What?"

His expression tensed. "What Banyon said, about fighting against her magic—that she's not a goddess, she's just a damn powerful witch with a magic knife. I hate to admit it, but I think he was right. It hurts like hell sometimes. But the pain of resistance comes in waves. The longer I've stayed away from my boss from hell, the less frequent the waves are becoming."

My heart skipped a beat at this unexpected news. "So, you're free?"

"Let's not get ahead of ourselves, Drake. So far, this is only an experiment."

Even so, I found the news that he'd spent three weeks away from Valery deeply encouraging.

Behind the podium, there was a large screen that showed the Empire's official crest. After the speeches, when the queen and Viktor moved over to the press room, the party guests could remain in this private room and watch the question-and-answer session from the comfort of their tables. And at that point, I could make my move—without the queen to interfere, I could mingle freely, find allies where I could. Now that I knew everyone had the potential for magic, I didn't have to work from a list. I just had to find the most sympathetic ear.

Of course, Elian could change everything with just a few simple words and make my mission unnecessary. But I couldn't count on that.

"Good evening to you all," the queen said, as poised and elegant as someone who hadn't just coldly sentenced two people to death-by-heir. "Thank you, my friends, for joining me here tonight for a celebration that marks the beginning of the Queensgames—our great, honored competition of strength, courage, and endurance."

Elian will change his mind, I thought, only partially listening to the queen's speech. *He has to. Give him enough time and he'll see that it's the only way.*

Another voice, that pesky doubt that hadn't gotten the hint that it wasn't welcome in my head anymore, had a different opinion.

Why would he? If I found a way for him to manage his problem, then he's back to being a pampered and spoiled prince, totally in control of his new life. The queen's manipulative enough that I wouldn't put it past her to find a way, find a story, that could reintegrate Elian back into the public eye as her heir. Why would he give that up?

Good question, Doubt.

The queen was still talking, clearly enjoying the sound of her own voice. "I would like to begin this night by officially announcing that Regis Ambrose will be stepping down from his position as prime minister in order to focus on some important personal matters."

My brows shot up, and I sent a look at the prime minister in question, who was doing a very poor job of covering up his shock at the queen's words. Was this news to him?

"Thank you so very much, Regis." The queen turned to look at him, a thin smile on her lips. "Thank you for agreeing to temporarily fill in after the loss of our beloved Louis Drake last year until I found a permanent replacement for this very important job. Your work and dedication won't be forgotten anytime soon."

There was a murmuring at the tables, as guests whispered to each other. Ambrose drained his latest glass of wine, and Celina sat stoically next to him, a pleasant smile fixed upon her lips.

Had my best friend been keeping something from me?

Contrary to her father, she showed no surprise at all at this shocking announcement. I had to wonder if Celina had said something to the queen to put doubt in her mind about Ambrose's trustworthiness.

Ambrose would never speak up against this decision now that it had been made public. His days as prime minister, and his grasp on a stolen title and place of power within the Empire, were officially over.

It wasn't true vengeance, but it was pretty damn close.

"I still want to kill him," Jericho muttered to me, as if reading my mind.

"Oh, me too," I agreed. "No question about it."

"Now, back to the Queensgames," the queen said brightly. I searched for some sign of the young woman I'd seen in the echo, a princess in love with a warlock, secretly pregnant with his son, whose life had changed in a matter of minutes. But I saw nothing. Maybe her time with Banyon had been only a momentary distraction, the whims of a spoiled teenager who'd enjoyed flirting with danger and rebellion for a few exciting months.

My feelings toward the queen had been all over the place, with that pesky doubt raising its head far too often. I'd started to believe in her again, despite her past decisions. Over the last couple of weeks, I'd begun to lean into the comfort of her lies.

And then she'd shown me who she was really was, and I wouldn't ever forget that painful lesson again.

"The Queensgames showcases the boldest warriors from the four corners of the Empire who are given the chance to display their battle skills for the entertainment of all. Let's take a look, shall we?" Queen Isadora then waved a hand at the screen behind her, and it lit up with footage from the last thirty years, and fourteen previous Queensgames. Swords clashing. Sand flying in the faces of fierce rivals. The cheering crowd seated in the massive, open stadium, with the sun shining brightly on their faces. A splash of blood, just to show how high the stakes were, but no death featured in this highlights reel, which finished with a clip of Viktor, his arms raised as high champion, as he stood in the center of the field, surrounded and cheered on by his adoring fans. The camera moved in to show a close-up of his handsome face. Many would interpret the emotion in his eyes as the pride of accomplishment, and the glory of victory.

But, despite his practiced smile, I now saw the grief there.

I reached down and took Jericho's tense hand in mine. His eyes were fixed on the screen.

"He would have helped you escape that night, even if the queen didn't give him that mission," I told him, my voice low. "You must know that now, don't you?"

His jaw was a tight line, but he jerked his head in a nod. "Yeah. I know."

This was probably one of the harder admissions that the Blackheart ever had to make. The truth sure could be complicated.

After the highlights were over, the queen continued to talk for a frustratingly lengthy amount of time about the history of the Queensgames, how it had been her father's idea, but he'd never had a chance to start it before his death.

Right, I thought. *He'd been too busy keeping a lid on the Royal Secret.*

"My father," Queen Isadora said, "had intended the games to

be an opportunity for prisoners to earn their chance at freedom, but I knew that it was much better to have willing volunteers, honorable fighters who would be role models for all of us."

"What a pile of horseshit," Jericho muttered as the audience applauded politely.

I watched them, my gaze moving over the faces I recognized from Banyon's list. But now I knew that there weren't dozens of potential magical bloodlines here at the party. *Everyone* here was from a magical bloodline, whether they knew it or not. The enormity of the truth threatened to overwhelm me, and I still had to process everything I'd learned and what exactly I could do with it when I had no real proof.

It was then that the queen's gaze met mine from across the room.

Shit, I thought. So much for trying to stay in the shadows.

Her words faltered for a moment. My heart jumped in my chest, but I refused to look away from her and forced myself to defiantly stand my ground.

I know the truth now, I thought, narrowing my eyes at her. *And your secret is definitely not safe with me.*

Queen Isadora raised her chin. "Many of you tonight are, I'm sure, curious to know more about my own recent victory. It's something I haven't spoken about publicly before tonight, but this is a night of celebration. It's been sixteen years since the tragic palace fire ended so many lives. Sixteen years that Lord Zarek Banyon has been a constant threat against my empire and its innocent, law-abiding citizens. The threat is now over, and thanks to my hardworking and loyal army, we can finally claim victory over the darkness that has cast a shadow over the Empire of Regara all these years."

I hated her. I hated that she was so smug and self-congratulatory, and that she clearly didn't see me as a threat in any way. I looked forward to the day that I would personally wipe that smile off her lying, royal face.

"At the Queen's Gala," she continued, still holding my gaze, "I was very pleased to share a special exhibit—composed of statues, artwork, and artifacts—that had been stolen by the warlock, retrieved during the raid on his compound. These, I believed, would serve as a metaphor of what this evil man had stolen from all of us over the years during his lengthy reign of terror. Many have asked me when he will be executed, but I've made the decision to spare his life."

Gasps of surprise sounded out across the audience, one of which came out of my own mouth.

"What the hell is she doing?" Jericho muttered.

"Zarek Banyon is gravely ill with a disease caused by the darkness of his evil magic, which has eaten away at him over the years—body, soul, and mind. This disease has stripped away his once-deadly magic, leaving him as harmless as one of his stolen objects of art." A cool smile played at her lips. "I thought it would be fitting to present to you all tonight my new art display, which will be available for viewing here at my palace indefinitely."

She gestured toward a black curtain that covered the wall opposite to the podium, which dropped to reveal a small room, separated from the banquet hall by a thick pane of glass. In this small room, seated upon a chair, was Lord Banyon himself.

"No," I whispered.

I guess I now knew what the queen's big surprise was for the night.

The sight of the queen's new "art display" brought half of the party guests to their feet with shrieks of fear and outrage.

Queen Isadora held up her hands. "I promise, you are completely safe. Just like the Queensgames, this shows that even the fiercest and darkest rival can be defeated. How even destructive magic that once burned so bright can be extinguished. That there is a beginning and there is an end to every problem we face in our lives. And that we, collectively and individually, are stronger today than ever before, despite all that this villain has stolen from us."

Banyon had risen from his chair and now stood with his hands pressed against the glass, watching the queen.

"Look at you," she said, finally allowing a sneer to enter her voice. "My prisoner once again, who lives only due to my mercy. How do you like that, Zarek?"

Banyon said something in reply to her, but I couldn't hear him. The glass was too thick.

"What's he saying?" I asked Jericho.

"I think he's saying . . . *I should have killed you long ago.*" He nodded. "I mean, he's right. He really should have. All in all, this isn't exactly the punishment I would have chosen for the warlock, but it is what it is. Now, let's get the hell out of here while we have this helpful distraction, Drake. Rebel shenanigans can wait for another day."

A trickle of perspiration slid down my back, and I frowned.

"Is it just me or is it getting really warm in here?" I asked uneasily.

Jericho wiped his sleeve over his forehead. "I thought it was this ridiculous uniform, but it's definitely hotter than it was a few minutes ago."

Suddenly, before our eyes, the art display burst into flames. Someone screamed as fire rose up behind the warlock, his hands still pressed to the thick glass barrier.

Only a moment later, the glass shattered into a million sharp pieces, and Lord Banyon calmly stepped out of his public prison.

TWENTY-FIVE

The queen stared at the warlock in shock as he moved toward her, while the party guests all scrambled for the exits. I noticed that the door handles were bright orange, molten hot. Anyone who touched them burned their hands, screaming in pain and staggering backward.

Banyon had sealed the banquet room shut with fire magic.

The queen stumbled back from the warlock, her face sickly pale. "You're powerless!" she cried out as a circle of flames trapped her where she stood. "You have no magic left!"

"Issy, Issy, Issy . . ." Banyon said, shaking his head. "For someone who lies as much as you do, you have always been ignorant to deception in others. Clearly, I have plenty of magic left."

"You're dying!"

He smiled thinly. "I certainly was. But I've been in remission for over two months now and getting stronger every day. A miracle, don't you think?"

She shook her head. "You showed no sign of this for weeks! Not even during your interrogation."

Banyon spread his hands. "And miss this opportunity to see you face-to-face in such an impressive venue?" He swept his gaze across the party guests, now all on the opposite side of the large room. "You see me as your enemy, but I'm not," he addressed them. "I'm more of a friend to you than this creature of darkness you call your queen. She has lied to you, and her predecessors have lied to you for generations, for centuries. The time for lies is over. I believe there are millions of mages in the Empire, and many are here tonight."

I stepped forward, my heart pounding. "You're wrong," I called out.

Banyon raised a brow, locating me standing alone, in front of the crowd that bunched around the doors. "Am I?"

I nodded. "It's not millions. It's billions. It's *everyone*. One hundred percent." I cast a dark look at the queen before returning my attention to the warlock. "I saw the echo you've been searching for. The secret is that magic in born inside of everyone. There are books at the queen's Summerside home that prove this."

Jericho whistled quietly behind me. "You could have given me a heads up on this bombshell, Drake."

I shrugged. "Sorry," I whispered to him, "it's been a busy night."

Just then, someone grabbed me and I shrieked as I felt the sharp jab of a knife against my throat.

"Get on the ground, warlock," High Commander Norris ordered Banyon. "Or your daughter dies, right here and right now."

Banyon faced the commander with a hate-filled gaze. "Just like you killed Eleanor," he bit out.

"Just like," Norris agreed.

Jericho already had his own knife out and pointed at Norris, but I raised my hand to stop him.

"Jericho, no," I said.

He froze, his expression now uncertain. "Damn it, Drake."

He could kill Norris, but even a Blackheart wouldn't be fast enough to stop the high commander from slashing my throat. He knew it. I knew it.

Banyon's hands lit up with fire as he regarded Norris. "You will die tonight, one way or the other. You and Issy."

I yelped as I felt the bite of the blade and the hot trickle of blood. As I looked around the room, I caught Celina's gaze. My best friend's eyes were wide with fear for me, helpless. It was better for her to stay back. I didn't want her to get hurt.

Then I searched for Valery, finding her standing at the front of the frightened crowd. Her arms were folded across her chest, and she watched our standoff with guarded interest. She wasn't going to do a damn thing to stop this. True to form, she had no loyalty to either side of this battle.

"Down on the ground," Norris barked out, nodding at both Banyon and Jericho. "Or the girl dies."

Banyon shook his head. "You are grasping at straws now, an old man kneeling before a queen who rules over an empire of lies. It's over." He swept his arm toward the party guests, and the doors swung open. "They have heard the truth tonight and they'll share it with the world."

The guests didn't hesitate to take the opportunity to escape.

"Let me go," I growled, clutching Norris's forearm.

"Foolish girl," he replied through clenched teeth. "You had it so good here, and the queen valued you, but you refused to be grateful for everything you've been given. The queen should have let me question you when you got back, and all of this could have been avoided."

"She really should have," I agreed distantly.

My fear had opened something new and unfamiliar inside of me, like a door I didn't know was there. I became hyper-aware of the candles on the tables, the flickering flames. The fire that burned inside the broken display. The fire that circled the queen as she gathered the silky material of her gown closer so it wouldn't be set ablaze.

The fire—it called to me. And I remembered what Celina had said about discovering that her element was water. It felt natural, like a part of her that had always been there.

The fire was a part of me. And I had no memory magic anymore to block my access to it. It was more of a subconscious thought, a passing wish, of summoning the fire to me, but it obeyed my command in an instant as my last echo had, coating my hands, my arms, like a brush of warm silk.

A brush of warm silk that lit the sleeve of Norris's uniform on fire. It took him a moment to register what had happened, but by then the fire had burned through the thick material and begun to scorch his flesh. He gasped, immediately releasing me and dropping his blade, batting at the flames. He managed to douse them just as Jericho moved in front of him, the Black-heart's hand coming over the high commander's face as he shoved him across the room.

Norris hit the ground hard, the back of his head smacking against the floor, and his eyes rolled back into his head.

Jericho shared a look with Banyon and shrugged. "He's all yours when he wakes up."

"Thank you," the warlock replied.

"You're welcome."

Celina quickly came to my side, searching my face. "Are you okay?"

"I just lit somebody on fire," I told her, then nodded. "I'm pretty good, actually."

She laughed nervously and grabbed hold of my hand for support—either mine or hers. Probably both.

Other guards had approached, but flames rose before them to hold them back.

Banyon scanned the banquet room before he turned to the queen, his hands still ablaze. "Now that that rude interruption is over, we can continue. Sixteen years, Issy. And here we are again. I was sure you'd have me executed the moment I was captured. Agatha . . . I don't blame her. I may have done the same thing in her situation. She loves her daughter—would have done anything to save her. And I know you'd do the same for Elian. Your precious heir."

"Your son," she managed, then shielded her face when his fire burned brighter and hotter. "Please, Zarek! Spare my life. I'll do anything you want. Anything!"

"All I want from you now, Issy, is to watch you die. But don't worry. The pain will be over far sooner than you deserve."

She screamed as the flames around her rose higher, his

fists blazed brighter, but her death didn't come.

Jericho had the warlock's fiery wrist in his grip. "You don't want to do this."

"Let go of me, Blackheart," Banyon snapped.

"I spent sixteen years wanting to kill you," Jericho growled back. "You stole my parents from me—and the life I should have had. You got to play the starring role as the bad guy in my mind; my entire focus was always on how to get big and strong enough to take you out someday. After that, I had no plans, no goals. Nothing. But Drake's made me realize something—I want more than that. I want a future. I want to leave my pain behind me and start to build something new."

"And, what? You think I want the same?" Banyon asked, his brows drawn together.

"Maybe I do. Queen Isadora ruined your life and you've wanted her dead for years. I understand how that feels. I also understand how much better it feels to make a different choice. The queen's done—don't you see that? What you've said, what Drake's said . . . it's over for her. Maybe not today or tomorrow, but soon. Just like Ambrose over there, cowering in the corner, probably pissing his pants right now." Jericho sent a dark look at the former prime minister, who was wringing his hands from a safe distance away. "Don't worry, I haven't forgotten about you, asshole." Then he focused on the warlock again. "Bottom line: why would you put your old girlfriend out of her misery so easily?"

Banyon stared at Jericho for another intense moment before the flames surrounding the queen extinguished.

"Thank you," the queen gasped at Jericho.

He rolled his eyes. "If you're thanking me, lady, you weren't listening to a damn word I just said."

I watched as the queen attempted to compose herself, brushing off the front of her gown, and patting her hair back into place. She waved off the guards as they approached, weapons drawn. "Well, there's a lot to consider here. I agree—that changes will have to be made. Not all at once. The citizens of the Empire could never handle such a great shock. The truth will be rolled out in stages, over months. Years. Perhaps a decade from now, we can finally see the results of this proposed shift in perception. I am willing to discuss the matter further."

As I tried to think of a reasonable comeback for that ridiculous proposition, the screen began to display a view of the press room, as Viktor took his place behind the podium.

"Good evening," he said. "As outgoing high champion of the Queensgames, I had a speech prepared to give to you. A pretty good one that my beautiful fiancée, Celina Ambrose, helped me write. But I'm going to give my time over to someone else who has a few very important things that he wants to say."

He stepped out of the way, and Elian took his place.

My mouth fell open.

I heard a pained screeching sound and realized it had come from the queen.

"Hello," Elian said, his black eyes focused on the main camera. "Yes, some of you might recognize me. I am Prince Elian. Sixteen years ago, my mother, Queen Isadora, claimed that Lord Banyon murdered me. But that was a lie. I drowned, and my mother had a warlock bring me back to life with death magic to preserve her family legacy. She's hidden me from the world ever since. There are many family secrets I intend to discuss today—that Lord Banyon is my biological father, and Josslyn Drake, my half sister. But the most important is a claim that, by now, some of you will know. And I'm here to confirm it's true. We are all born with magic within us. Magic is life and life is magic. Every single person in the world—we all have the ability to summon elementia. And it's time that this secret is known. Now. Are there any questions?"

I started to laugh, a sound that was only slightly unhinged given the situation. Elian had done it—he'd just irrevocably changed the world with a handful of words. And I really couldn't have said any of them better myself.

"Issy," Banyon said, raising a brow. "Shall we go to the press conference together or separately? I have a few questions I'd like to personally address."

The queen shifted her gaze from the screen to the warlock. She had the most disappointed and hopeless expression I'd ever seen on anyone's face. And for a moment, just a moment, I almost felt bad for her.

No, that was a lie. I didn't feel bad at all.

"I should probably check on my father," Celina said to me.

"Did you say something to the queen?" I asked her. "Is that why she fired him?"

She shrugged a shoulder. "I may have put a bit of doubt in

her mind about his drinking. That he's miserable. And that he hates his job. And that he may have murdered your father. It's all true, right?"

"That's a whole lot of true." I searched her face. "Are you okay with this?"

"No, I'm not okay with any of it, Joss. I can't believe that my father would do any of that—that the man who raised me is so despicable. But, when I marry Viktor, hopefully I won't have to see much of him anymore."

"You're still marrying Viktor?"

She gave me a small grin. "I am."

"So, you do love him."

"More every day," she confirmed.

I hugged her. "I'm happy for you."

She hugged me back tightly. "By the way, if you disappear tonight, I'm going to personally hunt you down this time. You can't help to drop a bomb like this and not stick around to also help with the cleanup. And there's going to be a lot of cleanup."

"I'm not going anywhere," I told her. "I promise."

"Glad to hear it." With one last squeeze, she let me go. "Maybe we can practice our magic together." She grimaced. "That sounds so strange, doesn't it?"

"It really does," I agreed. "But it kind of sounds good too."

Celina slipped away and I turned to find Jericho, only to see that he was now speaking with Valery. I closed the distance between us as quickly as I could.

"Time to go," the witch told him. "As exciting as all of this has been, I have some business back in Cresidia that I'll need you to handle personally. Your unplanned leave of absence, if that's what this has been, is officially over."

Jericho didn't move.

"That's a command, Blackheart," she said sharply, and I watched as Jericho winced.

"Yeah, that definitely still stings," he said.

"What stings?" Valery hissed.

"Resisting your marks. But practice makes perfect. We're done, Val. Consider this my formal resignation, effective immediately. You go your way; I go mine. I think I've served my time—two years is enough payment for what you did for me."

She shook her head, genuinely shocked at Jericho's words. "You mean, giving you a second chance at life?"

"A third, too. I died again a few weeks ago but managed to pop back up. If there's a fourth, well, I guess I'm going to have to take my chances, won't I?"

Valery's impatient gaze fell on me, and she sighed. "Oh, I see. This is because of you, isn't it?"

"I have no control over Jericho's decisions," I told her. "But I support them fully and completely."

"You would choose a seventeen-year-old girl you've known less than two months, one who could grow bored with you at any given moment, over continuing to work for me and all the perks that being a Blackheart gives to you?"

"I mean, put that way . . ." Jericho said, frowning. Then he nodded. "Absolutely, yes. I choose her. Anyway, let's not make this weird, okay? Bye, now."

"Jericho!" Valery called after him when he turned his back on her. He ignored her.

I hooked my arm through his. "Nicely done."

"Felt good," he agreed as we began walking away.

"Bold move. And brave."

"Thank you. I like to think so."

"Especially since she's someone who could kill you with a touch as easily as she brought you back to life."

His steps slowed. "Thanks for the reminder."

"However, I think if she wanted you dead, you'd already be dead by now."

"Here's hoping."

As much as I disliked Valery, I honestly didn't believe she'd use death magic to kill Jericho out of petty revenge. Along with annoyance at his ability to resist her command, I could have sworn I'd seen something else in the witch's gaze.

Respect.

"If she does try, she'll have to go through me first," I added.

"Yeah, you're definitely a badass." He laughed. "So, now what, Drake?"

"For starters, do you mind escorting me to a press conference that will easily go down in history?"

He raised a brow. "Why? Do you have something to say?"

"Oh, plenty. But I always have plenty to say."

"No argument there." A smile played at his lips as we left the still-smoldering banquet hall behind us. It felt like I was walking away from the carnage after a war, which I guess made a lot of sense.

"Do you really think you can resist going back to Valery?" I asked.

"I'm going to try like hell to do just that."

"Two years as a Blackheart and nothing to show for it but superstrength, enhanced healing abilities, and the ability to survive death."

"And incredibly good looks."

"Incredibly," I agreed. "So, that's not bad, is it?"

"Not bad at all," he said. "I did manage to grab a souvenir on my way out, though." He pulled the golden dagger out from his black Queensguard coat.

My eyes widened at the sight of the blade that had, not so long ago, impaled my hand. I rubbed my thumb over the scar on my palm. "Jericho, you stole this from her?"

"I borrowed it. Indefinitely. Before you reminded me of the 'touch of death' possibility. Still, I'm standing by my decision." He shrugged. "I figured a witch I recently met might find this a handy weapon to have in her arsenal."

"Who, Tamara?"

"No. Think blonder. And shorter. And much more sarcastic."

I considered this. "I'm not shorter than Tamara, but I am blonder and more sarcastic."

"If you don't like daggers, I'm sure you could sell it on the black market. An ancient, magical knife like this would fetch a fortune."

Jericho placed the dagger's hilt in my hand, and I looked down at it with awe—a legendary blade that had once allegedly belonged to an immortal goddess from another world.

"It is shiny," I said.

"Very."

"And I do still have some debt from a combination of too much shopping and not enough money. This would definitely help with that."

"It's all about priorities."

I closed my grip around the hilt, feeling the weight of the dagger. "We could split the profits. Eventually. But let's hold on to it for a bit until the dust settles."

"I like the way you think, Drake."

I grinned. "Then it's a deal."

Jericho regarded the mass of reporters and photographers waiting outside and inside the palace press room. Elian was still behind the podium, answering an endless string of questions with Banyon now standing at his side.

The former Blackheart gestured toward the throng. "Back to your normal, glittery life. I mean, without being normal or particularly glittery in the slightest."

"It's glittery enough for me," I told him.

"Glad to hear it," he replied. "Go get 'em, Drake."

When he leaned over and kissed me, I smiled against his lips.

The past was over. I was focused on the future now, especially when it came to Jericho Nox. The possibilities were really endless, and I couldn't wait to explore every single one of them.

A moment later, a microphone appeared in front of me, and a frantic-looking reporter beamed at me. "Josslyn Drake, given the shocking revelations tonight, everyone eagerly awaits your statement on the future of the Regarian Empire."

I knew that changing the world wasn't going to be easy, even with the truth on our side and a handful of people I knew I could trust with both my life and my deepest, darkest secrets.

Still, I couldn't lie. It felt really great to be back in the spotlight.

ACKNOWLEDGMENTS

The Echoes and Empires duology has been a treat to write, and I hope that you enjoy it as much as I enjoyed bringing Joss and Jericho's story to the page.

Thank you so very much to Eve Silver, who's not only a gifted author, but also my dear friend who's been a huge, huge support over the last decade and a half as we've surfed these fiction-writing waves.

Thank you to my wonderful editor, Gretchen Durning, for her invaluable help, guidance, and patience. To Jim McCarthy, who's been my rock-steady, rock-star agent since day one of my publishing career.

Thank you to the incredible team at Penguin Teen/ Razorbill for everything they do. To my fabulous publisher, Casey McIntyre. To Kristie Radwilowicz, who designed both beautiful covers for this duology, and Leilani Bustamante, who created the gorgeous illustrations for them.

I am eternally grateful to my family and friends . . . my mother and father, Cindy and Mike, Bonnie, Elly, Nicki, Maureen, Tara, Julie, to name but a few. Thank you . . . I love and appreciate you all.

And, as always, infinite love and gratitude to my readers. You make it all worthwhile.

21982320834447